Gravity and Rust

Gravity and Rust

Brian Quinn

Twenty-two tales of fiction, parody and personal mishap

Pp
Penny Post

Published in 2025 by Penny Post Limited, www.pennypost.org.uk

A CIP record for this book is available from the British Library.

Printed in the UK by 4Edge Limited

ISBN: 978-1-8382580-1-6

As ever, for Penny, Michael, Dominic, Allie and Toby

Many thanks to all those who gave me encouragement, advice and practical support in preparing this book, with particular thanks to Ollie Keen, Christopher Turner, John Williams, Etienne Hawkins, Kylie Sanderson, Mark Christopher, Becca Lacey, Owen Jones, Michael Quinn, Chris Clack, Chris Bessent and Alex and Emma Milne-White: and – above all and once again – Penny, without whom...

Contents

The Unforgettable Jeeves

I don't think PG Wodehouse ever visited East Garston or anywhere else in West Berkshire, nor set one of his stories there. If he did, there seems to be no record of it. But I suppose he might have done...

IT'S A RUM THING, life. There it is, ripping along like billyoh, all rose petals and trilling larks and what-not and the next minute it whacks you for six. I mean to say, take the other morning. I was finishing my eggs and b and sipping a cup of Mr Souchong's finest when Jeeves shimmered in.

"What-ho Jeeves," I called cheerily

"Indeed, sir. Mrs Gregson has just telephoned to remind you about the Boy Scouts' party tomorrow."

This was a disaster of the first water. Jeeves' reference was to my aunt Agatha, as fearsome a relative as can be found in a month of Sundays, or a week of Thursdays for that matter. In the dim and distant she had cornered me in her lair and bullied me into agreeing to give away the cups to a troupe of the vilest of vile Boy Scouts in, of all places, Maidenhead. Add to that her attempts to lure me into matrimony with her even viler secretary, Arabella Flockington, and you will see how the flaming fires of hell appeared balmy by comparison. I leaped out of bed.

"Jeeves, we must away!"

"The bags are packed, sir."

"To the jolly old Queens Arms."

"I have already booked the rooms, sir."

So that's how we found ourselves snugly ensconced in double-quick order at the QA. All in all it's one of my favourite inns, a mere ninety minutes from the lights of Mayfair and, more importantly, well out of reach of the tentacles of sundry aunts.

Its precise geographical location, seeing as you catch me in such an expansive mood, is in a village called East Garston. This suggests, even to my poor brain, the idea of a West Garston lurking somewhere nearby: presumably – and here I feel the old cogs are really turning upstairs – somewhere to the west.

If so, I've never been able to find it. Perhaps the locals like to keep it to themselves and bribe the Ordnance chappies to keep it off the map. West Garston may be crammed full of fellows like me with aunts like mine, using it as their bolt-hole at times of crisis. In short, it was their "night's cloak to hide them from sight" as some brainy bird once observed. I can sympathise with that.

Anyway, back to the old QA. Freddie and Sue, I have to report, are a very decent pair of coves. I have managed to forgive Sue for trying to marry me off to a rich widow of the parish, a crisis from which Jeeves only extricated me almost as the wedding march was being played.

Moving on down the list, it's also an absolute mine of info about local turf conditions. We Woosters are well known for our sporting instincts and there's little that pleases me more than picking up a red-hot tip for a long-priced winner in convivial surroundings. They also do a very decent nosebag in the dining department. All in all, it's as civil a place as one could hope to find.

I left Jeeves to unpack and sauntered across to the bar for a quick snifter. Imagine my surprise when the first person I saw was Buffy Frobisher. He was leaning into a generously sized G&T and looking as miserable as a policeman who has just had his helmet pinched.

I gave him the usual "what-ho" and slid into the adjacent berth.

"Bertie," he croaked. "I've forgotten it."

You should know that Buffy is always forgetting things. He has a memory like a leaking sieve. I suppose sieves always leak but you get my drift.

"Forgotten what, old fruit? Tell me all."

The long and short was that, some days before, Buffy had heard a dead-cert being tipped on the wireless from a racing cove who was apparently always spot-on in steeplechases. Buffy usually forgets to go to the bookmakers, or to bring his money, or to collect his slip. This time he had forgotten the name of the horse.

"Forty to one, Bertie," he mumbled. "And I've got fifty smackers. That would make…"

After a short silence, we both agreed that it would make a decent pile. I then recalled that I had fifty smackers or thereabouts in my pocket-book. The only problem was nailing down the name of the animal in question.

At that moment I saw a familiar domed head passing through the restaurant. "Ahoy!" I called. Jeeves changed course and glided towards us. "Excellent. Rally round, Jeeves. You remember Buffy? He has a problem."

"I am sorry to hear of that, sir."

Buffy started to lay the matter out in his usual tangled manner. "There we have it, Jeeves," I said some minutes later. "Does any solution spring forth in your giant lobes?"

"Perhaps Mr Frobisher could check tomorrow's runners in the sporting press in case a name suggested itself."

"I've done that twenty times," said Buffy dejectedly. "Well, nineteen at least. My mind's a blank." Poor old Buffy's mind was always a blank but it seemed kinder not to mention this.

"In that case, sir, I confess to being at a loss. I will give the matter my attention. And, if I may say so, sir…"

"Yes, Jeeves, what is it?"

"The waistcoat, sir." He averted his eyes slightly.

I looked down at the canary-yellow cloth that swathed the Wooster chest. "What's wrong with it?" I asked testily. "It's one of my finest."

"Yellow waistcoats, sir, are only being worn this season by provincial actors of dubious morals."

"I'm sorry you think so. Nonetheless, the waistcoat stays. That is my final word in the matter of waistcoats."

"As you wish, sir."

We ate well that night – I with Buffy in the restaurant on a mouth-watering rack of lamb, a hunk of Stilton and some very approachable claret, Jeeves at the bar doubtless on huge platefuls of succulent fish to feed his brain. I tottered off to my well-earned rest at about eleven. Jeeves escorted me to my room and ensured I got pointed towards the bed with the minimum of damage.

"Any thoughts on the Buffy conundrum?" I asked him sleepily.

"The problem is certainly a challenging one, sir. Let us hope the morning may bring results."

I don't know what results the morning brought Jeeves, but it brought Buffy and I to a bracing nine holes at the local course. It seemed my Christian duty to take the old chap's mind off his troubles. Yet no good deed, as some wise fellow once observed, goes unpunished. Two shocks awaited me on our arrival back at the inn at two o'clock.

The first was that my motor-car had vanished from the parking lot. The second was that the fifty pounds had vanished from the pocket-book in my room. I popped straight round and rootled out Freddie in his bunker.

"Your man went off in the car about half an hour ago," he told me. I paused for thought. Jeeves, a thief? It was rum in the extreme. I steered my way into the bar and ordered a large brandy. Buffy went off in search of a wireless so he could glue his shell-like to the race commentary.

Apart from Jeeves' treachery, two other points now struck me. Point one was that, with no money, I had no means of paying the bill. Point two was that, with no car, I had no means of mounting a quick escape from the consequences of point one. The sword of Damocles, or some such weapon, was hanging over me.

I had got as far as thinking about train timetables when there was a whoop from the next room. Buffy dashed in.

"I've remembered it, Bertie!" he shouted. "It's called 'Unforgettable'. And it's leading by six lengths! All is saved!" He started to dance a jig.

"Yes, but look here, you chump – that's all very well, but the race has started! You can't place a bet *now*. Anyway, who would you bet *with*?"

At this cold logic the poor old duffer reeled backwards like a wounded stag. He tottered against the bar where Sue was standing, a large B&S at the ready. Buffy drained it. "My God, Bertie," he said, "you're right." Then he slid down onto the floor.

At that awful moment, Jeeves appeared. I swivelled round and fixed him with my coldest of cold stares.

"Good afternoon, sir. Is Mr Frobisher unwell?"

"He remembered the name of the horse, but I've just pointed out that it's too late to pop any of the folding under its saddle. But what I want to know is..."

Jeeves coughed lightly. "There, perhaps, I can be of assistance, sir." He produced a slip of paper. "Unforgettable'" it read, "to win in the two-fifteen at Newbury, at forty to one, £50 wagered, pp B. Frobisher."

Buffy and I goggled at it for a few seconds.

"This morning, sir, while you were still asleep, I fell into a conversation with a gentleman who knew the tipster who spoke on the wireless, a Mr Brookes. It seems that Mr Brookes is a well-known radio personality." Jeeves gave a slight shiver, then pushed on with his narrative. "It transpired Mr Brookes lives locally and my informant was kind enough to give me his address. Finding you out, I took it upon myself to visit him and ascertain the name of the horse he had prognosticated..."

"The horse he had *what*, Jeeves?"

"Prognosticated, sir, to win. I was then able to place the bet in Lambourn in, as they say, the nick of time." He handed the betting slip to Buffy, who was now looking like a startled frog. "I was compelled to take the motor-car, sir. The matter was critical and admitted of no delay."

"But hang it all, Jeeves, where did you get the money from?"

Jeeves coughed again. "I took the liberty of borrowing the sum from your pocket-book. Of course, Mr Frobisher will now be in a position to repay you – perhaps, I might suggest, sir, with interest."

I glanced at Buffy to see if he had taken this last point in. It appeared not. "But what if the horse had lost, Jeeves?"

"There was little likelihood of that, sir. I was able to speak to the jockey on the telephone. He assured me that the race was, as he expressed it, 'in the bag.'"

"How did you manage to speak to him?"

"He is my cousin, sir. Will there be anything else?"

At this juncture, Freddie padded up to me with a telegram. I read it.

"Jeeves – not a moment to lose! Aunt Agatha has smoked us out and she's motoring here to kidnap me to be sacrificed by the Boy Scouts of Maidenhead. She'll be here by tea-time!"

"Indeed, sir." And with that, rather than dash about seeing to the valises, the blasted man walked coolly into the reception area.

Ten minutes later we were rolling down the highway towards Great Shefford, Boxford and points east. "What was that back there, Jeeves?" I ventured. "Did you need a bracer before the voyage?"

"Indeed not, sir. I thought it wise to apprise Mr Frobisher of the fact that we were going for a drive but would be back to take tea with him at four."

"No fear, Jeeves! Not were it served by all the sultry maidens of the Orient."

"Quite so, sir. But Mrs Gregson will be arriving at the Queen's Arms at that time in need of a man. It occurred to me that Mr Frobisher could take your place with the Boy Scouts. It is unfortunate I forgot to warn him of her arrival, for I know he finds Mrs Gregson as daunting as you do."

"'Daunting' barely comes close. Jeeves, once again you have excelled yourself."

"Thank you, sir."

"That waistcoat," I said after a long-ish pause. "Second thoughts and so forth. Perhaps you had better do with it what you will on our return."

"I have already given it to the gardener at the Queen's Arms, sir."

"I suppose it was a bit loud, what?"

"It was unforgettable, sir."

The Tragedy of King Starmer I (Part One)

Of all the subjects Shakespeare dealt with in his plays, few would think that welfare reforms would feature strongly. That's what I thought too until this lost (and, I'm assured, genuine) fragment came to light…

Act 1, Scene 1

King Starmer's Council Chamber in Westminster

KING STARMER My brothers; sisters; councillors; my friends
Welcome all. We are conjoined for one clear purpose:
To seize this nettle of our public purse
Whose solvency's not better, but far worse
Since we won the troublèd, tear-stained crown
And pledged ourselves to bring bread prices down;
To make our merchants fat; our justice swift;
To level up the common weal's great rift;
To staunch the flow of gold our kingdom blew
On that great folly, known as HS2;
And end the bitter strife of the Crusades –
All failed, despite the promises we made.
LADY REEVES My liege, as I've said many times before
The hungry wolves are howling at the door.
To put the matter plain, the well is dry
Though every day, from dawn to dusk, I try
To resurrect the state of our fair realm
To how it was when Blair was at the helm…
KING STARMER My lady, you do over-reach your rank.
We say again, so all may know our mind,

We will not have that base name spoken of
In our hearing: or from this council
The speaker of the same I shall expel.

LORD STREETING And "Brown" is banished too?

KING STARMER Yes, him as well.
So, now we've got that straight, we must now bend
Our minds to how we possibly can spend
More than we earn, or ever can afford
On this first matter: buying more new swords
And spears, and implements of war
To meet King Maga's clearly spoke intent
That this increase to more like five per cent.

LADY COOPER Forgive me, liege, but last time that I checked
King Maga was not ruling here: respect
Is owed, but not a slavish "yea"...

KING STARMER Easy are those words for you to say:
It is not you who's summoned to his lair
To hear his rants; pluck parchments from the air;
And nod, and smile, and shake his sweaty hand
While he ejaculates his latest plan.
No, my councillors: i'faith we're caught
Between two millstones: first, the fraught
Alarums and excursions of this world:
The Saracens and Slavs, their flags unfurled;
Then Maga's whims; the Europe that we've lost;
And promises we made, despite the cost.
I mourn the pomp and gloire that we are missing
And all the while, we've got no pot to piss in.

LADY REEVES That's millstones more than two, my Lord, I think.

KING STARMER Prithee, save thy number-skill, and ink
For the figures which I pay you well to write
In the Exchequer. The question's this:
Who's left to plunder?

Where can Morton's Fork next plunge: for we're bereft
Of cash – who else has money left?

LADY RAYNER The rich, my lord – there are a few still here
Who can be used to right these base arrears.
In Gerrards Cross, in Harrogate and Hale
And Alderley Edge and Stanford-in-the-Vale
They throng like lizards on a sun-baked wall.
I sense that few would notice it at all
If lavish sums were lifted from their purse.

KING STARMER And that, red sister, leaves us all far worse
Off in the eyes of those whose smile we crave:
The bankers – and, what's more, earn us the hate
Of the G-seven: or do I mean G-eight?

LORD LAMMY Another problem too, my Lords, it seems:
Most are non-dom: whatever that might mean.

LADY RAYNER We owe it to this land: what part of "soak
the rich" do you not understand?

KING STARMER These arguments I've heard: I shall now set
Our policy immutably in stone, so all is clear.
The rich, be they annoyed, can up and go
To Monserrat, or Sark or Monaco.
The poor, however, have no means of flight.
They must needs spend each damp and freezing night
In this cold isle – they are thus our aim.
The old as well, and those who're sick or lame.
Our royal purse has not the depth to cure
All the sour troubles of these days.
That might have once been so – but, alas:
That time has now long passed.

LORD LAMMY Alas, indeed: this time is deep corrupt
This heavy blow…

KING STARMER Pray do not interrupt me
In full flow.

LORD LAMMY Forgive me, gracious Lord: it shall be so.
KING STARMER Where was I? Ah, yes:
Know therefore, that we no longer can
Mend the weal of those who shrink or shirk
(as some – though not I – say) from honest work.
The system needs, above all else, reform
(Though note my lower-case) – the raging storm
Will break us else in twain: we must prepare
For dread events. The poor must pay their share.
It seems to us, we profit through neglect:
The less they have, the less they will expect.
LORD STREETING Know then that we have agreed a plan…
KING STARMER Leave it to me, my lord: We surely are
Still fit to speak our mind? Or do you feel
The day has come to see your King replaced?
LORD STREETING Apologies, my lord: I spoke in haste.
I retract my words, and I abase
Myself before you: watch now how my tongue
Inches forth towards the royal…
KING STARMER Don't overdo it, Streeting: just keep mum
'til I require your speech. That precept goes
For all of you as well: I'll love you less
If, from Master Chaucer's printing press,
I read one word of confidence unleashed
What's said here, stays here: am I clear; capiche?
LORD LAMMY Full clear, my Lord, to lady each and man
But tell us please: pray what's the cunning plan?
KING STARMER I have this very day instructed our clerks
In Whitehall to prepare a writ
To specify what we will no longer cover
Of the costs that these base knaves
(as some – though not I, note) would call them.
We do henceforth require they haul them

Selves out of their idleness and sloth.
This serves two ends: and know you all that both
Are mighty pleasing to us – so:
We help these folk to stand on their own feet
And, in the process, keep the bankers sweet.

LADY RAYNER But, my lord, many of these are hapless:
Blind misfortune has smote them many times.
Surely we would be twice unworthy if we now
Added further blows from our own hand?

KING STARMER We note your views: they were both clear and terse
Though would have been improved by rhythmic verse.
However, we are not concerned with blame:
Their langour or bad luck cost us the same.

LORD STREETING Well said, my lord. I was a poor man's son...

KING STARMER Enough already: please just see this done.

LORD STREETING That I will, my liege, and that right soon.

KING STARMER And so, we meet here, one week hence, at noon.
(Aside) Now I shall repair myself to sup
I can no longer keep this rhyming up. (Exeunt)

Act 1, Scene 2

King Starmer's Palace in St Pancras

Enter King Starmer and McSweeney

McSWEENEY My lord, I bring thee fearful news
A base rebellion is stirred across this land from sea to sea.

KING STARMER Rebellion? What knavery is this abroad?

McSWEENEY Several earls and ladies, good my lord:
Bangor, Barrow, Brent and Battersea
Bootle, Bexleyheath and Bermondsey
Have marched this day – and they are not alone;
For also, in this challenge to your throne,
Are Blackpool, Bournemouth East and Bleanau Gwent

And joining them, in this most foul intent,
Are Bracknell…
KING STARMER Do these rebels all begin with B?
McSWEENEY Why, no: they're listed alphabetically.
KING STARMER I get the picture: we'll be here all day.
On whom can I rely in these fell times?
McSWEENEY I'faith, my liege, it's very hard to say.
KING STARMER What moves them thus to treasonable deeds?
Whence comes this rank disloyalty
That tests my kindly patience so?
McSWEENEY My lord, they claim to represent the poor
And the afflicted: by that instruction
You recently did bid your scribes to draft
Regarding all the succour and the aid
That you did lately give, and now withdraw.
The rebels say that won't support this writ
KING STARMER What, not at all?
McSWEENEY No, not one little bit.
And there are more bad tidings I must bring:
That Masters Caxton, Guttenburg and others
Of their ilk and kidney have printed diverse tracts
Which circulate most freely. These slanders ring…
KING STARMER Such as? Good Sweeney, name them for your king
McSWEENEY Er – "why's he picking on the poorer men?"
And "time for regime change at Number Ten."
KING STARMER This must be met head on, this very night.
McSWEENEY A U-turn, Lord?
KING STARMER Indeed, I think you're right.
Please draw some parchment hence and draft your best
Charmed and weasel words to good effect
That will cause some of them to halt this strife.
We shall pause this measure:
Then discuss anew.

I leave the words and details all to you.
Oh – good Sweeney, also add this phrase:
"We know a change is needed right away
But must be done the Plantagenet way."

McSWEENEY And if they wonder why the matter
Was embarked upon with intemperate haste –
Not my words, lord, I feel that I must stress
I'm quoting from young Master Caxton's press.

KING STARMER Tell them – what? That I was sore distracted
By such heavy burdens of this realm that none can know.
"Uneasy lies the head that wears the crown":
A perfect phrase, methinks – please write it down
Lest some base playwright claim it as his own…
I like it well…

McSWEENEY My liege – your reason must be known.

KING STARMER Indeed – what neatly serves this circumstance?
Ah yes – discussions with the noble kings of France
And Aragon, Castille, and Italy
And the Duke of Greater Germany
About King Maga's latest crazed crusade
And whether we'd send arms, or whether aid:
All these matters, turned our royal mind
Quite from this welfare thing we'd left behind.
Yes – tell them that, should anybody ask.
It's widely known that men can't multi-task.

McSWEENEY A very cunning swerve, again, my lord,
That will unhorse them yet.
But, one thing, sire, if I may make so bold,
What next steps with the matter of the gold
That this was meant to save? Does Lady Reeves
Have orchards full of magic money trees?

KING STARMER We mint some more, and keep the matter vague
Just like the last king did in that fell plague.

McSWEENEY Indeed: my Lord; well said; it shall be so.
And just one further matter 'ere I go:
Although the ship of state's now pointing shoreward
What tactic do we call on, going forward?
KING STARMER This rabble throng will surely melt away
Before the words you'll write, and I will say.
But other storms will break, and fires burn
That can't be smothered by a swift U-turn.
So this I say – and mark me well again
No matter how the rebels frame their claim;
No matter what the force of Caxton's stories
We double down, and blame it on the Tories. *(Exeunt).*

How the Pangolin Got His Scales

I don't know if Rudyard Kipling ever wrote one of his Just So Stories *about a pangolin – but I suppose he might have done…*

IN THE BEGINNING, Best Beloved, in the high-and-far-off times when all animals were in their proper places, there lived a Pangolin. He wasn't ubiquitous and nor was he migratory – not him. He was indigenous to the hot, green Jungle of Yavdavipa on the Sundaland. There he spent his days and nights and the short dusks and dawns in between (for the Jungle of Yavdavipa was, you should know, in the high tropics). He was not crepuscular and nor was he diurnal – not him. The Pangolin was nocturnal, sleeping when the sun beat down through the monkey-chattering trees and hunting for insects during the deep, dark night.

In these high-and-far-off times the animals of the jungle were different from how they now appear. The Tiger was a yellowy-sandy colour with not a stripe to be seen and had claws as delicate as ever-there-was for scooping small things out of their shells. The Coral Snake had no venom, the Babirusa no tusks and the Anoa no horns. As for the Pangolin, he was not crusty-scaly as he is today – not him. He had sharp claws for digging but was soft and sleek and smooth as smooth can be. That was the way it all was, back in the high-and-far-off times in the Jungle of Yavdavipa: do you see?

One day a Man arrived. He carefully pulled his caique onto the beach and made it fast with a rope. Then he walked up towards the hot, green jungle and the first thing he saw was Pangolin asleep in the shade of a Rainbow Gum tree.

"Good morning," said the Man. His name was Wu Han and he thought himself 'scruciatingly clever.

Pangolin opened one eye. "Good morning," he said and introduced himself. "I haven't seen you before. What are you?"

"I'm a Man," said Wu Han. "Where can I find water? I've just sailed across the sea and I am as thirsty as ever was."

Pangolin got to his four feet and led Wu Han towards a river. Wu Han bent down and drank. When he turned round, the Pangolin had gone to sleep again, this time in the shade of a Melati bush.

"Are you ill?" asked Wu Han, poking Pangolin with his foot.

"No," said Pangolin. "I am nocturnal but I am never ill."

"Never ill?" exclaimed Wu Han. "Do you never get the colic or the canker or the croup, nor suffer from breakbone or boneshave?"

"Not that I am aware of," replied Pangolin.

"What – not dropsy or distemper, nor small pox, red pox or scrum pox? Have you never had quinsy or lockjaw, nor the flu or the ague? No gout, spasms, palsies, grippes, fits, fluxes nor scrivener's palsy?"

"I have never been ill," Pangolin said, "nor have the other animals."

"What animals are these that never get ill?" asked Wu Han.

"There is Tiger and Babirusa and Sea Snake and Anoa, and not forgetting Black Macaque, among others," said Pangolin.

"I would like to meet these animals," said Wu Han.

"We are all here at dusk. The nocturnals are waking up and the diurnals are going to sleep: but we must all drink." And with that Pangolin curled himself back up under the shade of the Melati bush and went back to sleep.

Wu Han walked back to the beach, pondering his good fortune. He judged by the sun that it was an hour before dusk – for you will remember that he thought himself 'scruciatingly clever. He went to his boat and got out a large sack and some stout rope.

An hour later, Wu Han was back at the stream: and there, as Pangolin had said, were Tiger and Babirusa and Sea Snake and Anoa, among others (and not forgetting Black Macaque). Pangolin introduced them to Wu Han, who bowed low.

"O, Animals," said Wu Han, "Pangolin here says you are never sick. Never the rickets nor the sloes or scrofula? Never the scurvy?"

"Not that I am aware of," said Tiger.

"Never apoplexy, nor amnesia, nor worm fit?"

Then Tiger and the other animals assured him that they had never been ill, not once. "Excellent," said Wu Han: and out of his sack he pulled a net and threw it over them – the nocturnal, the diurnal and the crepuscular, all together, like so. Then he got a rope and pulled that round the net: and before you could say Jawi Rinca, all the animals were wrapped up as tight as tight could be.

"Now," said Wu Han, "you will all come home with me. We Men have many sicknesses. I am an apothe-cary and will use some parts of you to make us well again."

So then he dragged them and pulled them and pushed them in the net down to the beach and onto his boat. The animals wailed and growled and hissed and looked at Pangolin and said, "this is *your* fault."

At last they arrived at a town on the other side of the wide, green-blue sea. Wu Han pulled the net onto the beach and put the animals into cages which he lined up next to each other. People gathered round, all full of 'satiable curiosity.

Then he produced a big book whose pages rustled when he turned them. They were filled with writing and diagrams and tables of figures and pictures with coloured inks that shimmered in the sun. It was bound in dark green leather and had a brass catch that fastened it shut with a snap!, like that, when he closed it. This, he explained, was the *Hakeem Davaai* – and that means a Book of Cures and Healing and was the kind of book you must specially *not* touch.

Wu Han then spoke to the people. "These are magical animals who never get sick," he said. "A small part of each of them will give you all health." He explained that they didn't get the breakbone nor the pox and they didn't get ague, nor colic, canker or distemper; nor morgellons, nor miasma; nor the mumps or the measles. All the people gathered round and stared at Wu Han, and the book, and at the animals, muttering to each other.

Then other men in other caiques arrived with other animals in nets and soon there was all manner of cages and crates lined up. There were Caimans and Crabs, Turtles and Tapirs, Pandas and Pumas; there were Cheetahs and Anteaters, there were Bats and Boas and Blue Macaws – yes, there were, all these and more.

All these men knew Wu Han. Some called him Yi-Sheng and some called him Tabib and some called him Ishi-San and some called him other names that were long and complicated and – for he was an apothe-cary – most deferential.

The people gathered round the animals and prodded them and poked them in their cages. Wu Han explained how the pineal gland of this one would cure the dropsy and how the liver of that one would ward off the grippe: how the paws of this one, if boiled just so, would be an admirable antidote to the ague and how the tail of that one, if dried just so, would be a remarkable remedy for the rickets.

So it went on, with Wu Han consulting the *Hakeem Davaai* and telling every person that, for whatever ailed them, there was a specific drawn from some part of these magical animals. And more people came; and more men came with more animals; and the town grew big; and the people who lived there grew rich; but none grew as rich as Wu Han.

The animals were crammed and rammed and jammed together in any old way. There were crustaceans from the Marshes of Sonnaput next to ungulates from the Great High Veldt of Nkobo; there were primates from the Forests of Manibar and Lan Xang next to marsupials from the far Antipodes. There were carnivores and herbivores, mammals and reptiles, the furred, the scaled and the feathered, nocturnals, diurnals and crepusculars: animals from all the four corners of the world pressed up so close to each other that none of them knew who they were or what they were doing – truly they didn't.

The animals looked themselves over in their cages (although many couldn't turn round properly as they were squeezed in so tight). It seemed to them that, by being pushed and squished and mashed and crushed against each other, they had each started to take on a different aspect. Tiger, who had been pressed up to Coral Snake, was now more stripey; on Tiger's other side, Babirusa now had long teeth – almost tusks, they were – while, beyond him, Anoa now found that his hooves had become cloven.

As for Pangolin, weeks of being pressed close to Coral Snake on the boat meant he was more bendy and more scaly than ever before. "I am not the same Pangolin as I was in my ancestral hunting grounds," he lamented. And all the other animals were thinking much the very self-same thing.

And that was not all, Best Beloved: for the animals, who had previously been of a co-operative and accommodating disposition, now found themselves possessed of the most fearsome and 'rascible tempers. Coral Snake developed poison in his fangs, Tiger found his claws could do more than scoop small things out of their shells, Anoa could jab with his sharp new horns, Babirusa could poke with his strong new tusks and Blue Macaque bite with his big new teeth. And there was such spitting and clawing and jabbing that it was all Pangolin could do to roll himself into a ball until he was showing only his hard new scales and wish that everything and everyone would leave him alone.

And so it went on, Best Beloved – all the animals were shifting in their shapes and changing in their natures, all because of Wu Han and his 'scruciating cleverness.

The day came when a sickness befell the people that was unlike any sickness that had befallen them before. There was such wailing and sweating and coughing and sneezing and all manner of other febrilities and expectorations that the Great God Vardaresh was disturbed in her meditations and asked the Middle God Ganglip to discover what was upsetting them so. Ganglip, who was having a sand bath, sent for the Little God Rafila.

"Oh Rafila," said Ganglip, "the sweating and coughing and sneezing and suchlike is causing great upset and disturbance. Pray thou descend to the people and establish the cause of this distress." (The Gods, being grand and formal, always addressed each other in this fashion, it being hallowed by time immemorial.)

"Oh Ganglip," replied Rafila, "that I shall."

So Rafila descended, disguised as a fisher-woman, and observed the people a-coughing and a-sneezing and all of the animals crowded together in their wrong places. She returned to Ganglip and to Vardaresh. And after they had had a pow-wow and a parlez-vous and a vichaar-varmesh and a diskusi and confabulated with each other, it was decided that Vardaresh would descend most formally to give judgement on the muddle that the people had got into.

So Vardaresh descended in a great cloak of all the colours of the Universe and with a roll of thunder manifested herself in the middle of the market. All the people who were still able to stand bowed and prostrated themselves in postures of the greatest abasement.

"Why are you a-coughing and a-sneezing and all, disturbing my meditations in this shameful way?"

"We are sick," cried all the people. "There is a great sickness among us, O Greatest God."

"Humph. And from whence did this sickness proceed?"

"From the animals, O Greatest God. The animals were brought to make us better but they have made us worse."

"Humph. And from whence did these animals appear?"

"From diverse foreign places across the seas, O Greatest God."

"Humph. And by whose hand did these animals arrive?"

"By the hand of Wu Han!" they all cried.

"Fetch him hither," commanded Vardaresh.

"He is sick, very sick," said the people, "a-coughing and a-sneezing and all manner of other febrilities and expectorations."

"Nevertheless," said Vardaresh.

So Wu Han was fetched, a-coughing and a-sneezing as the people had said, and Vardaresh regarded him with her four pitiless eyes.

"You are not, as you believed, 'scruciatingly clever, but a greedy and foolish man," she said at last. "These animals have no parts that can be curative to you. Matters have not been ordered thus. By your hand, things have been mixed which should have stayed separate and things have been altered which should have remained the same. Thus the sickness has come upon you."

Wu Han threw himself on the sand in a posture of the greatest abasement. "Oh Greatest God Vardaresh, tell me what I must do fully to right this wrong."

"The wrong cannot be fully righted," replied Vardaresh. "It was made by man and man must live with it."

At this, there was a wailing and weeping and trembling of the people. Vardaresh raised her hand and the noise was stilled.

"However, I tell you this. These animals must be returned to their ancestral places – to the Low Veldts, the High Veldts, the Jungles, the Plains, the Mountains, the Oceans, the Prairies and the Tundras from whence they came. Everything has its proper place and its proper space and there it must remain. That you must do – Vardaresh has spoken."

"What about the sickness?" asked Wu Han. "Can you cure this, O Greatest God?"

"I cannot. It was made by man and man must live with it. You are a sociable and talkative people but I must tell you that you must shun each other and mask yourselves for a year and a quarter and a month and a week and a day if you want to abate the sickness. But it will always be amongst you and at any time it might return."

"O Greatest God, the animals have changed," said a woman. "Tiger now has claws and Coral Snake a sting and Anoa horns as sharp as sharp can be, and all of them are in a terrible temper with us. Can you cure this and return them to their ancestral states?"

"I cannot. These changes were made by man and man must live with them. Be sure that henceforth Tiger will claw you and Coral Snake will poison you and Anoa will gore you and all the other animals will use whatever means they have to visit their displeasure upon you, this day and every day. You have earned yourselves the enmity of the world: and 'scruciating clever though you think yourselves to be, the world will have its revenge."

At this, Vardaresh whipped her cloak around her and vanished (with another roll of thunder), leaving the people in a state of great consternation. Before long, they surrounded Wu Han, still abased upon the ground. "It's *your* fault," they all said.

So Wu Han returned all the animals to their proper places, starting with Pangolin and Tiger and Babirusa and Sea Snake and Anoa, among others (and not forgetting Black Macaque) to the Jungle of Yavdavipa. But, as Vardaresh had said, they were changed from their ancestral states. The Tiger had claws, the Coral Snake a sting, Barbirusa tusks, all to use against Man and his 'scruciating cleverness.

As for Pangolin, he is still nocturnal but now has, as well as sharp claws, a wondrously bendy back and hard scales all over his body, all from rubbing up next to Coral Snake in the net for ever so long.

So, Best Beloved, if you ever visit the Jungle of Yavdavipa and see Pangolin asleep under the shade of a Rainbow Gum Tree and ask him for some water, do not expect him to help. He will just roll himself into a ball, as tight as tight can be and, if you try to unroll him, Pangolin will scratch you with his sharp claws.

If I were you, I would get back into your caique, sail back across the wide, green-blue sea to your ancestral hunting grounds and leave Pangolin and the rest to theirs – do you see?

The Looking-glass Pool

CHARLOTTE SHUT THE barn door and looked back up at the farmhouse. Lucas and Mr Arrowby wouldn't be back from the top field for half an hour at least and her mother and her sisters would be at the sheep fair in Lockbridge until dusk. For now, she had the place to herself.

Kicking a stone so it spun in an arc before clattering into a milk churn, she walked down the chalky, flinty path towards the bridge, just beyond which was the gate that marked the edge of their property.

The late afternoon was overcast and with a keen breeze that cooled her face and caused her long and rather untidy crimson dress to billow against her legs. She kicked another stone; then for no particular reason turned and scanned the view. It was almost as if she were about to meet someone – though, as far as she was aware, she wasn't.

Charlotte's thoughts had been put into a whirl by a book. As only she and Kate ever appeared to read anything, it was a growing mystery to her why there were so many books in the farmhouse. There was one room at the top of the house, into which no one but her ever seemed to go, which contained nothing else.

She'd thought of asking her mother, but feared that would betray a secret and perhaps cause the books to be removed. Maybe it was something to do with her father, whom she hadn't seen for five years. This was another subject which wasn't mentioned, except occasionally through hissed conversations that stopped as soon as it was noticed she was listening.

Another stone went flying.

She paused again, now only twenty paces from where the brook passed under the bridge at right angles to the path. She was vaguely aware that some books were appropriate – she said the word again to herself as she had recently learned its meaning – while others were not.

What the rules might be, however, she had no idea.

Dickens; Edward Lear; AA Milne; GK Chesterton; Thomas Aquinas; Willa Cather: hobbits and angels, goblins and unicorns; the good, the bad and the indifferent: all were selected randomly and pored over to reveal at least some of their secrets.

No one book completely made sense and some were left half-finished. As a result, separate insights and preoccupations were taking shape within her which sometimes left her thoughts crackling like a bonfire long after she had turned the last page.

The book she had just finished had been one such.

She walked to the bridge and turned right, following the brook for a few hundred yards until it vanished into a copse. There it slowed and widened and formed a pool that Charlotte was still young enough to regard fiercely as her special place. Ringed with ash and beech trees, surrounded with ferns and edged with bullrushes, it was entirely hidden except from the sky.

Fifty feet above the water, the break in the canopy created a circle of light which, depending on the weather, the season and the time of day, seemed to alter not only the colour but also the physical properties of the water.

To Charlotte's particular delight, the pond was constantly flowing from one hue or form into another. From being perfectly reflective of a cloudless sky one moment, it would then change to deep green or murky brown, often overlaid with shimmering patterns that appeared, if only she could focus on them, to be revealing objects moving in the water or in the sky high above the trees.

It was, Charlotte thought, as if the pool were reflecting something from somewhere else, a mirror of deeds she could only fleetingly glimpse. She had named it her "looking-glass pool", vaguely aware that the phrase was old-fashioned. Today, in light of the book she had just finished, the name seemed particularly right.

She sat down in her special spot near a gnarled willow tree. Legs crossed and chin settled in her hands, she carefully watched the images flow before her, willing something to happen.

Eleven years of life on the farm had taught her patience, which was allied to an innate inner calm. It was none the less provoking how the most interesting variations in the images seemed always to be at any point other than the one she was staring at. Like the objects in the Sheep's shop where Alice had ended up buying an egg, everything was happening somewhere else.

She forced her eyes to change focus so that she was seeing things she was not directly looking at. This required effort and was at first painful; but she gradually found that her field of vision was becoming wider.

After five minutes she was forced to relax her gaze and wipe her eyes with her crimson sleeves before re-applying herself. This time, she found it easier to see, before the image again blurred.

Once again, she wiped her eyes.

"You're going to have to look more carefully than that," said a voice from near her feet.

* * *

Charlotte could see nothing that might explain the voice. She felt very calm.

"Who are you?"

"You can call me Fisker," the voice said. "That's close enough. What's your name?"

"Alice," Charlotte said.

"No it isn't."

"No, it isn't," she admitted, feeling foolish. "It's Charlotte. Can I see you?"

"That's up to you."

Charlotte continued to stare-without-looking, this time scanning the reeds by the edge of the pond. Then she thought she caught a twitch of whisker and, as she pulled her gaze away, a pair of white front feet.

"What are you?"

"You would call me a rabbit."

"What are you doing?"

"I'm just here, talking to you. What are *you* doing?"

Charlotte realised that this was a conversation that, like reading a difficult book, would require work.

"Rabbits can't talk," she said, deciding to start with something simple and see where that led.

"Not where you live, perhaps," Fisker said, "though one can never be certain of anything."

"So, you're from another world?"

"Well, yes and no. From what I've seen, there are many different parts of the same world. Or they could be different worlds – I prefer 'existences' – that are connected. It's hard to be sure."

Charlotte thought about this for a moment, her head still in her hands. She'd reached a point of static equilibrium where she could see Fisker reasonably clearly as long as he didn't move. This seemed to make the conversation moderately normal.

"And yet you're from…from somewhere else."

"Yes. Yes, I suppose we could agree on that."

"I just read this book," Charlotte said in a rush, "and it was about a looking-glass world where everything changed quickly and the girl couldn't tell what was going to happen next and had to…had to make everything work, make sense of it, somehow. In the end it was all a dream. But dreams aren't like that. Not *my* dreams. They go – oh, I don't know, crazy, and I often get frightened. I'm not frightened now. So does that mean this isn't a dream?"

"Perhaps it doesn't matter."

"So, is it magic?" Charlotte hadn't wanted to use the word but now it had come tumbling out; and, with it, many other questions that she couldn't arrange in her head. She wasn't frightened – no, *that* wasn't it; but she was, well…

"You have beaches here, don't you? Deserts? Imagine someone said there was one special grain of sand and you had one chance to find it or something terrible would happen. If you knew which grain you were looking for, and where it was, and were able to spot it, and you did – would *that* be magic?"

"No," Charlotte said slowly. "But it might *look* like it."

"Exactly. Most magic is just the result without the explanation."

Charlotte thought about this. "I can see you, sort of. People might say *that* was magic."

"They might. But it's just a question of looking and thinking. You can do that. Many can't."

There was a brief pause while Charlotte looked and thought.

"Charlotte," Fisker said in a different tone of voice, "I… that's to say we, need your help."

Adults – if that was what Fisker could be called – often "asked for help" which generally meant "do this". The rabbit's request was different.

"With what?"

"Sometimes things get into the wrong places," Fisker began carefully. "You, for example, could fall into my 'world', as you call it, just by stepping into the pool, if I let you. So…"

"You said 'things,'" she interrupted. "Do you mean animals?"

"They can be. In this case, yes. But they could be…there are other things that aren't. They're, well – I hope you never get to meet them."

"Like nightmare things? But real."

"You're perceptive." Charlotte made a mental note to look the word up when she got home. "But that's why you're here, why we're talking at all. In any case, this is an animal, or we're pretty sure it is. We don't have any like this here normally. It's creating havoc."

"How do things get in? And out?"

"There are edges, places where two different existences touch and slightly overlap. I'm on one now, as are you. But you can't just go in. You need to be let in by someone on the other side. A balance of forces, of wills."

Charlotte had just started doing algebra at school so kind of got this. "So, someone let this thing in? Why?"

"Curiosity, boredom. Malice, perhaps. Not many have the ability to spot the edges. And it came from your existence because of where it was first seen. Terrifying thing."

"Can't you…can't you kill bad things, animals that come in?"

Fisker seemed to be shaking his head. "It doesn't always work. When you're outside your existence, things work differently. It might make matters worse. There was something a long time ago which…" Fisker stopped himself.

"Where is this animal now?"

"In a box about two feet away from me," Fisker said. "It was caught and nearly took someone's paw off. Anyway, it's here – growling."

Charlotte realised she ought to be feeling frightened but she wasn't. "What do we do now?"

"Step into the water in front of where you're sitting. You won't get wet and you'll be able to breathe. Go right under. Everything will look different. I've not opened an edge from your side before so I don't know what it looks like. From here, they're like a closed oyster shell. You need to pull it open and reach inside."

These instructions were given in such a matter-of-fact way that she was into the water before Fisker had finished talking. As her head vanished beneath what would in normal circumstances have been the surface of the pond, his last few words were clearer but boomy, as if he were talking in a large cave.

She was bathed in a strange, shimmering light. For a moment, she could make out nothing except a kind of haze and, quite close and also a long way away, a still paler outline that might have been that of a large white rabbit.

The light bubbled and changed, much as the surface of the water did; one moment icy blue, then hundreds of shades of green like every leaf in a forest, then a kind of buttery yellow that reminded her of the autumn sun.

In front of her she saw what Fisker must have been referring to. It wasn't an oyster shell, although Charlotte wasn't sure what an oyster shell looked like. It was a small door.

Suddenly, everything seemed ridiculously easy.

She pulled it open and found herself looking at a forest, like and yet utterly unlike anything she'd seen before. There were colours, frightening in every way, quite unknown to her. She only had a second to cope with this before the doorway became filled with a tangled mass of orange fur and claws and teeth.

"Coming through!" Fisker shouted, his voice now clear.

She felt a scratch on her cheek and something soft pushing past her. And then she was back on the bank, quite dry but slightly breathless, with a very familiar animal rubbing itself against her bare legs.

"Are you all right?" Fisker said, now restored to his previous position half in and half out of the water, or whatever the pond comprised.

"Yes!" Charlotte said. "Oh, Fisker – it's a cat!"

"Is that what it is? Absolutely terrifying creature. Don't let it come back here, will you?"

Charlotte smiled and rubbed the ginger animal behind its ear. From seeming to be about the size of a large dog when it came through the edge it had now shrunk to normal size and was purring loudly.

She laughed. "I don't think it *wants* to come back."

"Good."

"Can I keep it, I wonder?"

"Why would you want to do that? You'd have to ask *it* about that, though. Not our problem any more."

"Can you talk, puss?" she asked. It carried on purring. "It doesn't *seem* to be able to talk," she said, slightly sadly.

"It may do yet," Fisker replied.

"What can I call it?"

"How about 'Cheshire'?" Fisker suggested. "If you want to keep it."

"Oh, I do. We had a cat on the farm but it went away. It was so good at killing all the mice in the barn and..."

"Well, quite," Fisker said in a hurt tone.

"Why Cheshire?" Charlotte said quickly.

"I think you've just read a book that, perhaps, helped you find me.

There's another one you should read. You might meet some people you know – Cheshires and…white rabbits, and so forth."

"How lovely," Charlotte said, now fully an eleven-year-old girl again and almost clapping her hands with glee.

Then a wave of something older washed over her: the knowledge that friendship and love is inevitably followed by separation and loss; that things change, wither and become in unexpected ways different and various; or fade away, like that moment with the boy and the bear at Galleons Lap…

"So, you read our books?"

"Or you read ours. Some things are universal."

"But not colours."

"You noticed that? No, they aren't. I find your world scary as well. That's why I've got these glasses on."

"Fisker!" she called. "Will I see you again?"

"Why not?" he replied. "I can be found in unlikely places, as can you. We just have to look."

The cat was now on its hind legs pawing at her thighs with delicately velveted claws. She picked it up.

"How did you know I was lying?" she asked. "When I told you my name, I mean."

"I can only tell you how *I* saw it: but you seemed to shift slightly. There was suddenly a shadow behind you, as if you were cut out from your background which, for a moment, you didn't fit."

Charlotte nodded, almost beside herself with a fulfilment and a purpose she had never dared to expect. She felt as if her heart would burst.

"Good-bye, Fisker," she said.

"Good-bye."

And that was that.

The light was fading as she made her way back to the farm. It didn't seem in the slightest bit odd that the cat was following her.

"Cheshire," she said as they reached the buildings. "In a moment you're going to have to meet my mother. I'm not sure what she'll think about you. So, if you can understand me, it would be a good idea if you found a mouse in the barn and brought it in. As a present. Dead, if you don't mind. I'll wait here."

Cheshire looked up at her and glided off. Two minutes later he was back, a plump mouse between his jaws, around whose mouth were several grains of wheat from their precious harvest.

"Good choice," Charlotte said.

"So you found him at the brook?" her mother asked in the kitchen five minutes later. Cheshire was working the room: pouncing at shadows, rubbing against any leg or outstretched hand that was offered and generally making himself agreeable.

"He's a good mouser." Charlotte said.

"Aye," her mother said; high praise from someone normally so sparing of it. "Has he a name? I assume 'he', being ginger."

"'Cheshire'," Charlotte replied.

"That so? You seem sure. Who told you of that?"

"A white rabbit," Charlotte replied

Her mother gave a dry smile. "Like in the book."

"Which book?"

"You know which book, my girl. Up in the top room."

Charlotte hardly dared breathe. From across the table, she could see Kate's eyes fixed on them. Her other sisters paid them no particular attention.

"You look like I didn't know. Why do you think they're there? For reading. For those to find who will, or" – and here she glanced at her other three children who, really, might have been in a different world from this conversation – "or not, as the case may be."

"I..." Charlotte started, before deciding to speak for Kate as well, "we thought you might mind."

"Don't be soft. Pushing them down your throat, that's what does harm. Let those see as can. Wonderful things to be found if you look." For the first time, her mother stopped fussing with saucepans and turned to give her a full look. "As I reckon you've learned."

She watched, and didn't watch, her mother from the corner of her eyes as she'd earlier done with Fisker. What she had said rang true. It also looked right: there was no shadow, no cut-out behind revealing a darker place of deception.

Later that night she wandered, restless, in her room. Cheshire, who had refused to be separated from her, was sprawled on the eiderdown, his purr almost making the bed shake.

She looked out of the window, seeing the white roses that grew around the frame illuminated in the last light of the day. She wished that they were red – oh yes, a deep, mysterious red: like and yet unlike the deep, mysterious, nameless colour she had glimpsed in the pond.

She sat down and set out the cards for patience, which often calmed her. Tonight, though, nothing could settle her emotions. Although these were heightened, they were not running out of control.

The episode had been a curious vindication of something she had long suspected: that magic, or mystery, or what you will, hovered in every unexpected place.

She turned over another card. Yet again, it was a heart, this time the knave. She studied his impassive, side-on face and its reversed reflection on the bottom half of the card; like and yet unlike. By looking and not looking, she could see some difference try to show itself. It wasn't lying, that much she could tell.

She shuffled the pack together and, on an impulse, turned over the top one. The knave of hearts again.

Yawning, she climbed into bed and opened the book she had found earlier, without seeming to be looking for it, in the top room.

'Alice was beginning to get very tired of sitting by her sister on the bank…'

She felt her own eyes close and she shut the book again. This was better read when there was no danger of mistaking it for a dream.

She reached for the bedside light, as she did so glancing down at Cheshire. He had elongated himself so that, from nose to tail, he appeared almost as long as her.

He stretched further and looked at her. Her last impression, as she pressed the switch, was of his head looming up unthreateningly towards her; the rest of his body fading into shimmering and ambiguous colours like those on the surface of the pond; and his mouth widening into a benevolent grin that almost split his ginger face from ear to ear.

The Application

I don't think Franz Kafka ever visited West Berkshire or, even less likely, fell foul of its planning system – but I suppose he might have done.

THE ROOM WAS long and, at the far end, faded into gloom. Others were taking their seats at benches and tables arranged in three sides of a rectangle. K had been told to sit on a stool at a small table on which there was nothing but a pen, an inkwell and a blank sheet of paper. The brightest light in the room pointed towards him so that every time he raised his eyes he was hit by the glare and had to squint.

The twenty or so people were engaged in muttered conversation, no word of which K could catch. The bench and table facing him were raised on a dais. Two people were seated but the middle space was empty. Far above him, an iron bell tolled the hour. As the last peal died away, the door at the far end swung open.

Everyone got to their feet and bowed to the newcomer. K, who had been given no guidance, was unsure if he should do likewise. He half stood up but found his legs had gone numb. He crashed down in his seat; then stood up, more successfully, just as everyone else was sitting down.

He wiped a bead of sweat from his face. The meeting had started and he still had no idea why he was there.

A letter had been delivered to his house the morning before. "You are summoned," it read, "to Room 102 at the Central Offices of the County of West-West at 5pm on 3 March." That was all. There was an official stamp and an illegible signature with "Chairman" printed below it. There was no reference number, no contact details.

For the rest of the day K had brooded over the letter. He had thought of showing it to the Doctor, the only person in the village with whom he felt much affinity, but something held him back. Few people regarded him with anything like favour. He wasn't even sure what the Doctor felt about him. Their social meetings to drink tea and play chess had recently become less and less frequent. Nor did K know what he would think of this letter which, in its single sentence, conveyed all the signs of official displeasure.

On the appointed day K arrived a good hour early. "Wait here," a guard had said, pointing to a small, dank courtyard. Eventually a woman in grey uniform had appeared and asked him to confirm his name. After doing so, he offered her the letter, which he had read, folded and re-folded many times.

"Why am I here?" he asked.

She made a dismissive gesture and motioned him to follow. Through several corridors they went, she striding, he trotting after her, still hopefully clutching the letter. She ushered him in to Room 102 and pointed to the chair. "For you," she said, then swished out.

The man for whom everyone had risen stuck a small gong with a hammer. "The committee is in session," the thin voice of the Clerk piped up. K noted this detail hungrily: so, this was a committee – but of what?

Peering through the gloom and glare, K noticed other details. In front of each person was a card on which was printed their positions, though not their names. The man with the gavel was the President. On his right was the Vice-President; on his left, the Clerk. He could also make out First Councillor, Senior Officer and Sergeant. This last confused him: was this a military committee, or was Sergeant ceremonial? He nodded to himself; rather stupidly, it must have appeared to anyone who had been observing him, as if he had gathered useful information.

There was more mumbling conversation which again K could not decipher. Then for the first time the President looked at him.

"Applicant K," his voice boomed down the room, "identify yourself."

K's brain froze. Must he produce a document proving that he was both K and Applicant K? He had no such document. Eventually he raised his hand.

"Mr President," K said, "can you tell me why I am here?" His voice seemed both faint and shrill, exactly the combination he had been seeking to avoid.

There was a stunned silence. The President produced a pair of spectacles. By a strange transference, K could see the man more clearly once he had perched these on his nose. He was thin and wiry with large ears and piercing eyes which were now focussed on a point just above K's right shoulder.

"Because you were summoned," the President's voice rapped out.

"Yes, but…"

"Silence!" the Sergeant barked.

The members turned to their papers. Every so often the Clerk would squeak a page or paragraph number and, as one, the members would turn to appropriate parts of the documents, each time sending up small clouds of dust. They would then confer, occasionally shooting glances towards K.

He considered again asking why his presence was required. He could not, however, think of any way of accomplishing this that would be more successful. Why should he risk compounding the error against the slender chance of learning anything to his advantage? Using the few facts he possessed, he was calculating probabilities of outcome, weighing one unknown against another; slipping, unwittingly, into the manners of the muttered conversations that were so inaudibly taking place before him.

Inaudibly: yet not quite: for, every now and again, a word or phrase caught his ear. "Policy 13"; "Condition B"; "retrospective". "Klamm" was also mentioned – a person, perhaps present and perhaps not – whom the others held in great esteem and probably fear. He craned his head eagerly forward like a dog.

This continued for about two hours. Shortly after the clock had again struck the hour the members put their files away, rose to their feet and bowed while the President left. Once again, K was slow off the mark. They all filed out after him, none of them giving him so much as a backward glance.

The side door through which K had entered opened and the same grey-clad woman appeared. She motioned for him to stand up and follow her. "Be here again at two o'clock tomorrow afternoon," she said over her shoulder.

"Yes, yes – but why?"

"Because that is the order of the President." She stopped and turned to face K. "It is his wish that you attend. Is that not reason enough?"

"Well, yes…but what is the issue for which I am required?"

"That is not my concern," she said as they moved off down the corridor. "You will be informed of everything you need to know at the appropriate time."

That evening K went to see the Lawyer. The Lawyer was not well known to him but they had had dealings a few years before over a matter concerning a hedge. As he knocked he realised he could not recall on which side the Lawyer had acted nor if he had been successful.

He knocked again. A light went on and the door opened. The Lawyer, who was drunk, had no idea who K was. K explained where they had last met. Realisation of sorts finally dawned. The Lawyer clapped him on the back, led him into his drawing room and poured him a glass of vodka.

"Of course," he said. "Goodness me – you're a good fellow, I'll say that. I well remember that business with the well last year – who was it? The Miller, that's right. We showed him, didn't we? It's good to see you, I must say. Sit down, my friend, sit down. What was the man's name? No matter. Well – here we are! Goodness me!"

He prattled on in this vein for some time, beyond the point where K could say the Lawyer had him confused with someone else. More vodka was poured. K, who was of an abstemious turn, felt it wise not to protest. Eventually he diverted the conversation to the matter on his mind.

"Goodness me," the Lawyer said as K offered him the letter, groping for his spectacles. "Room 102, eh? Well, it could be worse." This was the first remotely good news K had received. The Lawyer reached for his cigars, offered one to K (which K politely refused), lit it and briefly vanished behind a cloud of smoke.

"102? Goodness me, let me think...that's the one normally used for...planning I think – let's go through the others – 106 is legal, 105 finance, 104 is...Klamm's chamber – well, you won't be dealing with *him*, I hope. Room 100 – yes, 100 is political. 101 – well, the less said about *that*...102 – planning, that's it! Sure of it. 102. There you are." He took another draw on his cigar and another gulp of vodka and sat back in his chair, beaming at K like a small, fat child.

"Planning?" K asked, bemused.

"Yes! You're building something, yes? Applied for permission – actual, implied, potential, retrospective, it doesn't say, but..."

"I heard the word "retrospective" mentioned."

"Well," the lawyer said, tossing the letter down on the table, "That's the nub of it. They're considering your retrospective application." He poured more vodka. "There you are." And he patted K on the shoulder.

"But I haven't applied to build anything," K said. "Retrospective or otherwise. And no one has told me anything."

There was a silence during which the Lawyer looked first at K, then at the letter. "Well," he said at last in a less animated tone, "if that's the way of it..." He drained his vodka and shambled to his feet "It's getting late, old fellow. Look – wonderful to see you, but...well, I have a client tomorrow, early. Goodness me, is that the time?' he added, though there was no clock in the room. "Anyway..." he made to pat K on the shoulder, as he had done many times, but withdrew his hand. "Good to see you." he manoeuvred K out of the room and to the front door. "So..."

At this point, words completely failed him. He gave K a ghastly smile and a strange salute that could have meant almost anything. Then, with as much politeness as his changed manner permitted, he shut the door in K's face.

"Goodness me," K said to himself as he walked down the drive in the twilight. He was both encouraged and alarmed by the interview. On the one hand, he had learned something about the reason for his summons but he was also now aware his situation was equivocal. The Lawyer's change of attitude – K allowed himself a small laugh at that. The man was clearly out of his depth and unwilling to offer an opinion on what was clearly a misunderstanding.

He felt heartened for a while: until the suspicion grew that such a misunderstanding would surely be a matter any lawyer could easily explain. He had seemed...K refused to accept the idea but it floated around the edge of his thoughts – he had seemed *frightened*. But why? Clearly the committee had K mixed up with someone else. He had made no application. His house, his only house, had stood where it stood for over two hundred years. Well – there you are! A misunderstanding. K would explain it tomorrow and that would be that.

The following day K arrived full of hope and was again ushered into his seat. A plan had been placed on the President's table. From what he could make out, the drawing seemed familiar.

During a pause, he put up his hand. "Mr President," he said in a stronger tone of voice than he had managed the day before. The faces looked up and regarded him coldly. "Mr President, I would like to have the reason for my attendance clarified. I believe there has been a misunderstanding."

K immediately realised he played a poor hand: for if he had no idea why he was there, how could he also think it was because of a misunderstanding? The President seemed to see these thoughts. He put his glasses on and appeared to be about to say one thing: then changed his mind and took them off again.

"Applicant K," he said. K instinctively stood up. "The matter on which you have been summoned, concerning which you seem to be both ignorant and curious..." – he paused as if expecting sycophantic titters from the benches on either side of his, which were supplied – "concerns an Application to Renew, reference 19/996554/HAU, on the site of the building known as Kafkar Herrenhaus in the village of T–."

"That is my house," K replied. "But I have made no Application."

"Yet we have it here." The President held a bundle of papers and treated K to a mirthless smile.

"May I see it?"

"The assumption is you are familiar with it. The court cannot waste time re-visiting such matters."

"The court? I thought it was a committee."

"A committee with judicial powers to consider the Application."

"I have already respectfully told the…the court I have made no such Application and that it was unknown to me until a few moments ago that an Application had been made."

"That is not our concern."

"By whom was this Application made?"

"Irrelevant," the thin voice of the Clerk cut in.

"May I see the Application?"

"Permission denied," the Clerk said.

"Be seated," the President said. K subsided into his chair.

Over the next hour he was occasionally asked questions – "who is your agent?"; "what are the internal dimensions of the proposed extended living area?"; "how can Policies 13 and 43 be consistent with Condition J?", none of which K could answer.

Shortly after five o'clock, the President put down his pen and pushed the papers away with the air of a man who had finished a satisfying meal. "The Accused will stand."

K was thunderstruck. Who was the Accused?

"K, the Accused – stand," the Clerk piped.

K shambled to his feet.

"The Application, being retrospective, involves the question of whether permission be granted for works which have already taken place," the president intoned. "Application 19/996554/HAU, on the site of the building known as Kafkar Herrenhaus in the village of T–, involves the construction of a three-storey house of one hundred and eleven square yards with five bedrooms…etcetera. The details are in the file. The question is this."

For the first time, he gave K a glance which suggested a relationship that was, if not one of equality, then at least admitting of the possibility that, through discussion, some way could be found out of the difficulty which the wisdom of the court had exposed. K momentarily relaxed: then recalled that he was no longer the Applicant, but the Accused.

"The question concerns the oast house," the President continued. "This is the aspect of the proposal which causes the court the most concern. If this were demolished, well…" he made a gesture with his hand that suggested compromise; even hope. "You must demolish this structure. Then – well…"

"Mr President, gentlemen of the court – there is no oast house," K said.

"Yet the Application clearly states this has been constructed," the First Councillor said.

"In which case the Application, which I have neither made nor been allowed to see, must be wrong," K said.

"Are you saying that the court is wrong?" the Second Councillor asked.

"No, no," K stammered, "but…"

"In that case," the First Councillor interrupted, "you concede the court is correct."

"I am saying," K retorted, "the court is proceeding correctly but…"

"Good," the President put in. "In which case, do you agree that the oast house will be demolished? It is on this matter, I assure you, that the entire issue turns."

"It is, sir, impossible to demolish something that does not exist."

"You do not need to accept the matter as being *possible*," the President replied. "You only have to accept it as being *necessary*."

K thought quickly. "I could build an oast house, then demolish it. Would that satisfy the court?"

"Build it without permission?" the Senior Officer asked. "Out of the question."

"But the court asserts that one *already* exists without permission," K said. "If the issue is one of demolition, this would address it."

The President tapped his finger on the table. "But that would leave the question of the *original* oast house. You may build and demolish as many oast houses as you choose but this problem remains. Due process is not to be cheated. For the final time, are you prepared to demolish the oast house?"

"As I have explained," K replied, "that is not possible."

"Noted, "the Clerk squeaked. "The court will now deliver its verdict." The members leaned forwards into a huddle.

A sense of dread overtook K at the traps into which he had been lured.

The huddle separated. "The decision of the court will be suspended until tomorrow at 10 o'clock," the President announced. "The court will rise." The same bowing was repeated and within a minute K was left alone in the room.

Perhaps because the meeting had finished earlier than usual, the grey-suited woman was not there to usher him out. K went out of the door and, instead of turning left to the exit, looked to the right. There was a row of doors with numbers on them. The first on the right about twenty yards further down was, K presumed, the main entrance to the room in which he had spent much of the last two days. The Lawyer had been right, for it bore the number 102. Other similar doors stretched away from him until they became lost in the corridor's unlit gloom.

K's heart leaped. One of them was Klamm's! What was the number the Lawyer had said? 104, that was it. Klamm – of course! He was by all account a man of power; a great man. Surely he could intercede? At the very least K could put his case and know that he could have done no more.

He hurried down the corridor and saw that 104 was at the end. In front of it sat a man wrapped in a fur coat. K wondered if he too might be a supplicant but, as he got closer, he sensed in the man a proprietorial air, albeit one of little power.

K tried to adopt his most assertive tone. "Well," he said, "This Mr Klamm's room? 104 – yes, I think so."

The man nodded slowly.

"Well, my man," K went on, rubbing his hands in what he hoped was a masterful way, "Is he in?"

"He may be."

"Surely you know?"

"It is not a question of whether I know, nor of whether he is in. I am the Doorkeeper."

"Are you here even when Mr Klamm is not in?"

"I am always here."

"If I wanted to see Mr Klamm, is this where I must wait?"

"Yes."

"But you do not know if he is in nor, if he is, when he will come out?"

"I am the Doorkeeper," the man replied with simple dignity. "You see, I am not without power. No one may enter without my leave."

"I shall wait a while. My time is precious, but..."

The Doorkeeper gave a shrug neither dismissive nor encouraging: he simply shrugged.

"Is there such a thing as a seat, eh? A chair, something like that?"

The Doorkeeper pointed and K saw a stool against the opposite wall. He moved it nearer the door and sat down. "Well, here we are. How long do you think I'll have to wait, eh?"

The Doorkeeper gave another shrug.

For a while, K tried to keep up a conversation but the Doorkeeper would not be drawn. As the evening set in, K found his chin slumping down to his chest and he fell into a fitful doze. He was awakened, by what he knew not, perhaps several hours later. The Doorkeeper was in the same position.

"Goodness, I fell asleep," K said unnecessarily. "How much longer, eh? It's getting late, I think." The Doorkeeper offered no opinion. A couple of minutes later, the iron bell started to chime. "Nine o'clock already," K said as the last peal faded away. There was a silence.

K felt imprisoned by the Doorkeeper's self-absorption. "Look here," he said, fumbling in his pockets. "I'm a busy man. I can't wait here all night for this gentleman Klamm. Now – you seem a good fellow. Here's some gold – see!"

He held four coins in his hand. He turned them so they glinted in the light of the dull lamp above the doorway. "I need to see Klamm, just for two minutes. Everything can be explained in two minutes. Or I can write him a note, a quick note, if he's not there. You see? All I need is for you to let me in. Then I'll be out of your way, and you can do..." K's words tailed off. So that the Doorkeeper could do what? There seemed to be nothing that K's presence was preventing him from doing.

The Doorkeeper took the coins. "I'll accept these, but only so you feel there was nothing that you failed to do," he said.

"So you will not let me in, after I've paid!"

"I did not ask for payment. All I can say is that, if you are to enter, it will be by this door."

K pondered the remark. "Is there another door?"

"Yes."

"Which Mr Klamm uses?"

"Yes."

"You did not tell me that!"

"You did not ask."

Tiring of this sophistry and annoyed, yet again, by his misjudgements, K stalked away and eventually emerged into the dark courtyard. He turned up the collar of his coat and started to walk home.

The following morning on his way back to town, K saw the Priest in the village square talking to a farmer. Although he had never cared for the Priest – moreover, only a few months before they had had an argument about a point of doctrine – K raised his arm in greeting. Both men turned away as if they had not seen him. K went on his way disquieted, thinking of the Lawyer's abrupt change of mood two days before.

At ten o'clock, K was back in Room 102. After the usual preliminaries, The Sergeant, a florid man with epaulettes and crimson trousers who had so far taken no part in the proceedings, stepped forward. "Prisoner K," he said in a loud voice, "be upstanding."

K shuffled to his feet. He was Prisoner now; Applicant, or Accused, no longer.

"The judgement of this court," the Sergeant continued, "is that retrospective application reference 19/996554/HAU, on the site of the building known as the Kafkar Herrenhaus in the village of T– be refused. Moreover, because of the prisoner's wilful refusal to demolish an illegal structure, the entirety of the aforesaid dwelling and outbuildings are to be demolished and all contents removed and sold as chattels of state and church. This process will begin immediately. The Prisoner is to be remanded until this is completed. Leave for appeal is not granted."

For a moment K was unable to formulate his thoughts. All he possessed, as well as his unfinished life's work, were in Herrenhaus Kafcar. It was all he had ever known.

"But I made no application!" he shouted. "What have I done wrong? There is no truth! This is..."

"Silence!" the Sergeant shouted.

The President struck the bell. "The meeting is concluded," he said. "Lead the prisoner away."

The Sergeant and Under-Sergeant moved towards K and grabbed him roughly, one at each arm.

"This is an outrage! I shall talk to Klamm – yes, the great Klamm! I have paid for my audience. Klamm will know justice. I demand to see Klamm!"

The participants, who had been in the act of leaving, paused and turned to face him. Even the Sergeants loosened their grip. K thought this to be a turning point in his case. Foolishly, he began to grin.

Wrapping his robes around him, the President walked slowly down until he stood a few feet from K. He smiled thinly, showing yellowing teeth, and shook his head. "You fool," he said. "Have you understood nothing? The court does not search for truth nor provide justice: it follows process and delivers verdicts. As for Klamm, what do you know of him, mm? What?"

"Klamm is a great man. I will ask him..."

"Ask, then. Ask now. I am Klamm."

At that point, K felt his legs crumple.

Six days later, K was released. His steps traced their way back to the village. On the way, he met peasants going to work in the fields, men he knew of old. Everyone turned their faces from him. Finally he reached his home.

Not a brick remained. The stable, the two outhouses, the greenhouse – and, of course, the glorious house – were gone: not so much flattened or razed but carefully removed so even the ground seemed untouched. Amidst his shock and sorrow, he could only remark on how total the work had been. He and his entire life had been excised from the world as if it had never been. His eyes blinking, he was forced to confront, and then almost admire, the majesty of the process which had accomplished this. His thoughts were otherwise turned to stone.

A rough fence, which he did not dare cross, had been thrown around the property. At the far side, he could see the Priest supervising the loading of some final items onto a cart. He turned to face K and, unlike the day before, allowed his glance to lock briefly onto K's: long enough for K to understand from whence his doom had come. The Priest turned away, got in beside the driver and they vanished down the track. K was left alone to survey the lone and level land.

After a while – it may have been two minutes or half an hour – K bestirred himself. He needed to go. Where? He had no idea. "Well," he said out loud, "that's that. Goodness me. What now? Well…"

His eyes filled with tears: not so much for his loss but for the process of which he was ignorant and which had defeated him in such an implacable way. It was not the sorrow so much as the shame that now crippled his soul: and so he turned hopelessly from this reminder of his failure, blinking and trembling as if this shame would long outlive him.

British Democracy in Action

I'M NOT MUCH of a political animal. Sure, I take an interest in what our rulers are up to. I even find myself writing about it all. General elections get me hooked, in much the same way that do World Cups. However, I've never belonged to a party not got involved in activism: not for me, the cut-and-thrust of the committee room, the whispered conversations in corridors or the feverish plotting. This last activity appears to be the main requirement of political activism and probably the one that yields the most tangible results.

Above all, it's the factions that got me. Back in the 80s, several of us used to frequent a pub in Brixton Road which was the favoured haunt of a number of left-wing groups. My friends Patrick, Paul and Mark, all of them journalists, used to play 'spot the leftie' there. This involved eavesdropping on a conversation at a neighbouring table, guessing which group they belonged to and then putting it to the test by asking them. To me it was a blur. I liked the beer and my friends but I couldn't keep up with the conversation. I'd have been much happier talking about football or how to write the perfect middle-eight for a song.

On one occasion, at the height of a particularly savage period of the Troubles in Northern Ireland, the conclusion of one round of spot the leftie resulted in the leader of the challenged group – almost inevitably, a middle-aged man with a beard – saying they were from Troops Out. Patrick, Paul and Mark nodded sagely. Perhaps because I wasn't nodding, the leader fixed me with a searchlight gaze. I felt that I should say something but the phrase meant nothing to me. "Troops out of where?" I asked dumbly.

I did, however, experience at first-hand one of the major political moments of that turbulent and very political decade. This was the Bermondsey by-election, held on the 24th of February 1983. Many folk of my generation would need no reminding about this event. As democratic processes go it was a spectacular and vitriolic spectacle. I think that this, more than anything else, put me off organised politics for life. Politicians whimper now about the 'loss of faith' in our political process. My own dates back to this election, which took place before many of them were born.

To anyone who wasn't around in the 1980s, it's hard to over-stress how polarised life was. Thatcher v Foot and the government v the unions were the main acts but there were plenty of side-shows. One of these was being waged within the Labour Party itself which was deeply split between pragmatic opportunists and a hard-left faction who believed that life's inequalities could only be remedied by dogmatic government intervention on a colossal scale.

Michael Foot, the Labour leader at the time. was a man of genuine intellectual and personal accomplishments. In 1983, however, with the Falklands war recently won, he was completely out of his depth when trying to combat Thatcher. The hard-left versus hard-right division between the leaders meant that the two main parties were probably further apart than they had ever been before: or, for that matter, since.

The by-election was triggered when the incumbent, Bob Mellish, who had been elected with a huge majority in 1979 – staggeringly, his eleventh consecutive victory, the first being in 1946 – professed himself disenchanted with Labour's lurch to the left. He jumped ship to take up a lucrative post with the London Docklands Development Corporation, which was about to transform many parts of east London, including that part, into something utterly unrecognisable to its long-time inhabitants. The grotesque political pantomime that followed was amply to justify all Mellish's fears about the troubles in his party.

In Bermondsey, Labour's leftwards drift was demonstrated by its choice of candidate. Peter Tatchell was radical, young, Australian and gay, any one of which would have made him unelectable in most seats (including, as events were to prove, this one). This defect was obvious even to Labour's leadership which tried to block his nomination.

The local party paid no attention to this and selected him. One of Mellish's cronies, John O'Grady, was persuaded to stand as the 'real Bermondsey Labour' candidate. The split in the Labour Party was made public for the first time: a nasty, visceral, tribal division which went to the heart of our national life and which has not been healed to this day.

Two 'Labour' candidates would have been confusing enough. In fact there were to be four, with an Independent Labour and a National Labour Party, whatever they were, also deciding to stand. There would have been five but the fifth one got into a muddle with his nomination form and wrote his occupation in the box that was meant for his party. As a result, in addition to the other uncertainties the ballot paper posed there was a candidate standing under the surreal banner of 'Systems Analyst'. If any of these people weren't left-wing enough, there was also a Communist and – cranking the dial up still further – a Revolutionary Communist.

I don't want to give the impression this was all dominated by the left: far from it. The National Front was out in force in every sense of the phrase. So too was New Britain, whose candidate was a self-professed racist, fundamentalist Christian and supporter of capital punishment for a wide range of offences. New Britain had a few years before merged with the United Country Party which had been run by the astronomer Patrick Moore. You might want to bear that in mind the next time you watch a re-run of *The Sky at Night* (if such things exist).

Oddest of all, though, was the Independent Patriot Lady Birdwood, a woman whose views on class, race and sexuality made the other right-wingers seem positively mainstream. Deluded to the point of incoherence and notable mainly for a collection of spectacles that Elton John would have envied, she had left first the Conservative Party and later the National Front because she felt each had become too working class. She was involved in some of Mary Whitehouse's famous blasphemy actions. She was a member of many virulent anti-communist groups, 'communist' in her case probably covering anyone under sixty who didn't have their own pack of foxhounds.

Most extraordinarily, she devoted much energy over several years in attempting to persuade the government to enforce King Edward I's Edict of Expulsion of the Jews of 1290 which, she claimed, had never been repealed. During the campaign she accused the National Front candidate of being a socialist, a slur which must have confused him as much as it did all the voters. What she was hoping to accomplish in a constituency like Bermondsey can only be guessed at.

We're not finished yet, not by a long chalk. Way ahead of his time in some ways was a man standing under the banner of Anti-Common Market and Free Trade: one can't help thinking that the 15 votes he polled (which, amazingly, didn't put him in last place) would have been increased were he to have been around in 2016. There was a candidate for the Ecology Party, which I think later morphed into the Greens. Of course, this being the '80s, we had Screaming Lord Sutch in all his top-hatted and self-serving wackiness. There was also a United Democratic Party Candidate, the UDP being some sad and confusing offshoot of the Conservatives.

Oh, I almost forgot: there was a Conservative candidate as well, Robert Hughes, who survived this debacle and rose to become a government whip before being forced to resign after an affair with a constituency worker.

Finally there was the Liberal candidate, Simon Hughes (no relation), another man who later became embroiled in a sexual controversy to the detriment of his career. (No Lib Dems in those days: that change, involving a merger with the breakaway SDP, was to be another result of Labour's troubles).

This, then, was the galaxy of political talent, the carnival of rage, hypocrisy and ambition, that was laid out for our choice and consumption. The candidates spanned the entire British political spectrum, indeed went some way beyond it at both ends. There were sixteen of them, which was then a record.

It would have been seventeen but for the fact that the Democratic Monarchist, White Resident and Road Safety candidate Lieutenant

Commander Bill Boaks (a man whose achievements included having roller-skated from London to Paris) was unable to participate after being knocked down by a taxi shortly before the nominations closed. Like so many aspects of this by-election, truth was a good deal stranger than fiction and often just as difficult to believe.

The main actor in the drama was, of course, Peter Tatchell, whose campaign was principled but ineffective (a common combination) and not helped by a barrage of abuse from every quarter. Indeed, he was the one unifying factor in a particularly divisive battle. All the other candidates loathed him, or professed to, and strove to outdo each other in the way they put this loathing into words.

There were then few laws against hate crime. Were there to have been, it's unlikely many of the other candidates would have been at liberty come polling day. He claimed to have been assaulted over 150 times in those few weeks and was threatened with death so often that he slept with a fire extinguisher, a stick and a carving knife by his bed.

Whatever one thinks of his views, no one could deny that he displayed considerable courage and determination (and continues to do so to this day). Indeed, he later said that it was this "baptism of hell" which made him determined to continue the campaigning which has become his life's work.

His homosexuality was then a particularly easy target. Even Simon Hughes – who much later came out as bisexual – was happy to cash in. An anonymous leaflet featured a picture of Elizabeth II alongside one of Tatchell and asked "which Queen will you vote for?" It also helpfully printed his address. It was wrongly claimed that he'd taken time off from the campaign to attend a gay Olympics in Sydney. O'Grady mysteriously accused him of "wearing his trousers back to front." One national newspaper offered £3,000 to anyone who could produce a sex-scandal story about him. Another re-touched a photo to make him look like a drag queen. The gay-loony-left card was played for all it was worth.

Vilified by the press and crucified by the other candidates, Tatchell was also unable to make a sufficient connection with the so-called traditional Labour voters. These would, he believed, flock to him because of the causes he espoused, which he felt to be self-evidently just and true.

Mellish had been a very different kind of politician; a hard-nosed local from a family of dockers who had distinguished himself in the war and become a tough and effective whip and minister under Harold Wilson. A militant young antipodean encouraging mass civil disobedience and promoting gay rights was hardly a like-for-like replacement.

For decades, the population had voted for Mellish. Now everything had changed. Yuppies were moving in. Unemployment was high. Immigration was causing concern. The docks had died and something unimaginable was about to replace them, Militant Tendency, Labour's strongly left-leaning faction, had taken over the local party. Thatcher and Scargill cast their long shadows over the land. The world was slipping anchor. Who would look after the area in these shifting times? Not, the local public decided, Peter Tatchell.

The most telling criticism of his campaign came to me from a story I heard (by someone who claimed to have been there although nothing about that election can be taken as truth). There was a particularly deprived area of the constituency called, I think, the Sullivan Estate. When addressing a public meeting, Tatchell was, so the story goes, keen to stress his credentials. "I *live* on the Sullivan Estate," he told his audience, "so I can understand your problems."

"Bloody hell," one man at the back said to his friend. "If he can't get himself out of the Sullivan Estate, what's he going to be able to do for *us*?"

Meanwhile, the other candidates contributed their own hideous background noise. The result was a screeching six-week symphony of hate played in sixteen different keys.

As all of this was long before the internet and social media, the war of words was conducted through leaflets – hundreds and thousands of them. I could probably have wallpapered every room in my flat with the ones that came through the letterbox (though I only got as far as doing this in the toilet). One I had thrust into my hand in Lower Road by a National Front activist. I said "fuck off," or something similar: quite mild invective by the standards of the campaign. He snarled back at me. The occasion had made monsters of us all. I was pulled away by my friend before anything worse happened.

The campaign seemed to go on for months. When polling day finally arrived. Labour's support collapsed and Simon Hughes swept home with nearly fifty-eight percent of the votes (he retained the seat until 2010). Tatchell got just over twenty-six percent.

All the other candidates lost their deposits. The confused man who declared himself as standing for 'Systems Analysts' got eight votes. Ten other candidates failed to get into triple figures.

I don't know if it's a record that this constituency (allowing for various changes of names and boundaries) had only two MPs in sixty-six years. If it's not a record it's certainly pretty impressive. The voters of Bermondsey are nothing if not loyal.

One day during the height of the campaign, I got off the East London Line (as it was then called) at Surrey Docks station (ditto) and closed my copy of *Europe's Inner Demons* by Norman Cohn. This book had as one of its premises the fact that marginal groups in society, including the early Christians, gypsies and, in particular, the Jews, were demonised by being accused of a range of crimes almost too horrible to contemplate, cannibalism and infanticide being top of the list. I'd recently finished a medieval history degree and found myself, not for the first time, recoiling from the horrors that we inflicted on each other back then. Life today, in 1983, was surely better, I thought. At least we've moved on from *that* kind of nonsense.

The train pulled away. On the opposite platform, spray-painted in bright pink in letters two feet high across twenty yards of advertisements and notice boards, were the words "Peter Tatchell Eats Babies."

Demonising our enemies isn't going to go away. Most of the time there's a thin veneer of civility and respect in our debates but, all too often, the crust breaks. It broke during the Brexit campaign and its protracted aftermath. Sure as hell it broke in Bermondsey in '83. In a lot of countries it's the norm.

That moment at the tube station taught me a valuable lesson: to hurt your enemy you have to hit low, hit hard and hit often. Politics is meant to be an elegant, though ruthless, alternative to violence, in the way that, in the middle ages, tournaments were an elegant substitute for war. Introduce someone from outside the pack, however, and all bets are off.

We pretend to be civilised but we're really only tribal animals with a thesaurus. Sometimes it shows all too clearly. Move on? We should be so lucky.

I would like to dedicate this reminiscence to my dear and late friend Patrick Fitzgerald who spent some time with me in the Bermondsey bear pit and whose wisdom and advice I still miss.

Lucky

I HAVE ABOUT sixty percent vision in my left eye. It should be zero percent. That it isn't is due to three amazing slices of good fortune, each a million-to-one shot that shouldn't have come off and yet did.

The story really started on an icy December morning in France in 1966 when, aged seven, I was thrown through the windscreen of a car. The accident ripped a dramatic two-inch gash just under my right eye and – more importantly as things were to prove – gave me an almighty whack just above my left one.

For practical purposes, the story starts in the early summer of 1986, back in the Thatcher days – she comes into this story too – when I was kicked hard on the left side of my head while playing football. It hurt but I thought nothing of it at the time. Three days later, however, I was forced to think about it again when, in the middle of a meeting at my office, my left retina detached itself.

For those of you who have worried about a retinal detachment I can give the reassuring news that it's completely painless. The visual effect, however, is extraordinary. It was as if I were suddenly viewing everything on that side of my head underwater and through a stained-glass window.

After a while, my brain refused to process these alarming and confusing signals. Perhaps to compensate, my right eye briefly became super-sensitive. I saw flashes of light and strange explosions of colour every time someone moved, as if this side of my head was caught up in an electrical storm.

By common consent the meeting was abandoned.

That evening I was having a drink with my friend Chris. With the insouciance of youth, I saw no reason to cancel. He's the kind of person who, if you describe to him a problem with a car, a cat or a computer will say, "ah, that's a..." and normally be right. He was this time. He drew a rough approximation of a dart board on a beer mat and asked me, using only my left eye, to shade what seemed odd. I did so. "You've detached your retina," he concluded. Feeling slightly self-important at this news, I ordered another round.

The next morning found me less chirpy. I went into work as usual mainly because an optician I'd used before was just down the road.

"I've detached my retina," I announced.

He gave me an 'I'll be the judge of that' glance and sat me down. After an examination he produced a sheet of A4 paper on which was printed a circle with a right-angled grid of lines, a rather neater but no more functional version of Chris' dart-board beer-mat.

"Shut your good eye," he commanded, giving me a pencil, "and shade in the bits of the paper where the lines are fuzzy or not straight. Do it as carefully as you can." I did this. Nearly half the circle was shaded. He then wrote a brief note which he stapled to the diagram. He put both in an envelope, sealed it and gave it to me.

"You're lucky," he said. Oh yeah? I thought. "Moorfields Eye Hospital is about three hundred yards up the road. You know it?" I did. "Walk slowly and carefully and give this to the reception in the Casualty Department." This was an alarming sentence to process at 9.15 in the morning. For the first time I realised there was something seriously wrong with me.

The Casualty Department was filled with people in a lot more distress than I was. I remember a builder with blood streaming down his face and a woman rocking back and forth with a tissue over her eye and occasionally screaming. An hour ticked by.

Pain-free though I was, my own reflections were becoming increasingly gloomy. I saw a call box and decided to share the misery.

I was between relationships at the time and the first two calls were to my ex-girlfriend and the person who, for want of a better phrase, I'd had my eye on for a while. Were I to have been able to look at her with two eyes I might have spotted what a fireworks display in a box she was going to prove to be: but that's another story. My ex was sympathetic, the new lady rather less so but this might have been because she felt that this was a demand for attention; which it was. I went back to my seat. Finally my name was called out.

The doctor was about my age. Having looked at my eye, he became quite excited: not the reaction I was hoping for.

Without apology or explanation he picked up the phone and dialled. "Tom – it's Mike," he said. "Could you come to B12? I think I've got another one."

There was a brief silence in the room. From the next-door cubicle I heard a doctor say, "Well, that's it, I'm afraid. It's irreversible."

Tom turned up a few moments later. Neither gave my eye more than a glance. Instead they started measuring my fingers.

I was in mild shock and in the control of professionals. In those days one did not challenge what professionals told you. If they wanted to measure my fingers then that was the way it was.

After a few minutes I was shunted out of the room. I sat down next to a man, also of about my age and whom I faintly recognised, who was cupping and blinking his right eye in much the same way I was my left.

"I've detached my retina," he said.

"Me too."

"It's a fucker," he said. This was the most sensible remark I'd heard for some time.

Being kicked in the head was my first bit of good fortune, for reasons I shall later reveal; working near the world-famous Moorfields was the second. The third happened now. "Mr Bird will see you," the nurse said to me and led me into a rather grander room.

Mr Bird was a silver-haired, middle-aged man who precisely matched my idea of a senior consultant at a major hospital. He gave me a brief examination, glanced at my notes and made a quick decision.

"I need to operate as soon as possible," he said. "You're lucky – I've had some cancellations the day after tomorrow." He described what he was going to do.

It seemed to involve using a laser to burn the back of my eye and the back of the retina, the scar tissue then spot-welding the two back together.

I didn't then know how new this technique was but he spoke about it as if he'd been doing it for twenty years. It was certainly an improvement on the treatment given some time before to someone I knew: she'd had to lie motionless on her back in a darkened room for three months. He asked if I had any questions.

Emboldened by his confidence, I mentioned the two young doctors measuring my fingers. What had that all been about?

His expression darkened. Flecks of lightning – similar to what I'd seen during the meeting the day before – lit up his eyes. "Could you excuse me a moment," he said and reached for the telephone. He stabbed the numbers and waited, drumming his fingers on the desktop. I hardly dared breathe.

The call was answered. Mr Bird turned away but the fact that I could only catch half of what he was saying made the effect all the more impressive. He was using a tone of voice quite different from the one he'd employed with me. This was the terrifying headmaster speaking. "…I've *told* you on *numerous* occasions…if you *ever*…I don't *ever* want to hear…*never* work in *any* hospital again…the *last* warning…do I make myself *perfectly…*"

He slammed down the phone and swung round to face me. Even though I had not been the object of this onslaught I felt I'd been raked with machine-gun fire.

"I'm sorry about that," he said, his urbane manner now perfectly back in place. "These two young idiots have this theory that retinal detachment in someone as young as you is linked to a genetic problem. This tends to result in preternaturally long fingers."

We both glanced at my hands. "Anyone can see that doesn't apply. Your fingers are long but quite normal for your height." He paused for a moment. "I don't think they'll be doing *that* again."

The scene shifted to a two-bed ward where I found myself with

Steve, the young man I'd briefly spoken to in reception.

"We're gonna get cut on Thursday," he told me. There was pause. "I've met you, man."

"I think so too." We pondered this for a moment. Then, about ten members of his family turned up, briefly turning the tiny room into a huge Jamaican party. One had brought a boombox. The TV was turned on and up. Robust jokes were exchanged. I was included in all this through necessity.

Eventually a nurse came in to tell us to calm things down. Steve seemed glad to see them all go. "Feeling a bit knackered," he said, flicking the remote control. "Do you like football?"

I said I loved it.

"Hey, the World Cup starts today." We watched a bit of the opening ceremony. "We can watch it with one eye each."

"One more than the ref." Bulgaria v Italy kicked off.

When I'd come in I'd thrown my clothes over the chair next to the TV. Just before half-time, Steve sat up and pointed at them with trembling fingers. "The trousers!" he shouted.

This was just the latest in the series of strange and alarming things I'd heard that day. "What?"

"Top Man! 'bout two weeks ago!"

I now remembered: I'd been shopping in Oxford Street and had bought these strange checked trousers from a man I now realised was Steve. The pattern on the fabric looked a bit like the diagrams I'd been asked to shade in by Chris and the optician. All these events seemed to have happened half a lifetime ago.

"That's it!" I said. "It's been bugging me."

"Me too." Steve said. He examined them morosely. "It's them that fucked our retinas." Looking at them now, shimmering into my one-and-a-bit eyes, it was impossible to disagree.

The next two days were dominated by a series of examinations I prefer to forget. The main articles involved were a pair of devices on the doctor's thumb and index finger very similar to the clip-on finger picks

I occasionally used – but have never been able to use since – when playing guitar. The purpose, I was told, was to draw an accurate picture of the back of my eye for the lasers.

Finally I was shown the result. It seemed identical in every respect to the one I'd drawn for the optician.

My mother came to visit, at one point coinciding with Chris, who had read up about my condition and was able to supply her (though not me) with information of what was about to happen to me.

"He's a very clever man, your friend," she told me when we were alone, "but he's a bit frightening. He knows so much." I agreed with her.

The horrors were not yet over. While I was on the stretcher outside the theatre, a perky young nurse came up with a marker pen and drew a cross over my right eye.

"What the hell are you doing?" I asked.

She laughed. "I'm just marking which eye they have to take out."

"Take *out*?" She shrugged as if this were just some form of words. "But it's my *left* eye they're doing!"

"That's right."

"But you've put the mark over my *right* eye."

Her expression clouded. She held both hands up and half turned her shoulders, still looking at me, as if for the first time struck by the fact that things are reversed when seen at 180 degrees. She started rubbing the mark over my right eye. It didn't come off. She spat on a tissue and tried again. Then she drew another cross over my left eye. "There," she said. "*That* should be clear, I hope."

Another nurse appeared and rolled up my sleeve. "Just a small prick," she said. The needle went in. "Count to ten."

"But it's my left..." Then I fell backwards into the night.

The waking up was horrible in a different way.

As the nurse admitted, in an operation only one part of the body is of any interest and the rest is twisted into all kind of terrible shapes. I could hardly move my right arm: Steve could hardly breathe. Neither of us could turn our heads. His bed was on the left and mine on the right so for thirty-six hours we couldn't even look at each other. The World Cup was the salvation and, one-eyed, we watched two days of matches.

On the second day, Mr Bird visited us. "You've both done very well," he said. "No problems." He told Steve he should make a full recovery. He turned to me. "Did you have a serious head injury about twenty years ago?"

"Yes," I said after a moment's thought, "I was in a car accident when I was about seven."

He nodded. "That makes sense. Nearly half your retina had peeled off and died," he said. "The brain is, perhaps unfortunately, very clever at disguising symptoms of things like this if they happen gradually. In another twenty years you'd have been blind in that eye."

He paused to allow this to sink in.

"Did you receive another head injury recently?" I told him about the football game the week before.

"Best thing that could have happened to you," he said. He stood up and shook our hands. "Good luck to you both. Come back in a month for a check-up. You can go home now."

"You better burn those trousers," Steve said as we got dressed. "Big bad luck." I can't remember what I did with them but I never wore them again. I never saw him again either, which I've always regretted: there was, however briefly, so much that we'd had in common.

For the next month I had to apply eye drops of Atropine four times a day, which froze open my pupil to aid the healing.

For the first couple of weeks I kept on with the eye patch but after a while gave it up. The effect for an onlooker was alarming. The eye was about two thirds its normal size. The bit that should have been white was red, while the bit in the middle that should have been bluey-green was, because of the Atropine, jet black. In Earls Court where I lived this kind of weirdness passed without too much comment.

It did, however, spook one guy I was talking to at a party towards the end of the month. I noticed his gaze flicking from one of my eyes to the other in a rather excited way. I was half-way through a sentence when he held up his hand. "Sorry, gotta ask – what drug are you on?"

Had I not been making much sense?

"The eyes, man! One's blue, one's, like, *black* – it's spookin' me out..."

"Atropine."

"Wow."

Many years later, I went to have a routine inspection of my left eye at a clinic in Swindon with a doctor of about my age. Finally, he switched off his equipment. "All seems fine." He hesitated, as if about to embark on a confidence. "If I may ask, was this operation done in Moorfields by Mr Bird?"

I confessed that it was. Could it be possible that the silver-haired consultant had lasered his initials into my retina?

"I recognised his style," he said with pardonable smugness. "I studied under him."

I wondered if his name was Tom or Mike and if he had at one time been fascinated by finger lengths but said nothing.

"How come you ended up at Moorfields?" he asked. I told him. "Do you know how lucky you were?" I said I didn't, although admitted that the word kept cropping up.

"I'm not surprised." He sat down. "At that time there were only half a dozen hospitals in the world that could do this operation. Three were in the USSR, one in France, one in the USA. Moorfields was the other. Mr Bird was the the best of all of them anywhere. How come he operated on you?"

"He had a cancellation."

He shook his head. "Lucky, lucky you. He was about the only person who knew what he was doing. Same sort of time, Mrs Thatcher had a detached retina. She went into a fancy private clinic. They screwed it up. She went virtually blind in that eye."

My mind went back to my awful, but successful and free, experience and tried to contrast this with what Mrs T would have said when confronted with a hefty bill for 20-0 vision. I shuddered. Lucky, lucky me.

"All OK?" Penny said when I came out of the consulting room.

"It's all fine," I said. "I've been lucky. I'll tell you in the car."

So, Mr Bird, this is for you. And Steve, my fellow detachee and brief trouser-sharer. Wherever you both are, I wish all the very best things in life to both of you. As for Chris, you still know so much. I just hope you don't have to diagnose anything else for me. Even Tom and Mike I've forgiven – though I doubt Mr Bird ever did.

My Life on Team Cat

THERE ARE SEVERAL such arguments – The Beatles or Elvis, football or rugby, Mac or PC, EastEnders or Corrie. They're not exactly opposites but can sometimes seem so. It's possible to enjoy both of each pair but everyone would have their favourite and wouldn't have to think very hard if asked to name it. The "cats or dogs" debate is right up there with these. The UK has about twelve million of each, so this can't be settled just on the stats. I have my own views on this: as, I'm sure, do you.

There are, I admit, things in favour of dogs. They're loyal, obedient, useful and (with one exception) trainable. They can find dead birds and injured skiers, guide blind people across streets, apprehend criminals, round up sheep and guard houses. Once adopted by an owner, the bond is hard to break and in many cases you come between the two at your peril. They were the first animals to be domesticated and have put their senses, teeth and claws at the disposal of humans ever since.

All they want in return is a good long walk, two square meals a day and a kind word every now and then. Give them these and they're yours for life.

What do cats offer in this vein? Absolutely nothing. You can't train them. They don't do anything useful except catch mice, which they normally leave on the bedroom carpet. They treat any home like a free hotel, departing sometimes for days or weeks at a time. They adopt new residences for no apparent reason. They spend much of the time asleep. They won't scare off intruders, fetch balls or do tricks to order. If you're looking for something that's going to add value to your household, you can cross cats right off your list.

A dog is like having a well-trained servant: a cat more like a permanent teenager. Fortunately, they are – unlike some teenagers – also supremely elegant and scrupulously clean.

On the debit side for dogs, they bite, bark and poo everywhere. Unless they've been groomed, they also often look like they've been sleeping in a ditch. Cats look as if they're about to go on stage at a major awards ceremony. And boy, do dogs stink. The only smell worse than a wet dog is a wet dog that's been rolling in its excrement. Why do they want to do this? Is leaving it in the middle of the lawn not enough?

For all their millennia of co-existence with us, no one has ever trained a dog not to poo wherever it happens to be at the time (often just outside our house). If you get a kitten, it will already have been toilet trained by its mum. She won't have taught it anything else: but this seems worth all of dogs' trainable advantages combined.

Cats also don't need supervision. We went to Australia for five weeks and asked friends to come in to feed the cats twice a day. We came back to find the house just as we had left it. Leave a dog in those circumstances and it would have eaten half the sofa before we'd checked in at Heathrow. We're dealing here with an animal so reliant on human company that, if deprived of it for even a few hours, it goes completely to pieces.

Neither relationship is equal, humans being the dominant partner with dogs and cats the dominant partner with humans. When she was a child, Penny had a sheepdog called Bella. One day she said "sit – stay" to the dog, went off to Newbury with her mum and came back several hours later to find Bella in exactly the same position.

Say that to a cat and, if you get any reaction at all, it will look at you with eyes as remote as planets, turn round and stalk out of the room. Short of physical confinement, there's no way a cat can be made to do, or refrain from doing, anything. Everything that happens is always exclusively on its terms. Rightly has it been said that dogs have owners but cats have staff; also that dogs suspect they're rubbish humans but cats know that humans are really rubbish cats.

Dogs are like the serfs, villeins and squires of the medieval world, fulfilling their allotted role generally without complaint. Cats, however, are the 'masterless men' who were then figures of alarm and terror – admitting no lord, recognising no bond of loyalty, wandering where they wished and generally threatening to undermine the fabric of a societal structure to which they are indifferent.

In their separate ways they are both really successful species, right up there with cockroaches and viruses. Unlike cows, sheep and pigs, they won't get slaughtered or pillaged for their milk or fleece. They're allowed the run of the house and get looked after when they're ill. They're not confined to cages, pens or tanks. Dogs, however, have to work for their corn. Cats don't.

Unique amongst any species I'm aware of, they have found the way of convincing us that we are getting pleasure from something that gives them far more. This is done by the purr, the noise developed for no purpose apart from interacting with humans. Wild cats don't do it. It's all they give back when being stroked to an almost orgasmic pitch of excitement. So rarely do some cats dish this out that it becomes all the more precious when it happens. In the art of playing hard to get, the cat has no peer.

You've also got to pay some mind to aesthetics if you're going to have such creatures in your house. Nobody looking at a dachshund, a pug or a Yorkshire terrier could claim that an evolutionary apex had been reached. The proportions between a dachshund's length and legs are wrong, end of. (Some friends of my parents had one so long that when they took it for walks they had to strap a pair of wheels round its midriff to stop its belly dragging along the Kensington pavements.) You look at some pugs out in public and it's not immediately certain that the owners have put the lead round the correct end. As for Yorkshire terriers, more of them in a moment.

Dogs have allowed themselves to be moulded into all manner of perverse shapes for god-knows-what human enjoyment. Some of them can barely walk, breathe or stand upright in a moderate wind. The old trope about dogs being like their owners is only possible because there are so many kinds of dog. In fact, the term "dog" is a bit useless. It encompasses everything from an animal that could fit in a jacket pocket to one with the proportions and temperament of a medium-sized bear.

The other thing about dogs is that they have absolutely no style. Have you ever seen a dog trying to climb a tree? Pathetic doesn't come close. They are what their breeders or owners have decreed that they become, on various scales ranging from tangled fur ball to crazed sprinter, from nice-but-dim to totally empathetic or from coweringly abject to tear-your-throat-out. In all cases they are also the product of how effective their owners are. A cat is just a cat. It's that simple and there's nothing you can do about it.

If cat owners resembled their cats, we'd all look like Viv Richards or Audrey Hepburn. When you say "cat", that's what you get. With a few minor variations, there's little to choose between any domestic breed and, aside from size, between them and their distant wild cousins. As with sharks, you're looking at something absolutely perfectly built for what it's designed to do. No improvement is possible.

Owning a cat is like owning a Ferrari: owning a dog is like having something that's part tricycle, part tank, part motor bike and part two-stroke lawnmower. If you don't like it, however, it doesn't matter – as long as you have a couple of grand to drop there'll be another model available soon, perfectly tailored for your unique lifestyle.

I think my own inclination in the matter is pretty clear by now. Let me close by giving you my earliest formative experience of dog-handling. Then, perhaps, you'll understand.

For many of my pre-teen years, summer holidays were spent in my uncle and aunt's farm in a tiny village called Spreyton in Devon. I was a timid, solitary and bookish child, none of which characteristics endeared me to my frightening uncle George. I'm sure he was a lovely man but I rarely saw that side of him. George had a Yorkshire terrier called Rosie, on whom he doted.

I had never been brought up with dogs and gave Rosie a wide berth. I found George's fawning on her embarrassing and her teeth-bared acts of bravado whenever I was near her pathetic, alarming and inexplicable in roughly equal measure. Whenever George witnessed our not being matey, he doubtless suspected me of wanting to cause her harm. All she probably wanted was a stroke and a kind word from a stranger. Mind you, so did I.

My aunt Patsy, my father's sister, was an ethereally beautiful but slightly vague woman. One day she hit upon what must have seemed the perfect way of integrating her shy seven-year-old nephew more fully into the life of the household. She asked me to take Rosie in one hand and a bowl of food in the other across the courtyard to the converted stable, off which George had what was called his business room. How could I refuse?

Picking up Rosie was unsettling. Compared to the lithe, muscled cats I was used to this was like holding a bag of dried twigs. Very carefully, I crossed the yard and got to the door. With the dog wriggling in one hand and the bowl unsteadily grasped in the other, I was a hand short. I tried to improvise. The door finally swung open. There was a slight lip in the floor which I hadn't prepared for.

I was hoping to achieve this task without drawing attention to myself. The next few seconds put paid to *that*.

There were four noises, which followed each other at roughly one-second intervals. The first was Rosie falling from my grip and collapsing on the floor with a strange thud-crack-plop that I'd never heard before. The second was a brain-fusing shriek from her, way out proportion to her size. The third was the sharp crash as the bowl smashed on the flagstones.

The fourth, which rapidly replaced the other three in my attention, was of the side door being thrown open to reveal Uncle George. He roared at me, all his fears about my dog-malice now confirmed. Crunching the broken bowl and spilled dog food underfoot he bent down and clasped Rosie to his bosom.

To my even greater alarm, it appeared to me that whereas she had previously had four legs, she now only had three. Where had the other one gone? The roaring continued until Patsy appeared and scooped me away.

I was in disgrace for the rest of the holiday. Rosie's front leg had not, as I had feared, snapped off but had been dislocated. So tiny was the dog, my mother told me later, that a matchstick had been used as a splint. This cemented in my mind the fact that dogs were absurd. Some might need a matchstick for a dislocated limb, others a sturdy cricket stump. Either way, I wanted nothing to do with them.

Some years later, I witnessed my mother being pulled off a moped by an Alsatian (not a sentence you read every day). This was in France, where owners tended to keep guard dogs chained up. If the chain broke, they would go at anyone they saw like a torpedo.

I've had dealings with several dogs since. Many have bitten me, looked as if they were going to bite me, killed one of our chickens, defecated on our drive or tried to lick me. I find all of these more or less equally repulsive. It's true that I meet them in a spirit of armed neutrality and so don't give them an even chance.

Above all, I always feel uneasy when I'm in proximity to one. I'm not its master so all bets are off as to how it's going to behave. Potentially, I'm just an enemy. I'm certainly not a friend. The essential thing about cats is that they don't give a damn one way or the other.

Applying all this to myself, I reluctantly have to admit that I'm more of a dog than a cat. I'm loyal and fairly compliant and obedient. I understand the need for hierarchies and processes. I respond well to praise and am apt to cower if whacked with a rolled up newspaper. I have plenty of self-doubt and can, as long as I accept their logic, generally accept clear instructions.

The part of me that I most admire, however, is feline. I've never been part of a close pack, like many of my friends have been or are. I don't always accept received wisdom at face value. Above all, I enjoy and often relish my own company. Intensely solitary experiences like swimming, writing stories and composing and recording songs make me come alive in a way that most co-operative activities can never accomplish.

Then, I see myself as The Cat that Walked by Itself in Rudyard Kipling's *Just So* story: after having either rejected or perverted to its own ends the deals of co-habitation proposed by the clever woman, the clever man and the clever dog, the cat announces himself to be his own master, waving his wild, wild tail and walking by his wild lone.

Perhaps that's why I like to be surrounded by them. After all, I see the dog-like part of me every day in the mirror, when I'm doing the laundry or when I'm putting out the bins. The cat-like part is more elusive and precious and so needs role models. When the cats are out, doing whatever mysterious and generally crepuscular things cats do, they provide it by their absence. Then I often feel it's the time to vanish up to my room, pen or plectrum in hand, and swish my wild and lone tail as best I can.

The Year of the Vulture

THE FIRST MINI car came off the production line sixty-five years ago. A celebratory article on the BBC website included reminiscences from past owners. They didn't ask me for mine: but, uninvited, here they are.

My first dealings with Minis were not auspicious. Before I was seven I'd had my hand slammed in the door of one and been thrown through the windscreen of another. Undeterred, I acquired another when I was about twenty-three. It was already in late middle age, a dull green thing which seemed lower to the ground than it ought to have been and which looked, even when it was clean – which wasn't often – scrawny and unkept. It smelled of petrol and mould and sour milk. It became known as The Vulture; perhaps not the most optimistic of nicknames. Then again, I reasoned, I'd already had all the bad luck with the brand that I might reasonably expect. What could go wrong this time?

So many things went wrong that I hardly know where to start. Let's kick off with the one that would have had the highest death toll.

As I soon discovered, The Vulture often didn't start on cold mornings. The street I was living in was a cul-de-sac off Offord Road which ran downhill to the busy thoroughfare of Caledonian Road. I learned I could unpark it with muscle power and then bump start it down the hill. This rapidly became normal, thus removing danger and caution from an activity that was full of one and demanded the other.

The event that would, were I a few inches shorter, have been known as the Caledonian Road Disaster, took place on a bitter February morning. I did the usual back-and-forth number at the kerb and soon The Vulture was, as usual, trundling down the road in a straight line towards the junction. Then I realised there was something terribly wrong with the situation. Apologies if you've seen this coming: what was wrong was, of course, that I wasn't in the car.

It may help if I explained that directly opposite the turning into Offord Road was a bus stop thronged with people and, behind them, the plate-glass windows of the local Sainsburys. There seemed nothing that could stop the car from ploughing into both.

I ran after it. I'm no athlete but accomplished some sort of record. I managed to grab the door handle and, after being half dragged along for a few yards, opened it and threw myself in. Like a grizzled soldier in combat, habit kicked in. Before I knew it, I was bump-starting the car as if nothing had happened. The whole incident had lasted perhaps ten seconds. To me it seemed vastly longer and was replayed in my mind, in slow motion, countless times afterwards.

As I turned in to the Caledonian Road I discovered that the hand brake was still partly engaged, which explained why I'd been able to catch it. It was probably the only part of the car that worked properly.

You might think that a vehicle which didn't like the cold would offer compensation by coping well with high temperatures. Nothing could be further from the truth. It would overheat in almost any circumstance, most spectacularly when the dial went from blue to red in about thirty seconds while I was driving up York Road. Familiar with this problem I kept a large bottle of water in the car and got out to fill up the radiator. What I'd forgotten – in fact, didn't until that moment know – was that water in radiators is pressurised and so can be hotter than 100°C. When the pressure is reduced the water turns to super-heated steam and roars out of the opening. It was a month before all the skin on my arms had grown back.

The heater also didn't work, so in winter I had to wear gloves, an extra jumper and often another extra jumper.

The problem with the windscreen wipers probably dated from when the dashboard caught fire on the Shoreditch one-way system, the cause of which I was too cowardly to investigate properly. A car without reliable windscreen wipers is almost useless in England. The Vulture's unreliability spanned the full range: both working, only the right working, only the left working or neither working were all possible options.

The first two were the most common which, each time, led me into a fool's paradise that the thing had somehow fixed itself or – this even less likely – that my own fumbling attempts at repairing it had succeeded. Specialist help and replacement parts were needed but I wasn't very well off and anything spent on this car seemed like money down the drain.

One night I was driving back from a party with my flatmate Robbie, whom we'll meet again in a minute. The rain was torrential. About half way down Regent's Park Road the wipers stopped working altogether. Fortunately I was sober and the two o'clock streets were almost deserted. We were about three miles from home. We waited for ten minutes. The rain got heavier.

Eventually we decided that if Robbie leaned out of the passenger window and shouted directions at me, and if I drove very slowly, and if nothing unexpected happened, we could make it. We decided to give it a go. At fifteen mph the windscreen became completely opaque. There was now also thunder which made it hard to hear his directions. His head, you will remember, was out of the window.

"What?" I shouted.

"The road's bending to the left…not *that* much – that's it. There's a traffic light coming up."

"What colour is it?"

It was that bad. By the time we got to Camden the rain had eased and we made it home without further incident.

The Vulture had already given me a few shocks. It was now my turn to give it one.

I mentioned that I lived in a cul-de-sac. This was used to dump unwanted cars, something that caused irritation to Dave next door. He tried calling the council but nothing happened.

Robbie, who soon afterwards was diagnosed as a paranoid schizophrenic, had a more exciting theory about them. At the end of the cul-de-sac was the railway; and, beyond that, the back of Pentonville Prison. The cars, so Robbie's believed, were getaway vehicles for a jail-break. He would stay up late into the night, recording the switching on and off of lights in the prison which were, he claimed, relaying coded messages to the accomplices. He once sent copies of his findings to the Home Office but did not, so far as I'm aware, receive a reply.

Whatever the cars were doing there they were certainly an irritation. One evening in the Hemingford Arms up the road, I, Dave, Robbie and a couple of other people hit upon what seemed the perfect solution. If we turned the cars over, the council would *have* to remove them.

Full of beer and certainty – a combination which has been the pre-condition of several worse disasters – we stumbled out of the pub and down the road.

It's surprising how easily five pissed young men can turn over a car once they set their minds to it. The first one, which had been there at least three months, was turtled in less than half a minute. We moved on to the next, which was smaller. From side to side it went…

"Stop!" I shouted.

"Wassamatter?" Robbie said.

"Ish my car!"

The next day, as we had predicted, the upended car had been removed.

I don't know if it was because of this trauma but shortly afterwards The Vulture's right indicators intermittently packed up. The exciting aspect of this was that, unlike with the windscreen wipers, I had no way of knowing if they were working or not. Often a horn blast from the vehicle behind me was the only clue. I got used to making hand signals. This was OK in the daylight or at simple junctions but worked less well on big roundabouts or in the dark.

That wasn't the only problem nightfall brought. The Vulture's head-lights were feeble enough but the rear ones were so pale as to be almost invisible from thirty yards away, and completely so from any distance when it was foggy. Driving back from Cambridge on the A10 on such a night I saw a huge pair of headlights behind me, getting bigger all the time. There was no other traffic. It seemed certain that the lorry driver couldn't see me.

I was gripped with a mounting sense of fear. When he was about fifty yards away he still hadn't slowed: but my guardian angel was alert and supplied a lay-by for me to pull into. I felt the leviathan thunder obliviously past and watched its tail lights – about sixteen of them – recede into the fog while I waited for my heart rate to come down to the low hundreds.

To add to the list, you couldn't get it into first gear. Having for a few days used a car with no reverse and, on one mad New Year's Eve, driven across central London in a car whose gearstick came off in your hand at every change, this wasn't a huge problem; or, at least, it wasn't on the flat. On a hill, however, particularly with passengers, the engine was so underpowered that once stopped it barely got going again.

All these problems severely reduced the journeys I could safely undertake. Darkness, rain, fog, heat, cold, hills and right turns all presented the car with serious or insuperable obstacles. Despite this, it once got to the Forest of Dean (and back) and even as far as Edinburgh (and back), both times with the wonderfully-named Ian Heavens. If The Vulture's flesh was weak, its spirit was certainly willing.

Perhaps The Vulture's greatest moment was during what might have been known as the Hampstead Heath Shooting. Late at night (again) and with three drunk and disorganised passengers, I came across some police cars on the Heath. Confused by the flashing lights and the paranoid state-clampdown outbursts from my friends, I thought that the policeman was waving me round an accident.

Having almost stopped, I started to pull away.

Suddenly there were spotlights and shouting and a voice in a megaphone telling the driver to slowly get out of the car.

"Put that joint out," I said, "wind up the windows and don't say anything." I slowly got out. Two policemen came towards me. One had a gun. There were several others behind them. Just beyond the ring of light I could hear police dogs growling and straining at their leads.

I learned later that they were looking for four people in a Mini who'd committed an armed robbery in Highgate. The officer questioning me must have realised they'd got the wrong guys. I reflected that if the car had had a first gear and I'd been able to accelerate away at a normal speed we'd probably all be dead. I doubt The Vulture's bodywork would have stopped any bullets. It was intensely cold. I started to shake.

"Have you been drinking?"

I hadn't. "No," I said.

He turned to car. "Has this thing got an MOT?"

It had. "Yes," I said.

Amazingly, he accepted both statements. He walked round the car, shining his torch through the windows. The frightened faces of Paul, Patrick and Mark peered back. I was glad they had had the sense to keep quiet. Having a bright light shone in your face by an armed policeman takes a lot of the bounce out of you.

"Are you *sure* this has an MOT?" the policeman was saying.

"Absolutely."

He gave the front bumper a kick. Amazingly it didn't budge. "Who's a clever boy, then?"

I couldn't think of anything to say to this.

He flashed his torch around a bit more, ending up with it on my face. "On your way, son," he said at last.

We drove off, slowly.

The last Vulture incident I can remember took place in Hyde Park one baking Sunday morning. For some reason I'd removed the front seat and then lost the bolts. I felt the gap added to The Vulture's odd charm as well as offering extra rear-seat legroom. The only passenger was my friend Patrick who was, on account of the heat, stripped to the waist and drinking a can of beer.

A policeman stopped us near the Serpentine. He took in the missing seat, the fire-damaged dashboard, the half-naked man, the lager. Were any of these things illegal, in a Royal Park or elsewhere? I could see his mind searching for precedents or certainties, but finding none. No words were exchanged before he waved me on.

It seems odd but I can't recall what happened to the car. Like a cat that decided to adopt me, it drifted into my life and then, a year or so later, vanished into the darkness. Maybe it's still sitting in the side street off Offord Road, waiting for the jailbreak.

When I started writing this I imagined it was going to be a savage critique of Minis in general and that one in particular. Now that I've finished I feel differently. I can't say that I miss it but I now feel a certain respect; even fondness. It was involved in – indeed was often the author of – many of the memorable incidents of those slightly crazy couple of years; but I see now that I was complicit in many of these and that The Vulture was not entirely to blame.

Writing about it has made me remember these times and, more importantly, the friends and fellow travellers, many now dead or no longer known to me. Finally, it's a useful reminder that sometimes objects don't work as they should and you just have to cope. I'm not pretending this has made me a better man. Certainly, and despite the myriad opportunities for self-improvement The Vulture presented to me, it didn't make me a better mechanic.

So, you BBC journos, is this the kind of recollection you were expecting (assuming you'd asked me to write one, which you didn't)? No? Oh well: it's done now. Smelly green Vulture and all who sailed in you, I salute you.

Why I Can't Speak German

WHEN WE'RE YOUNG, we're proud of reaching milestones that mark the progress towards what proves to be the mixed blessings of adulthood. Our first long trousers, our first double-figure birthday, our first kiss, our first solo visit to a cinema: all these things, not always in that order, celebrate another shackle of childhood being shaken off.

It's only later, of course, that one hankers for these carefree days. Many times since, in the throes of some financial, emotional or existential crisis, I have yearned to be returned to the imagined simple pleasures of childhood. Were this wish to have been granted, I would be at once counting the days until my tenth birthday or sulking at the unfairness of being told to eat pork chops. We're never happy. Perhaps that's what makes us human: or perhaps it just shows how rubbish life is. I don't know.

My first train set, for example, was something I had looked forward to for months before my eighth birthday. When the morning arrived I was so excited I could barely speak. Of all the pleasures that I've been lucky enough to experience I think this would be number one, certainly in terms of expectation being matched by experience.

To say that my day was spoiled when I was told that I was going riding in the afternoon would be a huge understatement. My aunt ran a livery stable in Wimbledon and fondly believed that an outing on a pony would be the birthday treat I most craved.

Somewhere I still have a photo of me sitting on this animal with an expression on my face that would have curdled milk. I have never been on a horse since.

I mention this episode because it shows what a strong effect an unwelcome incident can have. For example, I can't speak German. There may be other reasons for this omission but this is my version.

Two of the things I was particularly proud of aged about 11 were my new front teeth. I knew these were permanent (or so I thought) and that the painful but also wonderful sensation of having a milk tooth loosen until it demanded to be pulled out was now finished with. Unlike my other teeth they were of perfect size and regularity. These, I thought proudly, baring my fangs in a mirror, were the real thing. Teeth – what grown-ups have.

As it turned out, I had about three weeks to enjoy them. One Saturday afternoon, rising slightly higher than my opponent to head a football, the left one snapped off flush with the gum. The only immediate satisfaction I had was that it embedded itself in the other boy's cheek. I've forgotten his name but I'd probably recognise the scar.

My parents were summoned. This was a boarding school called Caldicott in Burnham Beeches. The staff didn't like parents wandering about except on advertised days as this would have interfered with the sadism and paedophilia that were the main reasons many of them worked there. An exception was made, however.

My mother was underwhelmed by my calm and – until I opened my mouth – unaffected appearance. "I thought you'd be all bruised and covered in bandages," she said. This was probably an attempt to cheer me up but it made me feel a bit of a fraud.

After an unpleasant month while the nerve died, the question of what was to be done reared its head. "We can't do anything permanent until his mouth has stopped growing," the dentist told my parents. "You'll have to wait until he's grown up."

This was absurd. I *was* grown up. I'd my adult teeth through. Now I would have to wait. It was *so* unfair.

He put in a temporary crown. Two days later it came out. He replaced it. That lasted a week. This went on for a bit until, for a year or so, the falsie was abandoned. I learned to speak without lisping by twisting my tongue to the right.

Before I went to my next school two years later, I insisted we try again. This prosthetic was slightly better as it fitted over the stump rather than just being glued onto it. When I felt it loosening I would do a strange thing with my tongue and lips for which there is no word I'm aware of. This had the effect of sucking the air out of the tiny gap and causing the crown to contract slightly so sealing it in place.

This was fine until I ate a piece of toast or coughed or did one of fifty other things that would work it loose again. From time to time it would break which would result in a few weeks of toothlessness, then a trip to London, then a few months of respite: then the loosening would start once more.

During one of these toothless episodes I acquired the nickname of 'fang'. Pretty obvious really and not too bad compared with some of the other sobriquets then in use. It probably wouldn't have bothered my if there hadn't been a language lab at this school.

This room had rows of booths, each one with a mic and a pair of headphones and was used for teaching us French and German. I am under no illusion that I have no natural talent for foreign languages. That I can speak French passably well is only because my parents invested all their savings in building a house there in which we spent many holidays.

German, on the other hand, I had no connection with. The language may have been one the lab could have helped me master, were it not for the fact that the first words in the course – uttered at a time when everyone in the class was still giggly and settling down – were 'let us begin'. The German for this phrase, which I will remember long after dementia has obliterated *eins, zwei* and *drei*, is *fangen Sie an.*

At this point, everyone would turn round, laugh, point and shout "fang!" A stronger boy might have used this as the spur to become fluent. Unfortunately I was not a stronger boy. I entered each session in the language lab with a closed mind and it never reopened until just before the end. I wished then I could go back to being eleven again and not break my tooth, or forward to eighteen when I'd have a proper replacement. As I couldn't do either of these things, I switched off. That's my story, anyway.

My proper coming of age happened when I was about eighteen and a permanent front tooth was fitted. I was now grown up, in this respect if none other. All went well until about fifteen years ago when the tooth suddenly fell out in, of all places, the deep end of the Hungerford swimming pool.

For a moment I couldn't work out what had happened. I felt something odd in my mouth and saw a silvery object spiral down and land near the grille at the deepest part of the pool. Then a disturbance, probably caused by me, made it move – and suddenly, it was gone.

I got out. The gap where the tooth had been felt about six inches wide. I got dressed and went to the reception desk.

"Excuse me," I said, "but I think my front tooth has been sucked into the filtration system." At least that's what I thought I was saying. With no front tooth, all those sibilants must have sounded like wind coming under a door. The receptionist looked at me as if I'd lost my reason. I tried again with much the same result.

Then I hit upon the plan of putting my finger where my tooth had been. He must have thought I was trying to make myself vomit. This was better, though muffled by my hand and so almost as obscure. The fourth time I made myself understood.

There was a pause while he considered this sentence, which must have been unlike anything he'd ever heard. Then he told me there was no way it could be retrieved. I went on my way, lisping and cursing.

The next step, I was advised, was an implant. If I'd known how expensive this would be I might have gone back to the lisping fang days. The final shreds of physical vanity still clung about me, however, so I went for it. This involved a number of trips to an implant expert in Reading.

Of all the truths which I have absorbed in my life, none is more useful or widely applicable than that which states that if you go to a dental practice with a fish tank in its reception area you are going to get ripped off. This one had two, and complimentary tea and coffee – another warning sign. I've blotted out how much it all cost: but at least I know that, live and on the hoof, I'm now worth a bit more than I was due to the titanium screw which extends some way up into my skull. In these days of metal thefts I perhaps shouldn't boast about it.

The day of the implanting arrived and Penny drove me there and settled down to enjoy the fish tanks and free coffee. I was told I was going to be given something which would keep me conscious but only just. As the anaesthetist was preparing the jab the dentist asked me if I was all set. I thought for a second. It was now or never. "Could you turn that music off, please?" I said.

There are quite a lot of genres I don't like. Opera, bagpipes and anything by U2 are close to the top; but in the gold-medal position is that ambient nonsense that wafts around the stave lines like a drunk man on an ice rink, never modulating and never resolving. I knew it would drive me mad.

"Oh," he said and put down his drill. "I find it rather calming."

I knew that picking an argument with someone who was about to knock me half unconscious and then start drilling in my mouth was a bad idea but I'd gone too far.

"I don't," I said.

He switched it off.

The needle dug into my arm: and I was plunged into a dark half-world which I have only visited in delirious dreams and have no desire to visit again.

I happen to have a fairly low pulse rate. One of the effects of this drug was to drop it still further. After about an hour – or it might have been three minutes, I don't know – I was roused from this pale nightmare by the dentist shaking my shoulder. His urgency communicated itself to me at once but the meaning was harder to follow.

"Brian, Brian, are you an athlete?"

Anyone who knows me will be well aware that I am not an athlete. It seemed an absurd question in the circumstances. Was it some test to see if I was still alive?

"No," I said. I thought about this. "I do swim, though." I considered telling him about the filtration system but couldn't face it.

He appeared satisfied with this reply. The fog descended again. I was dimly aware of a massive noise in my head but it seemed to be happening to someone else.

"Sorry about waking you up, earlier" he said after I had sort of come round, "but your pulse had gone down to about 25." I couldn't think of anything to say. Should I apologise? Most of my brain seemed to have turned to cotton wool and my legs didn't work properly. 25 bpm seemed about right.

The final stroke of genius was getting me to pay the last instalment of the money while I was still in this condition. I'm sure it was what we'd agreed but it was probably as well I couldn't take in the sum. Maybe that was the real purpose of the drug.

"All done?" Penny asked me. "Have you paid?" I giggled.

"Get in the car," she said.

So, now I have two front teeth, one of which probably cost more than the car in which Penny drove me back. I can say "I think my front tooth has been sucked into the filtration system," with perfect clarity but see no reason why I should ever again need to.

I cannot, however, say this, or anything else, in German. If ever I have to, and if using English or French won't do, it'll be back to the language lab, but this time paying more attention to *fangen Sie an* – and so we beat on, boats against the current, wishing to be at any point in our lives apart from the one in which we happen to find ourselves.

Operation Mercury

TOMMY PARKED IN the High Street where McClusky had said there were no CCTV cameras. Checking his false beard, he got out of the car and crossed the road towards Wesbury's supermarket.

Three staff members dealing with trolleys in the car park were, like him, identifiable by their yellow and black Wesbury's jackets. His was of a different design, denoting a higher rank.

"No loitering," McClusky had impressed upon Tommy the day before. "You've three targets. Go for the one nearest the store first then get out. Never look hurried."

Tommy hesitated, remembering the Tamworth fiasco: one target lost. He took a firm step forward.

"No issues," Tommy's report read. "Time on site: one minute twenty-four seconds. Targets: three. Targets hit: three."

* * *

"Nineteen this week," McClusky said to Mr Bertram the following day. They were discussing Operation Mercury in the long office on the top floor of Faraday's HQ; the 'bowling alley' as McClusky called it to himself. "Seven at Wesbury's, five at Springfield, two at…"

Mr Bertram nodded and stirred his coffee. He was staring out of the window, his mind fixed on the golf tournament on Saturday at which he hoped to implement his long-cherished plan to seduce the club secretary's wife.

With a sigh, he forced himself back to McClusky's list. "…and one for us. Northampton branch."

Mr Bertram continued to nod and to stir his coffee. He wondered if, were he to start shaking his head, he'd be able to continue the same smooth, circular motions of his left hand. Slowly, both movements stopped. He allowed himself five seconds to contemplate his mental image of the curves of Tanya Jefford's thighs before sternly focussing his thoughts on the man opposite him.

"And the response?"

McClusky handed Mr Bertram a document bound with a metal fastener. It related to reactions from the press departments of the other companies. There were several screengrabs of social-media posts and articles from local papers. Some made Mr Bertram snigger. He pushed the file back across the table.

"The results show the same pattern," McClusky said in his clipped lowland brogue. "An estimated twenty-nine hours of lost marketing time per target hit and an average drop in sales of point eight of a percent in affected stores."

Not for the first time, Mr Bertram winced at the military language before recalling that for twenty-two years McClusky had been a soldier; which was kind of why he was there. He felt like asking, though wasn't sure he wanted to hear the answer, how exactly McClusky had got these figures.

Instead, he repeated his milder question about why his subordinate was sure the sales fall had been the result of his work.

McClusky started reciting a rationale Mr Bertram had heard before. Complex algorithms were at work. "It's all a question of having enough past data to work from," McClusky explained.

For Mr Bertram, this led back to his previous problem: from where had this data about their rivals been obtained? Much was available to those prepared to wade through public on-line accounts: much else, he suspected, was not. All this had been in large part his idea. The feeling that matters were running out of control had been growing on him over the last month. Out of *his* control, he corrected himself. McClusky clearly knew exactly what he was doing.

McClusky paused, sensing that his superior's attention was again wandering. Mr Bertram looked up, so McClusky continued. How could he know that, superimposed on Mr Bertram's view of his rugged profile, was a vision of Tanya Jefford first refusing, then coquettishly accepting, a refill of Pinot Grigio?

"We also know that on at least three and possibly six occasions, the target companies have instigated disciplinary measures against managers assumed to be responsible who in fact weren't. So, plenty of confusion and costs. Two cases are set to go to court."

At the word 'court', Mr Bertram started paying attention again: but McClusky was standing up.

"There's a briefing in ten minutes. Would you like to be there?"

The question was formal and rhetorical, as both of them knew. "No…no," said Mr Bertram, giving McClusky a wan smile. "You, er… no."

McClusky made a strange gesture with his right hand that stopped short of being a salute and marched out of the office. Mr Bertram allowed his inner gaze to wander over the image of the nape of Tanya Jefford's neck where a stray lock of hair was, tantalisingly, apt to trail.

* * *

"'From April, parking will be forbidden after nightfall except for vehicles equipped with child seats'. What the hell does that mean?" Laura Bestwick, Wesbury's South East England Head of Corporate Affairs, tossed the notice on the desk.

"Go, on – read it."

Mike Manders, several rungs further down the ladder, picked it up with trembling hands. He had been responsible for appointing the Thatchbury manager, who now appeared to have gone insane.

"Read it."

"Erm…'vehicles' is spelled wrong," he began. "two 'ls'." He paused. "'Maximum', again wrong…er…'maximum stay not to exceed not to exceed…' don't know why that's repeated, 'the duration hours as specified from time to time.'"

He carefully put the notice down on the desk between them.

"Who's the manager?"

"Who's the…er…Jasper Sharpe."

"Sack him."

"What? I don't think…"

"Well, sack *some*one."

* * *

"So," McClusky summarised, "we've targeted stores with new managers who've recently gone on holiday, with bad or no car-park CCTV and with poor records of corporate adherence." He turned to the whiteboard and brought up a new slide. "So far, that's given us a hundred and eight successful targets out of a possible of a hundred and nine" – Tommy felt a sergeant-major stare rake towards him – "so, *almost* perfect. This is across four organisations. There have also been eight in our own stores for…"

"For camouflage," said Alex, to Tommy's left. McClusky nodded approvingly.

"Now…"

Tommy listened to McClusky's summary of the next phase. The point was to inflict maximum internal confusion and reputational damage with minimum effort. Perplexing and nonsensical notices about parking arrangements were just the start. The time had come to move from small-arms fire to something spectacular. "We need to turn from snipers to terrorists," he concluded.

Tommy glanced at the other three, hand-picked like him from among Faraday's lower-management team. They were nodding excitedly, their eyes shining. Tommy felt less certain and sickened by the military language which stirred unwelcome memories. In this respect he shared the doubts of Mr Bertram, whom he had never met. He joined the mute show of approval a second after McClusky had noticed his not doing so.

McClusky had been about to explain the next stage but had, with the caution that enabled him to survive many unexpected challenges, decided to hold fire. He had been having doubts about 'Tamworth'

Tommy. The problem was what was to be done about him.

"So," he continued. "As you were for the next three days, then we pause. Here are your detail sheets." He passed them around, giving all of them except Tommy a full-on man-to-man stare. "It's all in the timing," he reminded them as they stood up. "In, out, one minute tops."

* * *

It's all in the timing, Mr Bertram reflected. Given the way Max Jefford worked the room, he had a minute tops to make his opening pitch. Tanya was socially a slow starter, likely to hang back, gauging the mood of the event before deciding who to talk to. Max, on the other hand, dived straight in and was off, networking like crazy. This would be his chance.

Although he knew how pointless it was, he found himself running through possible opening exchanges, each more improbable than the last. As always, his thoughts were side-tracked, instead locking onto stockinged calves, silk-shimmering thighs and dark pink lipstick. He realised he was over-thinking things, and for all the wrong reasons.

The same could not be said about his reaction to Operation Mercury, which had in many ways been his own idea.

About three months before, he had been shown a notice that had appeared in the car park of their Crewe branch:

"Please note that from tomorrow car parking will is restricted in all bays all bays to one cars per bay, regardless of length except after closeing time of store and in other bays."

This had been written, in a hurry, by an over-enthusiastic deputy manager who'd got involved in argument with the owners of a Toyota iQ and two BMW Isettas who'd parked end to end to end, the last one protruding far enough to cause (allegedly) a Range Rover to clip the side of a delivery lorry.

Mr Bertram had casually mentioned this oddity to McClusky, whom he had recently appointed in a vague security and enforcement capacity which he had already started to regret.

Mr Bertram mentioned that he'd been impressed by how much negative publicity the notice had received. How much more disastrous, he suggested, were this to have been in somewhere like north Oxford, Harrogate or Tunbridge Wells where grammatical purity was particularly cherished. The following week he was astounded to learn that very similar notices had appeared in the car parks of three of Faraday's rival stores in these very places.

On being confronted, McClusky had said that wishful thinking could reasonably have been seen as order. Mr Bertram missed his chance to correct this Thomas à Becket confusion and, before he knew it, McClusky had created an elite team of industrial saboteurs whom Mr Bertram had only met once and had no desire to meet again. However, he'd signed the first payment authorisation and so was now complicit.

How this would all end he had no idea. Meanwhile, there was his vision of Tanya…

* * *

"Listen to this," said Maggie du Cane of Springfield: yes, Maggie du Cane; for the matter had reached senior director level. "This from the car park of our Ringwood store yesterday."

"'Without permission from from Friday,'" she read, "'parking forbidden in the car park park except three or more passengers parking and using car park/store during the closeing hours except on Fridays. To prevent abuse of parking. Fine: – £50.'"

There was a pause while her colleagues tried to digest the syntax.

"The give-away word here is 'closeing'. This was mis-spelled in the same way in the first one of these we saw, from Faraday's in Crewe five weeks ago. There have been six others we've seen with the same mis-spelling. Altogether, there have been about forty others we've heard about and probably a lot more that we haven't. The gibberish level is rising. Only five, by far the smallest number, have been at Faraday stores, by the way."

"So what you're saying..." the head of communications began.

"Exactly," Maggie du Cane said, who hadn't got to where she was by having people tell her what she was saying while she was saying it. "It's a conspiracy. Against all of us. By...well, whoever. It's cost us a lot of money, including two, perhaps three, wrongful dismissal cases. I'm going to stop it. I've doubled the security in all our car parks, especially where there's a new manager. That seems part of the pattern, here and everywhere."

"What about the other groups?" one of the other directors asked. "They shared their data with us. Should we not share our conclusions with them?"

Ethically, this was a good point: so Maggie gave this the two seconds of apparent consideration it merited. "No. We look after ourselves first. That's what I, what we, are here to do."

And, with an approving nod from the non-executives who were on the directors' remuneration committee, the meeting moved on to agenda item six.

* * *

So it was that, two days later, the already nervous and de-motivated Tommy found his notice-posting at the Springfield store in Basingstoke unexpectedly full of peril. Whereas normally no one paid him any attention, today there were five people, four menacingly in plain clothes but from their expressions undeniably of that place, advancing towards him.

There was a brief scuffle. Tommy had spent three years in the army before PTSD in Kabul knocked him sideways, so was able to evade the attempts at a citizen's arrest. The notices – "Parking forbidden during Ramadan except on Saterday and other days before closeing time or otherwise, fine £200" – were dropped. A camera flashed in his face.

Instinct kicked in. The mission was aborted. Escape by any means was now justified. He pushed a convenient row of trolleys towards his assailants and then grabbed the car keys from a woman who was about to get into a Fiat Bravo.

Gunning the engine, he accelerated out of the car park and turned the wrong way into the one-way street. Horns blared. Tommy swerved and made good his escape.

Two minutes later, more cautious instincts kicked in. He dumped the Fiat in a side street and made his way to the station, CCTV cameras recording his movements all the way to platform six.

* * *

McClusky learned of the debacle the following morning, a Saturday. As they had with Tommy, military instincts prevailed. The immediate problem had to be handled. Other considerations could wait.

He picked up his private phone, scrolled through the contacts and dialled.

"Mr Trench here," he said.

There were no pleasantries. Details, including Tommy's description and address, were exchanged.

"Now," McClusky concluded. "And whatever it takes."

An hour later, as he downed another scotch in the Star and Garter, McClusky wondered – again as Tommy had done in Basingstoke – if he had over-reacted. "Whatever it takes" could, and possibly would, encompass anything.

Had the time passed to talk to Mr Bertram? It had: just as Mr Bertram had earlier realised that the time to talk to anyone else about this insane project had also passed. McClusky had precipitated matters into an arena that Mr Bertram, with his middle-class and middle-management prejudices, could never understand.

In any case, Mr Bertram was where the buck stopped. He was the official instigator. Even so, the temptation to pull back was strong.

McClusky checked his pocket for his passport. One never knew when it would be needed. He had friends in many unlikely places and could easily disappear. He'd done it before. His time at Faraday's had been a pleasant and well-paid retreat from other problems: for don't think for a moment McClusky was his real name.

He picked up his phone and dialled the same number. There was no reply. By then, it was already too late.

* * *

There must have been a hundred people in the room at the Swayle Golf Club, Mr Bertram among them. There had been a half-glimpsed headline about a murder in London and another about an altercation in a supermarket in Basingstoke which had caught his eye and disturbed his thoughts: but his lust, as ever, had the upper hand.

And now, in the Sir Peter Corbett room of the golf club, there was Tanya in plain sight, even if his real enemies were, as yet, not. The initial speech had just finished and Max was, as he had predicted, about to start on his room-working routine.

You pompous jerk, Mr Bertram thought, watching the soon-to-be cuckold shake hands with two different people simultaneously.

Tanya was, as he knew she would be, standing back, reviewing the ghastly throng with a half-amused and quizzical expression which, in his highly charged state, conveyed to Mr Bertram an undercurrent of suppressed lust that nearly lifted him off his feet.

There – Max was off. Mr Bertram took a step forward towards Tanya, then another. He was three paces away when their gazes locked.

At that moment he saw in her something real, something that had not been part of his fantasy. Hs courage failed. Coming as it did, at the very hinge on which his life was to turn, he would remember it through all the dark years that followed but was never able to say exactly what it was.

Then he felt a strong hand on his shoulder.

"Mr James Bertram?" he swung round.

"Yes?"

"Inspector Peterson and Sergeant Crawley. We need to ask you a few questions about the murder of one of your staff, Tommy Johnson, last night. Sorry to interrupt your evening but your wife said you'd be here.

It should only take a couple of minutes."

The questions might be as innocent as they had seemed or they might not. Flashing one glance over his shoulder at Tanya's surprised and mildly shocked expression, he suddenly saw all the pale stratagems and failures of his life laid bare. The purely priapic seduction and the hopes of success through his accidental professional subterfuge were but two sides of the same dud coinage. He was brutally confronted with the knowledge that he was a failure, and a mediocre one at that.

So, he ran.

They overpowered him just as he was about to crash through the window at the far side of the room. If not pleased, then at least satisfied he had finally embarked on a course of action that was entirely in his control, he offered up his wrists for the handcuffs.

Let Him in

I'VE NEVER BEEN sure what I thought of old Humphrey Vance: well, I'm sure *now*, but I wasn't before. He was often in the Club, but I tended to steer away from him as I didn't share his taste for esoteric and recondite knowledge which formed the basis of his conversation. There was also the fact that I had, two decades previously, enjoyed an eight-year affair with his wife.

I never knew if she had told him about this, nor if he had discovered it by other means. People make all kinds of admissions, often years later, for reasons of expiation, revenge, malice or even boredom. Claire was living somewhere in South America and I had no means of asking her.

Sometimes I was sure he was studying me with an intensity that went beyond mere curiosity. In turn, I took to watching him: and was gradually to learn he subjected others to similar scrutiny. Thus I found myself becoming interested in him, and perhaps something more. Certainly, and by slow degrees, I found myself being drawn into his orbit.

I say "old" Humphrey Vance, but he was at most only a few years older than me. However, he conveyed a sense of age: less through appearance or mannerisms than by the impression of knowledge that seemed the product of a long lifetime's study. He did not wear his erudition lightly. There were few matters in which he would accept even the mildest contradiction. If the conversation strayed from the channel he had selected, he would affect a sardonic expression, which often put the speaker completely off their stroke, before weighing in with a withering comment.

"Well, that was what *some* people believed fifty years ago," he said last week, after a discussion – 'monologue' would be more accurate – about the afterlife, which one of the company had briefly diverted towards the early Crusades.

"The righteous have ever believed that their souls would be rewarded," he informed us. "Which was not a concept initiated by Pope Urban" – this with a pitying glance towards the conversational rebel. "But what of the unrighteous, however defined? Was there not the means for them to achieve paradise?" To this question, it seemed, none save Humphrey Vance had the answer.

His interest in the afterlife was starting to intrigue me, as it did others. When prompted to be more specific he shied away from the G-word, despite hinting at an intimate and immediate knowledge.

Ghosts. Without being so named, the conversation had turned to this subject the evening before. "Surely," a retired Judge opined from his seat opposite the fireplace, "if you accept the afterlife, you must accept some…crossover, if you will, between the two planes, however inadvertent. Yes," he added, boldly looking at Humphrey Vance, "I mean ghosts. After all, Jesus himself transitioned from one to the other, or so we're taught."

This last remark had over-cooked what had otherwise been a reasonably good point. Vance thought so too.

"Hardly a comparable case," he said with a saturnine finality. "If you accept a deity, you must accept some degree of unique omnipotence. However," he paused menacingly, "that was not my point. If you recall…"

After one too many glasses of wine, I found my attention wandering. I was thinking of my grandmother, the only person I've ever known with any credible claim to psychic awareness. She treated such tales as calmly as if describing a chance encounter with someone on a bus, which made them all the more believable.

Her precepts were equally matter-of-fact. Ghosts, she said, were not always what they first seemed and often you didn't recognise them as such until afterwards. You needed to let them in to yourself for them to reveal their true purpose and nature. Above all, you had to accept them for what they were and on their own terms, not yours. Their existence was stretched; ours was concentrated. They had a broader view and were vastly less interested in our preoccupations than we were in theirs.

Vance indicated that he had said all he was prepared to that evening, and the gathering broke up.

I'm rarely in the Club at lunchtime, but a few days later I had a meeting nearby which had prolonged itself. I took my time over a frugal and solitary meal, then strolled into the Members' Room for coffee. I was vaguely aware there were only half a dozen others there. Ten minutes later, I realised that this had shrunk to one. It was as if the scene had been cleared for us.

Vance made a casual but imperious gesture and I obediently crossed the room to join him.

For a while he said nothing, but appraised me with a mordant gaze which I returned with a bland smile.

"We've never been exactly *simpatico*, have we?" he asked rhetorically. "Perhaps in some ways we have too much in common."

It was impossible to know what he meant. Again I steeled myself not to react.

"None the less," he went on, after taking the smallest sip of port, "we've had some interesting discussions recently."

'I have listened to you talk', I could have replied. Instead, I merely inclined my head.

"I have a fascinating story to tell you. I have observed you are interested in matters which many call 'the supernatural', though more accurate terms exist."

I have no clear recollection of what then unfolded. In my few lucid moments since, I can recall only the sense of a gossamer thread being woven around me and draped across my senses. This comes as if from a dream: I cannot say if it more accurately describes what happened then or what I realised afterwards had happened. Incidents tinged with such mysteries have a way of annihilating, or at least confusing, the perception of time. This was my first experience of it, though not the last.

The next thing I remember, we were walking across Green Park towards his house in South Audley Street. It was a beautiful afternoon at the end of October: the last day, the last afternoon, of that part of my life.

"Many think," he said, as he paused while opening his front door, "that…'ghosts', if you will" – he offered a surprisingly warm smile to humour my inferred description – "are malicious. 'A sudden drop in temperature', is that not the phrase? 'A sense of deep foreboding'? Let me show you something."

He pushed open the door and I was transported into a place of delight.

Shimmerings of warm energy engulfed me. I was aware of small bursts of colour and musical tones that harmonised perfectly, wrapping me in something that approached ecstasy.

My other senses were ravished too, with the taste of sweet almonds, spices and a wholesome tang of citrus. My nostrils filled with the aroma of soft woodsmoke and violets. Everything I touched seemed soft and yielding, as corporeal as Claire's half-remembered body and yet rich with the promise of something eternal, satisfying a longing that, even during the best of times we had shared together, had been only hinted at.

This was, perhaps, paradise. I wonder still if that brief glimpse might have been worth everything that followed.

From the far corner of the room, Humphrey Vance was missing nothing. "This is my apparition," he said. "This is my truth. Do you welcome it?"

The question seemed absurd, the answer self-evident. I was in so many ways not myself. "Yes."

"Will you let it in?"

"Yes, I will."

With these words, my world collapsed.

It was as if the floor had vanished and I was falling into a place where my heightened senses were experiencing the opposite of the recent bliss. Discord, disgust and pain were all around me, and also within me: for I had been invaded by a force I had not the skill to repel.

My last sensation that day was of a dark laugh from far above: then, for an all-too-temporary moment, oblivion claimed me.

Since then I have lived a life undead, tormented by a presence within me that I can neither control nor expel. There are, as with a fatal disease, good days and bad days, but no promise of escape. Eight years have passed, during which I have been prey to something of such piteous and unchanging malevolence that I fear the condition might be eternal with death offering no respite.

In my few moments of calm, I recall my past life and yearn for its unremarkable and pale hues, enlivened by its one great indiscretion. Far more rarely, I am afforded a tantalising glimpse of the brief paradise I experienced before my fall. This normally presages a particularly brutal descent into the abyss, in which seconds pass as if hours.

Humphrey Vance died shortly afterwards, so I shall never know by what terrible spiritual alchemy he created the illusion of perfection only to cheat me into accepting his offer. Nor will I ever know whether his motives were personal or objective.

So: what *have* I learned?

In my lucid moments, I reflect that my transcendence took place on All Hallows' Eve at the very end of October, although my misery has now put me far beyond superstition. I also now know that my grandmother had been right: you don't always know what you're dealing with until afterwards.

I have also learned that, as by grandmother had told me, you have to let the ghosts in. As a result of a terrible trick, I had done just that. The problem was that I knew of no way to let them out again.

Mary's Supply Chain

MARY DYSON PICKED up the phone for what she hoped would be the last call of the day. The last eight hours had been relentless. Of course, buying on the vast scales she did, or organising others to do so on her behalf, was by its nature relentless. Items would be sourced, ordered and invoiced: they would be delivered, distributed and consumed; then, sooner or later, the strident cuckoo squawk would start again, beaks wide open, demanding replenishment. It was easy to feel she was accomplishing nothing.

As she dialled she realised she felt curiously light-headed. Exhaustion, clearly. She sat back in her chair, her head resting comfortably against the wall so she was more horizontal than vertical, and closed her eyes.

The number took some time to connect. When it did, it was to a ring tone that, for some reason, reminded her of her childhood. In fact, it sounded French.

She found herself wondering what would happen if she just stopped buying things. Next time the armed forces said that they needed half a million night-vision goggles, two thousand boxes of toilet paper or three tons of fish fingers – all of which she had handled this week – she could just say, "no: you don't really need this stuff." What would happen then? Could she just stop this incessant merry-go-round, or her little part of it?

The ring tone continued in its strange, dreamy way. The last idea developed itself in her mind. When she was growing up in a Berkshire village forty years when life had run on less hectic, though more immutable, rhythms: those of nature and the seasons, on which had been overlaid the various Christian festivals which had played a moderately large part in her family's life. Now everything ran to deadlines and schedules that had no particular logic, or even consistency. It was exhausting. She was exhausted.

The ring tone seemed to be getting fainter. Then it was answered.

She made her request but seemed to be reading from a script written by someone else in a language that she did not understand.

"I don't think that timescale is realistic," the man said.

Mary took a deep breath and suppressed the temptation to fling herself forward and bash her forehead against the desk. Today she had fired three procurement sub-contractors and was in no mood to be messed around.

"Why not?" she asked.

"Well…" the man said slowly. Mary had the image of him flicking through a hand of cards during a game of gin rummy, wondering which one to play.

"*Well,*" he said in a different tone, implying not indecision but the fact that the card was so obvious it hardly need be played at all. He played it anyway. "Covid."

Mary's hand gripped the receiver. "Don't try me with Covid," she said. "This time yesterday I was signing a deal for ten thousand sheets for the Nightingale hospitals. This afternoon I organised two years' supply of Ibuprofen for the RAF." She now had the image of herself playing a kind of one-sided blind whist, struggling and failing to recognise any of her opponent's cards – all of which appeared as red or black blurs – whereas he could see all of hers.

"Of course, the supply chain is broken," he said, as if she had not spoken. He was obviously gambling that she knew little about his supply-chain issues. In fact, Mary didn't and was instead wondering how much of her knowledge was transferable; also if an argument based on this aspect of the problem was going to accomplish anything. An equivocal response was called for. Now it was bridge they were playing: still at the bidding stage, still feeling each other out.

"…and, of course, there's Brexit," he added.

Mary sighed. The objections of Brexit and Covid, and the various supply-chain nightmares each had wrought, were fired at her like bullets each day. This was now like a horrible game of chess in which the opening moves by the opponent were so predictable that one almost fell asleep, switched off from the game until something more interesting came along. She realised she had switched off now and made an effort to re-focus. She found that she couldn't. Someone else seemed to be in control of her.

"...were all from Poland," the man was saying. "Or Bulgaria. A lot from Bulgaria, for some reason. Or was it Romania? Anyway, there were only two Polish people who stayed but now one is self-isolating. Of course all the Brits don't care to work our kind of shifts and want the minimum wage, plus bonuses, and..."

He droned on. Money, Mary thought, that was where they had got to. It came up sooner or later. Well, she could face that one out, just as she'd done with the fish-finger people this morning. Put them on the spot early on about what they wanted, then demand other concessions: get those agreed, then go back to the figure and chip away at that. It was a bit of a Danish Gambit but she'd made it work before.

She opened her mouth to say "so the price is the problem?" but no sound emerged. Instead, the man came out with a completely random move that put her on the back foot.

"...and then, there's Michaelmas coming up."

"Michaelmas?" she managed to ask; though her voice sounded odd: distorted; delayed; almost underwater.

"...which is a big weekend for us. Very big. End of September. End of summer, you know, or used to be. Still – Michaelmas. Everything's different after Michaelmas. It's the daisies, of course. That's what people remember about it. The daisies. The daisies usually..."

Mary had been privately educated at a school which had a Michaelmas term but had never been told, or bothered to ask, what this meant.

"...of course after that then it's unlucky to pick blackberries. Got the devil's spit on them, so people say. Don't believe it myself, but my sister told me..."

'The devil's spit'? What was the man talking about? Mary lived in Camden and could get blackberries, year-round as far as she was aware, from Waitrose. Her sister loved them, so when she came to stay...

"...but my sister didn't believe it when she came to stay. Nor did the doctor. Suppose she should have asked a priest. Mind you, she's a Catholic, but..."

Mary tried to recall what they were talking about, what she was trying to order, where they had got to. She couldn't. She needed to assert herself but she couldn't do that either.

But the man was off again.

"...of course, getting staff in the run-up to Halloween is next to impossible. It's the delivery problems, you see. Same with bonfire night. Do you have a pet? A lot of people think that fireworks..."

Mary wondered now if the call had been such a good idea. Her brain was frazzled with immense numbers, unfeasibly complicated payment terms and numerous contractual obligations. It might have been better to have gone home, opened a bottle of wine and seen what there was in the freezer. But, having started, she wasn't going to give up so easily.

"...then there's Christmas, looming on the horizon," the man was saying. "Booked up solid we are then. Solid. Not everyone likes turkey, or holly. Or crackers, come to that. My mother-in-law, for instance..."

She could, of course, just hang the phone up. She had no idea any longer what game they were playing. This was a call that should have been made earlier in the day when she was fresher and sharper. The Treasury's toilet paper had, compared to this, been child's play.

"...January's always difficult, obviously. Haven't got my desk diary for next year yet so no point asking me to book in anything for then – no, that's my joke. It's electronic now, isn't it? I could tell you what day my birthday will fall on in 2060 if you wanted to know..."

Mary didn't want to know but she found herself saying "Tuesday', though no sound emerged.

"...on Tuesday, as it happens," he went on. "Mind you my birthday's usually on a Tuesday."

Mary grappled with this for a moment, but the man had moved on.

"...plus the long-range forecast isn't looking too good for January, is it? Seems like snow – of course then there's February to get through..."

"*Février?*" she said sarcastically. There was a pause. It was the first thing she'd said for some time. But why had she said this in French?

"*...et vous m'appellez maintenant, demandant livraison en février?*" the man asked. "The thing about February, of course, is that..."

He was probably right, Mary thought – delivery in five months' time of whatever they were talking about was an absurdly short time-scale. She'd embarrassed herself, let the department down. The man didn't seem to have noticed, however.

"...such a short month, " he was saying, "hardly worth bothering with, ha ha. Before you know it – woosh, it's gone. A lot of people ignore it altogether nowadays. Not even a leap year..."

All the day's fish fingers and toilet paper and sackings had turned her mind into mush. Her doctor had told her last week she was over-working. So had her boss. She wanted to admit this now: she wasn't herself. But still the man droned on.

"...and then we're looking at Lent, which is obviously a complete bugger..."

Well, it was. Self-denial was ever the enemy of procurement. She heard the Apostles' Creed running through her head like water, accessed from constant childhood repetition: 'I believe in God the father almighty, maker of heaven and earth, and in Jesus Christ his only son...'

"...then there's Easter looming– always a busy time, people starting to think about, well..."

Had they really spanned half the year since the mention of Michaelmas? Had the whole of autumn and winter swung past in two minutes of disjointed chat and, here they were, breathing down the neck of next spring and *still* nothing agreed? Schedule, price, product, delivery terms – all were slipping away in the face of this man's peculiar recitation of the passage of the seasons.

"...though, of course, Whitsun is the big one – that's the day by which a lot of firms set their clocks, obviously. No sooner is that, and all its weddings, out of the way than you've got Mother's Day coming at you, all guns blazing. That's not so big for us, though. Well, it is and it isn't. Mind you, before and after, people like to have a change, know what I mean?"

Mary didn't know what he meant. She now seemed to be floating above the conversation. The man had turned into a lizard at the end of a long, dark corridor. His tongue was flicking in and out over a hand of playing cards in front of him which, though turned face-up, she could not read.

"...then there's July and August. Should be the boom months – but you never know what the weather's going to do and it's a complete write-off for any kind of planning as everyone's away. That's when the supply-chain problems really kick in, and if you add in Covid and Brexit..."

At the mention of 'supply chain', Mary snapped to attention. "Are you saying," she asked in her best professional tones, "that your supply chains will still be disrupted in eleven months' time?"

There was a pause: a different pause from before. The light in the room seemed to have changed. When the man spoke, it was in a different voice. "Excuse me?"

Mary said nothing for a moment. It was as if she had just woken up. The fact that her face was on the desk rather supported this. She thought quickly. "I'm sorry," she said, "I was talking to someone else."

"No problem, madam. So – what do you need?"

Mary told him. It now seemed so simple. The man repeated it back to her.

"So, a nine-inch pepperoni thin-crust, garlic bread and coleslaw, at 7.15pm. And the address?"

"Five Lock Gardens, Camden Town," she said.

"OK – I need the long number on your card."

The transaction over, she hung up the phone. What had all that other stuff been about? Already the details were fading but the essential procrastination remained fixed in her mind. What a nightmare. What a horrible insight into her life that had presented. The doctor was right: she needed to take a break. She stood up and reached for her coat. Just then, the phone rang.

"Mary Dyson," she said in her usual crisp tone.

"Er…Hello…er, Mary," a slightly undercooked voice replied, "We haven't spoken before. James Milton here from GFK's Accounts Department." There was a pause. Mary, now on the front foot again, said nothing. "Yes…I was wondering, that is…I was asked to get the payment details for the toilet paper you placed with Janet Hawthorne this afternoon. I've got the reference – PX349/3. The terms seem not to have been agreed."

Indeed they hadn't, Mary recalled. So grateful had they been to get the contract that Mary had been able to skate over the issue with her usual 'standard payment agreement' and 'best terms' which, of course, meant nothing.

"We need this," Alex went on, almost apologetically, "for the…the, you know, the contract."

Mary had only a faint sensation of the last so-called conversation. Now she felt well and in control once more, these dark prognostications could be ignored. The memory was pulling away from her like a receding tide, the rush and suck of the water on the shingle wiping the memory of the hectic high waters: but several phrases still remained. It seemed foolish not to use them.

"Payment?" she said in a dreamy voice, with an eye on the clock. Her pizza wasn't arriving for an hour so she had twenty minutes to spare for James, which should be about long enough. "Well, you see," she said in a regretful voice, "with Michaelmas coming up…"

Colour Blind

FIRST IT WAS motorway to Swindon; then A road to Gloucester; then B road to Lydney; then a road with no name or number through the dark and houseless woods of the Forest of Dean to Welsh Trefford, a village a few miles from the border.

Welsh Trefford is in England. Across the Wye valley is Trefford Inglis, which is in Wales. This paradox must give the local inhabitants – amongst whom were now my old friends Bel and Steve – amusement and satisfaction. 'Things are not quite as they might appear', might be another message: 'strangers beware.'

We arrived as a long September dusk was settling across the hills that surrounded their house on the outskirts of the village. It was a solid eighteenth-century dwelling set slightly back from the road. To the rear, I was to discover, were several outbuildings (one, with a strange faux-clocktower, painted an incongruously bright yellow) and a long lawn sloping down to a copse. This side of the house, where the other guests were gathered, was full of light and music. The front seemed shuttered and closed as if denying that anything was happening here, or ever had done.

There were fifteen or so of us. Most of us had been at university together. Socially I could not have been on firmer ice. However, I often feel the need to absent myself, in body or spirit, from gatherings of any size, if only for ten minutes now and then. Most people are able to lose themselves in a social function and become as one with it. I have never been able to.

This evening I felt a particular sense of isolation. The house, the garden and the event were all large enough to permit the occasional absence. At about ten, I retreated to a room full of books and browsed for a while. An hour later, I took a turn around the house, feeling both restless and also infected with lassitude. The village was dark. The front of the building was invisible. No lights were showing. More powerfully than on our arrival, it gave the impression of either having been here for ever or else not really there at all. There was something implacable and austere in its solitude. At the time, I felt no threat from it.

I sat in the garden and watched the familiar shapes of my friends and my wife flit back and forth past the window. I felt comfortingly close to them but also very distant. The effort of even the simplest conversational ploy seemed beyond me. Above me, the stars twinkled in a black, moonless and cloudless sky.

Five minutes later I was back inside, the moment forgotten.

That night, Penny went upstairs before me. When I got upstairs – we were at the top of the house – the room was dark. Throwing my clothes onto a chair next to the window I stumbled into bed. As I dropped off to sleep I sensed a heaviness in my head that was, I was certain, due to something other than wine.

I'm normally a good sleeper so when I do wake in the night it's often with a sense of unease. I felt feverish, though that hadn't been what had disturbed me. I'd been woken for a reason. My unease vanished, to be replaced by curiosity: for there was something odd about the room.

It took me a few moments to realise that, though it should have been dark, it was not. My watch told me it was just gone three. Feeling clear-headed and alert, I quietly got out of bed and pulled back the curtains.

Our room looked over the rear of the house. The lawn, the fence, the copse and the fields beyond were all flooded in a pale, lambent light that must have been the moon: but there was no moon to be seen, just as there had been no moon earlier. The lawn was not the dull green that moonlight normally reveals but gun-metal grey. This must be hoar-frost. I looked across the valley. Hills rose on every side, obviously creating a cold micro-climate. The yellow outhouse with its ornate tower was recognisable but barely distinguishable from the structures on either side of it. Aside from its faintly lemony tinge, and some similar hues on the edges of some of the shadows cast by the house and the trees, all the colour had been bleached from the still and silent landscape.

Then I saw the man.

He seemed to have emerged from nowhere, stumbling and looking over his shoulder as he hurried across the lawn. He left footprints which faded almost at once. He was carrying something in his arms. Within seconds he had vanished beyond the buildings to the left. The scene returned to its photographic stillness. I suddenly felt exhausted, as if I had been awake for days. I collapsed back into bed.

I awoke the next day with only a vague memory of the dream. I pulled back the curtains. My word, that shed was a violent colour: almost orange. Bel and Steve had only recently bought the place so I assumed it was something they'd inherited. Aside from this, the morning landscape was displayed in a range of subtle colours I'd not previously appreciated.

At about noon Steve needed to take a lawnmower back to a neighbour and I went along to give him a hand. After we'd got the mower out, he invited us in for a drink.

His name was Peter, in his mid-sixties, a tall man with longish greying hair and slightly hooded eyes. While Steve and Peter's wife Di chatted in the kitchen, we moved into the living room. This was overfilled, giving the impression that items had been recently added to a place that was already fully-furnished. Several paintings and photos hung on the wall, with more photos on the mantelpiece. The two alcoves either side of the fireplace were painted a deep, ox-blood crimson, the wall facing it faded gold and the others plain white. The double windows looked out over a garden which seemed as haphazard as the arrangement inside but in a more pleasing way.

I took all this in and then, more slowly, resumed my scrutiny. There was something that I had seen but also not seen.

We chatted for a while about this and that. He had lived in the area for most of his life. He had been born in the village. While talking, I continued my survey of the room. It was like the first part of a game of Pelmanism, before the cards are turned over.

"The problem with this place," he was saying, "is that the beer's wonderful but you can't buy a decent bottle of wine. I don't know why." His manner was affable but his eyes remained watchful. "Maybe I'm fussy. Here, try some of this. Not bought locally, I should stress."

He moved to the side table and poured two glasses of red. "It's Bulgarian, a Starosel," he said as he handed one to me. The name conveyed nothing. It was dark, almost black. I gave a sniff, more out of curiosity than a desire to be seen as a connoisseur. It smelled dark brown and musty. I took a sip. There was a bright burst of magenta on the back of my tongue. On the second sip the same sensation was repeated but the colour was paler. After the third it was gone. I realised I'd drunk about half the glass. There was a grey, bitter taste in my mouth of something stale and decayed.

Why had I been sensing the tastes as colours?

Peter was watching this with a thin smile on his face. "Different, isn't it? I could tell you all about the vineyard and the grapes and so forth but most people aren't interested in that. Are you?"

"Not particularly."

"No matter."

Steve and Di's voices couldn't be heard. It was suddenly very silent and very still. Outside, the sun drifted behind a cloud and a grey shadow rolled across the garden.

The view outside, which faced in the same direction as did the back of Steve and Bel's house a mile down the road, fleetingly resembled the tableau I had witnessed the night before. The colour seemed to have been stripped away. The room itself was fading. The grey world outside was engulfing me.

Peter, a few feet to my left, seemed transfixed.

Then the sun came out again and the world was once again drenched in colour.

From the next room, Di was laughing. It seemed to be the middle of a laugh. Somehow I had missed the beginning.

I felt as if I had been holding my breath in deep, dark water. I looked around slightly wildly. I wondered if I had in those few seconds done something foolish or indiscreet. I caught Peter's eye and saw no surprise there. If anything he appeared satisfied, as if something he suspected had been confirmed.

Steve appeared in the doorway. "We should be off."

I drained my glass and turned to shake Peter's hand. He looked me full in the face as he did so. At other times this might have been unsettling.

"Thanks for the drink."

"Not at all," he said. "*Very* nice to have met you."

More people turned up for lunch at Steve and Bel's, a pleasant but confused gathering spread over several rooms and the back garden. I glanced out of the window. What a colour that tower was. No one else had commented on it. I was going to mention it to Steve but was talking to someone.

I wandered into the garden and sat down. I was alone. There was not a breath of wind. Not a leaf moved. Then the sun went in.

As in Peter's house, the view at once bleached. Now the tones were inverted. The pale sky turned dark. The green grass paled. The only colour seemed to come from the clocktower, a washed-out yellow that hung in the air around it like a sickly halo.

I didn't see the woman at first. I noticed her only when she was halfway across the lawn, her head bowed and her feet slightly dragging. She seemed to be trembling. She was wearing a thick dress, rather thicker than the warm weather demanded. It looked grey but could, in the circumstances, have been any colour. Then she was gone, vanished through the wide archway in the hedge. I could see where she had walked because there were faint footprints on the pale ground as if she had been walking in snow. There was a noise like the slamming of a door.

Then the footprints faded and the scene was flooded in a thousand shades of green. The sun had returned.

"We're all going for a walk," Penny said. "Are you coming?"

I stood up. "Absolutely." The clouds were moving slowly but purposefully towards the sun.

Away from the house and in the woods and fields that surrounded it, the strange moment faded, as dreams do. I was left with only a nagging sensation of unease. For the next hour or so, we ambled in ever-changing groups across the early autumn landscape. The sun went in and came out a dozen times but I experienced nothing approaching the colourless vistas I'd seen twice that day. These dissolved the memory almost completely. By the time we returned at dusk and were cracking open the first bottles of wine, they had faded to nothing.

It was after midnight when I went to bed, my head thumping. Again, Penny was there before me so the stumbling around in the dark of the night before was repeated. Again, I fell asleep quickly; again I found myself wide awake just after three o'clock, the room suffused with a waxy light that seemed to come not from the moon, nor from the stars, nor from any lantern, light or candle.

Again, I walked towards the window. Before I reached it I glanced down and noticed the doll. It was on the chair where I'd dropped my clothes.

It was wearing a dress, blue and frilled at the edges in an elaborate and old-fashioned way. The legs were bare apart from a pair of woollen ankle socks, one red and the other green. The face, classically round and apple-cheeked, didn't have the normal bland half-smile of most dolls. It seemed rather to have caught a real expression, as if taken from a photograph. The emotion seemed one of surprise. I felt a curious reluctance to touch it.

I moved slightly and jogged the chair. The doll moved and the eyes opened, the over-stated eyelashes flickering once or twice before settling on some point just above and beyond my left shoulder. There was something real and not-real about it.

The overall impression was of something that had once had life but now had none, rather than a dummy created from plastic mouldings and balls of glass in a workshop.

Why I had not noticed it before was, perhaps, explained by seeing my clothes from today, and some of those from yesterday, on the floor by the chair. Clearly, in getting undressed that night before, I had dropped garments on the chair. Tonight, my second undressing had pulled some of them down, so revealing the doll.

Only partly satisfied by this explanation, I moved to the window. The scene was much as the night before. The familiarity revealed details that had previously eluded me. 'Scene' – that was the word. It was a tableau on which I was looking, constructed with the same formal symmetry as a painting from the Dutch Golden Age.

The lawn was perfectly framed by the borders. Behind these ran the hedge, with the opening in the centre. Beyond this stood the clock-tower and the outbuildings on either side. Beyond that was the copse, each tree blending into a harmonious whole; beyond that, the unbroken field on the downward slope of the valley. Rising to match these, on either side, were hills which, like the copse, gave the impression of perfect regularity.

These, and the sky and the field, merged together in ever-darkening shades of grey towards a vanishing point of total black.

It was both intensely real and utterly lifeless; simultaneously complete and empty. I might have been gazing at an artist's preliminary sketch to set the scene and to provide the dimensions and angles over which colours and characters could be deployed.

It was no surprise when the man appeared, again moving from right to left. At first, his progress across the canvas, carrying his burden before him, seemed identical to what I had seen last night. Then I saw it wasn't. Now I could see more of what he was carrying and forced myself to watch the scene to its end.

This revealed something I had previously missed: for, just before he vanished into the copse he half turned, as if checking he was not being observed. As he did so, I saw the child in his arms.

I also saw two other things. Firstly, the child was itself carrying something else that had a human shape. Secondly I was certain, from the angle of the man's head and the briefest of pauses before he ducked out of view, that he was aware he was being watched, and from this floor of the house. I had ceased to be an observer in this grey drama. I was now a participant.

Once again, I felt drained. The tableau shimmered with uncertainty. As before, I groped my way back to bed and collapsed into a fitful and slightly feverish sleep.

It was after ten before I awoke. Penny had long since got up. From three floors below I could hear the chatter of conversation, could smell coffee and bacon.

I stretched and dozed. Something was missing from the moment. I was aware less of a feeling of unease than of incompleteness. After a while I sat up in bed and rubbed my eyes. They felt gritty and sore, as if I had been up half the night. I got up and had a shower, after which I felt better but still light-headed. As I came back into the bedroom, drying myself, I noticed the doll on the chair.

It seemed vaguely familiar. I took in the blonde hair, the pair of red socks, the white dress and the bright blue eyes without any particular sense of having seen them before, certainly not in any world which touched on what I could see all about me: the cherry-red towel in my hand; the yellow T-shirt on the floor; the green lawn stretching under a clear, fresh azure sky down towards the copse that was already decked in the infinitely subtle golden hues of early autumn.

I was pouring coffee downstairs when Steve's phone rang. "Yes, he's here," He said. He passed the phone to me. "It's Peter. We went over there yesterday." I could tell Steve was curious as to why he was calling. I was curious myself and felt a flutter of apprehension.

"Peter, hello," I said.

"Hello. Brian, isn't it?"

"Yes," I reassured him. There was a pause. I wondered if that was all he had to ask me.

"Do you own a black mobile phone? Nokia. Quite, how can I say, old fashioned?"

"Yes, I do. I must be the only person on the planet who doesn't have a smartphone."

He chuckled. "Well, I have your old fossil here."

"I must have left it when we came over yesterday," I said idiotically. There was a pause. "Thank you very much. "Can I come and get it? I think we're going to be leaving quite soon."

"Now would be perfect." He could have said 'the sooner the better' with exactly the same inflexion.

Steve offered to take me but I said I could remember the way. It seemed important I should go alone.

Ten minutes later I was ringing the bell. Peter appeared. I wasn't expecting him to have the phone in his hand and he didn't. Instead he ushered me in. We walked through to the same room we'd been in the day before. We faced each other across the sea-green carpet.

"My wife will be out for half an hour," he said at last. It was as if we were keeping a lovers' tryst. I nodded. There was another long silence. I watched the shadows move across the lawn. The sky was largely clear.

Partly as a continuation of what had been occupying my thoughts in that house the day before and partly from sheer nervousness, I began once again to cast my eyes around the room. Once again, although the sun was still out, I had the sense that the world outside my immediate field of vision was fading away. I was looking through some peculiar optical instrument that distorted perspective and shredded colour, causing me to focus on things in a way and to a level of detail that normally would not concern me.

Beside me, Peter was taut with anticipation. This man, whom I had met twice and exchanged barely a hundred words with, had suddenly assumed some kind of sacramental role in my life.

Then I saw it. A small framed black and white photograph on the wall to the left of the mantelpiece. It was of a blonde-haired girl aged about six. It looked as if it had been taken about fifty years ago.

I walked towards the photo. I stared at it for a few moments. The face stared unblinkingly back, the expression one of slight surprise. "Who's this?" I asked.

"My sister," Peter said. I glanced at him. His voice now seemed less tense though I couldn't work out why this might be. "Sally." There was a silence.

There was still a gulf that needed to be crossed. It was hard to know where to start.

"I saw..." I began, then stopped. What had I seen, exactly?

Peter put his hand lightly on my shoulder. "Sit down. Would you like a drink?" I nodded.

He poured another glass of the dark red Starosel. I was interested to see if would have the same effect as the day before. It didn't. My senses seemed to have become vitiated. Peter himself was making do with water, though it could have been neat gin.

He turned and stared at the fireplace for a moment although there was nothing to see there. "Did you know that she...we, used to live in Bel and Steve's house, where you're staying?"

I felt a shiver run down my neck. "No, I didn't."

"We grew up there. She was five years younger than me." He sighed and quickly glanced at his watch. "My parents divorced shortly before Sally was born. My father left and Martin moved in." Again he stared into the non-existent fire. "Martin wasn't an easy man. He had...problems. Depression, bi-polar disorder – perhaps more. One didn't speak of such things in those days." He smiled grimly. "My mother certainly didn't. I think she thought it was all an illusion. A phase. Something neighbours talked up because they didn't approve."

He fixed me with a level stare. "It wasn't."

I said nothing. Nothing seemed to be expected of me.

"In the last year before she was...before she died, I could tell something was going badly wrong. I was twelve and was starting to notice how adults behaved."

He let out a long sigh and stared into his drink. "Of course, with a step-father like that you notice more quickly than usual. The family was falling apart and we didn't know why. My father, when we saw him, didn't know anything about it, or didn't seem to. Of course, I never said anything. What could I say? Where could I start? Things like that just didn't happen, did they?" He looked away again. "Then, when you reach a certain age you start – well you get involved as well. Complicit...at best."

I wondered if he wanted to be forgiven. I could not do this. I tried to meet his intense stare but it was focussed behind me, as if I wasn't there and he was looking at someone sitting about three feet further back.

I had a vision of flashing lights: all were white but, in a way I couldn't define, different kinds of white.

"Then there was Martin's blindness. Of course, that was a problem."

"He was *blind*?"

"No, no. He suffered from achromatopsia. Fabergé's Achromatopsia, to be exact."

"What's that?'

"Almost total colour blindness, like life in the old movies." He took a sip of his drink. "Achromatopsia is normally associated with being hyper-sensitive to light and having poor vision. With Fabergé, the rods are normal – in fact, there are rather more of them. Hardly any cones, though, which detect colour. Some yellow ones, maybe a few of the other two. So, more like watching *Casablanca* with a pair of slightly yellow-tinted sunglasses. Perhaps easier to imagine than normal colour-blindness."

I nodded. "Genetic, I suppose."

"Yes. A triple mutation, each one very rare. I think there have only been a handful of people with his condition. All male." He drained his glass; then paused with it half-way down to the table. "It's funny," he said. "That's the thing I most remember about him. Because of Sally's clothes."

He put the glass gently on the exact centre of the coaster and sat back in his chair. "You've got odd socks on."

I glanced down. "I know."

"Exactly. You know and you don't care. It doesn't matter now." He smiled, to show he was stating a fact, not making a judgement. "It did then. Martin *didn't* know but he *did* care. In those days, people noticed if things didn't match. Marked you down. If it was a child, they said the parents didn't care. Particularly in a village. Martin cared a lot. He knew he wasn't welcome in Trefford. People didn't divorce much then and the new partner always got the blame."

He paused. "In fact, *all* of us got the blame. Tainted. If you had a disability as well, that made it worse. You were the object of pity, and contempt. And fear. The evil eye. Anyway, he needed to prove he was a good parent to cover up – well, the fact that he very definitely wasn't. But he couldn't. Because of the socks."

He stood up. For a moment I thought that was the end of the conversation. "Would you like a top up?"

"Perhaps a small one." He refilled my glass and sat back down.

"When you can see no colours at all it's hard to disguise it. People latch onto weaknesses. Particularly children." He bowed his head.

"You used to..."

"You've got to understand," he said almost violently, "he was my step-father. I didn't hate him. I just couldn't understand what he was doing there, in our home, instead of my father. He tried to ingratiate himself with me in other ways, as I said. Give us something in common." He wiped his hand across his face.

I felt like doing the same. The demands of this confession – which I suspected wasn't over – were wearing me down. I wondered why he had chosen me. To make matters worse, I was starting to feel very unwell: feverish, light-headed and achy.

"I can't remember a great deal about him, to be honest. Blotted it out. But I remember the socks."

We were back with socks. I took a sip of my drink and waited.

"Sally loved bright colours. Red and green in particular. She had several pairs, knee-length. The kind young girls wore then. When it was his turn to get her dressed or take her out she used...*we* used to play tricks. Of course, he couldn't tell, could he? If she said they were both green, he believed her. If he managed to get two of the same colour on it was easy to change them. I'd heard about his colour blindness. She was entranced. Red and green – her two favourite colours at the same time. It wasn't her fault, of course. Nobody blamed *her*."

From the hall, a clock chimed the half hour. It was a muffled, dusty sound: old-fashioned, as chiming clocks always are. There was a faint whir as the wheels disengaged. Silence descended once more.

"It was a kind of quantum entanglement, these red and green socks. He had no idea of which was which until he was told. Bertlmann, wasn't it? The scientist?"

I shrugged, having no idea what he was talking about. He shrugged back, as if the remark had been just a passing whim.

"No matter," he said, with a mild wave of his hand. "The thing is, I got cunning. For a week or so I'd make sure she had matching socks. I could tell Martin was relaxing. Then I'd change them. He got her to tell him what colours they were but she turned it into a silly game. Do you have children?"

"Yes."

"Then you'll know how hard it is to get a straight answer out of a four-year-old. He tried not to get cross with her, I'll give him credit for that. He took it out on the rest of us, though. For me, it was a joke. A nasty one, I admit. He suspected but how could he know? For my mother, it must have been hell. Then, in winter, we'd switch to gloves. Same for a week or so then the old red-green switcheroo." He put down his glass and looked at me again, full in the face. "We gave the man no respite."

He gave me a cold smile. Any charm he had earlier used to engage my sympathy had evaporated. I felt in his power, unable to move. There was something chilling about his single-mindedness, even after half a century.

"But you have to use power sparingly, don't you? Not every day. It's like terrorism. Wait a bit, then go again. Each time is then like the first time, if you have the patience." He looked grimly at the fireplace. "Which I did."

I felt that unless I contributed something I was going to slide completely into his dark world. "My father used to have this thing he'd say at bed-time," I ventured. "'Is it going to happen now, or is it going to happen later; or is it going to happen when you've forgotten all about it and are thinking about something else...?' And then he'd tickle me. Worked every time."

Peter nodded slowly. "Exactly. It was the uncertainty that ground him down. That's what drove him to it in the end."

He stood up and walked over to the French windows that looked onto the garden. Then he sat down again and took a deep breath.

"It was freezing cold – a gloves day. The twenty-first of December, in fact. The winter solstice."

I was faintly relieved at this. By repute, these kind of events happened on anniversaries. Today was not the twenty-first of December but the twenty-second of September. This rang a faint and sinister bell in my mind. Of course – the autumnal equinox. My unfocused unease returned.

Peter paused, as if to let the implications of his last point sink in, then resumed the story.

"Earlier, Sally had gone out with colours all over the place. She thought it was wonderful. Someone had said something to him – no one admitted it later, of course – that must have hurt. How he was a freak, a wife-stealer, a rotten father. He didn't drink that often. When he did, he really went for it. And, of course, took it out on my mother." He paused. "She knew, I think, what was going on. With Sally and Martin – and me. She must have. She missed her chance to stop him. That gave him extra power over her.

"My room was on the top floor, on the right. Sally's was on the left. There were things being broken – screaming, crying. I got up and went halfway down the stairs. I heard him coming up and went into the bathroom on the landing below. He didn't see me. I heard him get Sally up. She started crying too.Then he came down. He must have been carrying her but I couldn't see. He went out of the house and slammed the door.

My mother was still screaming and wailing. I didn't know what to do."

There was another long silence. Peter closed his eyes. There was no question of his trying to remember what happened next: he re-lived that every day. He was gathering his strength. For fifty years he had held all this inside, revealing a bit here and a bit there. Now, for the first time, the whole thing was being acted out for my unwilling sole benefit.

"For some reason," he began slowly, "he didn't go out onto the road, towards the village, but out the back, across the garden. There's a path that leads through Lacey's Copse. At the other side there used to be a railway line that ran down to Lydney. Gone now. You'd walk along the track for a mile or so and there was a station between Trefford and Dryslade. It was dark, of course. He was carrying Sally. Running, probably, to catch the last train."

The white lights came back, flashed a couple of times in an angry way, and were gone. I felt as if I was going to retch.

Peter was talking again. "He probably didn't hear the train. The lights may have confused him. Who knows? Anyway, the train hit them. Both killed outright." He paused, then shifted in his chair.

I felt a sharp pain in my head as if I'd been shot.

"My mother heard the news about an hour later. Owen Walker came up from the village to tell her. She was quite calm." He looked at me, his expression utterly blank. "She thanked him, got up, went out into the outbuilding – that one with the clocktower – loaded a shotgun, put it in her mouth and…"

Peter stopped talking and remained perfectly still. Part of me wanted to say something to ease his pain. Then I realised I didn't need to. Somehow, he had already passed enough of it on to me.

I was at that moment struck by a more powerful and immediate sensation. My skin felt hot, my eyelids gritty, my throat sore. I put down my glass and sat back in the chair. The edges of my vision were blurred and flickering. Directly ahead were the windows leading to the garden. The sun went in and the shadows rolled across the lawn, the bushes, the wall to the right of the house, draining the life and colour from them.

The last thing I remember of that day was Peter standing over me, filling my narrowing field of vision. His mouth was twisted into a strange smile that might have been one of triumph: but the rest of his face wore a bleak expression that could have masked any emotion.

* * *

I have no recollection of how I got back to Bel and Steve's nor how I got back home. For some time afterwards I was neither fully conscious nor fully awake. The backdrop was of flickering lights, shivering sweats, intense, searing headaches and a swirl of images that fractured into ever-more complicated patterns, each demanding classification or resolution I could not provide. In the more lucid moments, these presented themselves one by one, as if on a broken television set. Mostly they swarmed around me like bats, combining and separating at will and jeering at me with voiceless cries of delirium.

I woke up from all this clear-headed and ravenous. I called out. Penny came in, smiled and sat down on the bed. She put her hand on my forehead. "Welcome back. You look better."

"I feel better. What day is it?"

Saturday evening. We'd left Trefford the previous Sunday afternoon.

I lay back and half closed my eyes. I tried to arrange the events of the weekend in my mind but failed. The clearest scene of all was the very last one.

All Penny was able to tell me was that I'd collapsed at Peter's house. A doctor had been called. I'd been to hospital, spent two nights there and gone home in an ambulance. I could remember nothing of this, beyond bright lights and a drip in my arm.

"Was I tested for poison?"

"*Poison*? Why? Not as far as I know. You had a fever."

I thought about this. Slowly I started to remember other things. The clocktower, the doll, the people walking across the garden, the tricks of colour – but what had I imagined, suggested to me by the things Peter had said, and what had actually happened?

After a while, I became fretful. As night fell the chaotic demons again gathered around me to resume their assaults.

I called Steve and told him I was trying to piece the weekend together..

I had met Peter twice, Steve told me. On Saturday he had no idea what we'd discussed as he'd been in the kitchen talking to Diana. The second time, when I'd collapsed, I'd gone on my own.

"Have you got his number?"

There was a short pause. "He's…they've gone away. Went early this week. I've no idea where. We don't know them very well." His words seemed rushed.

I thanked him and hung up. I lay in bed, trying to arrange what I could remember into two piles: things that had really happened and things that hadn't.

Into the first went most of the conversations with Peter, waking up on both nights, the walk in the afternoon, the woman on the lawn and the doll. Into the second went the night-time visions, the shifting colours I had from time to time experienced and some parts of what Peter had said.

There were also a number of impressions and briefer incidents that I couldn't classify. I had mentioned none of these at the time. Peter was away. It was all therefore down to me to sort out.

Then I saw there was one thing I could establish, I called back and Bel answered.

"I've been thinking about that doll," I told her, after she'd asked how I was.

"What doll?"

"The one on the chair, in the room we were sleeping in."

She laughed. "There's no doll there. Like you, we've only got sons."

I had touched it. I could still feel the smooth sheen of the plastic beneath my fingers, could remember the rustle as I ran my hand down the dress. More than ever I wanted to talk to the one person who could help anchor my recollections.

"A shame about Peter," I said.

"Yes," she agreed. There was a pause. "Fortunately the doctor got there in time on Monday. I don't know what he'd taken. He was raving, apparently. Awful." She paused. "Steve mentioned this?"

"Oh yes," I replied, "he said he was away." She seemed re-assured.

Steve had obviously been being kind to me. That he had felt the need to do so made me more alarmed. Whatever had happened had twisted not one mind but two. I wondered if this tragedy, the details of which I could only partly remember, was over. I felt fearful: inexplicably guilty; above all, terribly sad.

I had one more thing to ask. "How long have he and Diana been married?"

"What an *odd* question. Why?"

"Just interested," I said with a brightness I was far from feeling. "Trying to piece it together."

"Since you ask and since I know, not very long. He mentioned his having been a confirmed bachelor until a few years ago. She was a widow. Yes, I remember – they'd bought the house just after they got married. Did you know he grew up in Trefford, in our house, in fact?"

"Yes. He mentioned that." There was a pause. I could tell she wanted to ask me more but I had too much to think about. "Thanks. And sorry for collapsing on you last weekend. See you soon."

So, he'd told no one but me. A late-life marriage needs to avoid secrets. Probably he'd had no one else to tell.

I shivered under the duvet. What had passed between us had done so in a time of half-light to which there was no return. What I had unwittingly been given was now mine to keep. Even if he were prepared to discuss it, I doubted he would be a reliable narrator.

All those years it had been trapped inside him, until I had appeared, weak with a feverish susceptibility, a perfect vessel into which he could pour the contents of his long-fermented cup of sorrows.

For a few minutes, this almost convinced me. Then I saw that this assumption depended on the events having unrolled in a certain order;

and that I had been told things by him before I'd seen them for myself. I could now never be sure that this was the case.

I slipped into a fitful sleep, sure there was still one certainty that eluded me.

I was suddenly awake. Penny was asleep beside me. Moonlight streamed through the unclosed curtains. I looked at my watch. It was exactly three o'clock.

I got up and moved over to the window. One of the cats was lying on the chest at the foot of the bed, his limbs spread in an almost artificial pose of relaxation. I reached down and stroked my hand down his flank.

Then I knew what I had missed.

The doll *had* been real, as real as the cat. There was no doubt. Bel had known nothing of it but this didn't matter. I knew what I had touched and seen.

It was only later, as I again lay restlessly in bed, that the truth hit me. That Sunday morning, both the doll's socks had been red: but the first time I had seen it, on Saturday night, one had been red and the other one green.

Gravity and Rust

I'VE NEVER BEEN sure what to make of stories of the supernatural, fictional or allegedly otherwise. Often revenge is involved, perhaps from some unknown ancestor. Sometimes there are higher aims at work; at other times, very base ones. Whatever the motive, such tales should develop obliquely – so obliquely that one is not sure until afterwards, maybe long afterwards, what if anything has been going on. The event might change the narrator in some unlikely way. At the very least it should challenge any certainties they might have about their fragile yet self-confident humanity.

I won't pretend this story passes any of these tests. It happened several years ago one Sunday evening at the end of one of those dank autumn days that never really seems to get going. I was driving from Kingston to West Berkshire, a journey I'd done countless times before. My familiarity with the route, the warmth of the car, the surprising emptiness of the road and the fog – which one minute vanished into a few stray wisps and at others descended like something palpable – combined to dislocate my thoughts from the reality of my surroundings.

I had a nearly-finished song in my head. I've been writing songs since I was about 16. The results are rarely special. The majority I quickly forget. Some are all right. Quality isn't the issue, though. The thrill is getting a blend of words, rhythm and music which can, at the moment it's caught, send a shiver down my spine. The moment won't last – what moment does? – and is intensely private but, like any rush, it's worth it while it's there. Some songs survive though most flutter off and get pulled apart by the first gust of wind. That doesn't matter. The moment is all.

On this occasion I had something I thought was better than average. The title had come from a chance remark my friend Mark had made at the end of a rather boozy lunch a few weeks before. Somehow, this had provided the key for an idea for a song that had been slowly taking shape in the back of my mind for some time.

Many years before I'd had a magical day when on several occasions I should have come to harm or got rebuffed, yet everything had worked out to an extent I neither expected nor deserved. I had developed the fanciful notion that I'd been given a blessing, a free 24-hour immunity from life's slings and arrows; and that I had used it well.

The day came to loom over-large in my memory, creating a slight sense of dissatisfaction with much of what had followed. The blessing had turned, if not to a curse then to an accelerated vision of the disappointments that most days offer.

Perhaps writing a song about it was not the best way to shake such thoughts. Mind you, I'm far from sure if the 'I' in the song is me, nor even what the song is about. It seems to derive both from my reflections of the day and from the sentiments I wove around it. It was as if, for a few hours, I then simultaneously inhabited two parallel universes, one of which was partly my own invention.

I was running through the song in my head. There was a small problem with a chord change but a more serious one with the scansion. Then the solution came to me. It was simply a matter of stretching the second line. As well as freeing space for a phrase that needed including to balance the mood, it allowed the rhyme to hang suspended until it was released, to greater effect, two bars later than expected. It also, I now saw, echoed a similar pattern in the chorus.

With that, the whole musical and lyrical structure locked in place like the last turn of a Rubik cube. This was the only way it could be. The chord problem, I now saw, was a harmonic detail that would resolve itself. I was filled with a sense of calm and satisfaction, perhaps self-satisfaction. I had created something. The essence of the day and its long aftermath had been made, if not flesh, then something almost tangible.

At this point I was driving on a straight three-mile stretch between Bagshot and Bracknell on the A322 between the M3 and the M4. The road was surprisingly empty. A solitary lorry rumbled past in the opposite direction. As it passed I flicked my headlights back to full beam and was for a moment dazzled by the thick white mist that had sprung up around me. At that point I saw the hitch-hiker.

Hitching used to be very common. In my 20s I used to hitch all over Britain and France. On a Saturday morning the slip roads of the main motorways out of London and Paris would have perhaps a dozen people, each bearing their sign – 'Dunstable'; "Lyon'; 'Scotland'. I once saw one that simply said 'Anywhere!'

These days you hardly see hitchers at all apart from people who've obviously broken down, or car-delivery men ostentatiously holding dealer's plates to show they're respectable professionals rather than crusty psychopaths. It had been a long time since I'd stopped for a hitcher, or even seen one to stop for. I probably wouldn't have stopped for this one except that the road behind me was empty, the night foul and my newly enriched spirit benevolent. I flashed my lights and pulled onto the verge.

The door opened in a leisurely way and a muffled figure with a small but heavy-looking backpack got in. There was absolutely nothing remarkable about him. Clean-shaven, handsome in a regular and perhaps almost bland way and utterly self-possessed. Hitchers normally start gabbling thanks as they're yanking open the door. This one settled in his seat and fixed the belt before even turning towards me.

"I thought you might not stop"

"I nearly didn't." The road behind was empty but still I didn't pull out. "Two minutes earlier and I'd not have noticed you. I had something on my mind."

"All worked out now, fortunately."

I grinned. "Yeah, apart from a few details."

He nodded and almost beamed at me.

I gestured towards the backpack. "You can put that in the back if you want."

"It doesn't matter," he said.

"Okay." I checked the mirror. The road was still empty. For some reason I was reluctant to move. I revved the engine a few times. Finally I pulled out. The road was straight and empty. As before, the fog would suddenly lift slightly then redescend in almost sulphurous clouds. We drove on in a silence that was almost companionable. I seemed to have had part of my volition, the part that makes me talk too much, stripped away.

We reached the Win Bridges roundabout and I swung the car round the curve, effortlessly finding the shortest way across the empty junction. Some of my will started to return. My passenger shifted slightly in his seat.

"Where are you heading?" I asked. It seemed odd this hadn't come up before.

"Lambourn way," he said carefully.

"Me too. I live about four miles from Lambourn. I'll take you home."

He made a gesture of his hand as if this were of no importance.

Soon we hit another roundabout: Bracknell has a lot of them. Just as I pulled off to the left and slowed down fractionally on the curve by the Siemens offices, he spoke again.

"You've just caught up with yourself."

"What?"

"You wasted time picking me up. You've just made it up."

On one level this was just a form of words but there was something precise about the remark. The combination made it hard to decide how best to react. "Possibly. I wasn't noticing."

"Well, no."

"There was a Sherlock Holmes story," I said lightly, "I forget which. Holmes and Watson were on a train and Holmes calculated their exact speed from counting the distance between the telegraph posts. Of course, being Holmes, he knew how far apart the telegraph posts were on the LNER. Was it something like that?"

The passenger laughed. It was musical, almost seductive: all things I'd more associate with a woman. I was finding his personality, even from these short exchanges, overwhelmingly attractive. I sneaked a few glances but the face was hidden in shadow.

"No – just a figure of speech, I suppose." The self-effacement was surprising.

I felt a powerful urge to keep the conversation going.

"What led you to be hitching a lift back there?"

"It seemed like a place where you…where someone might stop. Plenty of time to see me."

I doubted that. His clothes were of an indeterminate colour impossible to define in the gloom of the car but they couldn't be called particularly visible.

"Had your car broken down?"

"No, no. I just suddenly had to be somewhere."

"You were lucky I stopped, then."

"*You* were…" he checked himself. "You were very kind to do that."

The exchange had been inconclusive. The answers had been evasive – no, that wasn't right. They had been restrained. The small indiscretions didn't seem to imply reluctance. Diffidence, perhaps? Overall, the impression was of someone who was trying to conceal from a small child the details of an elaborate birthday surprise.

If not fully at the time but certainly afterwards, I was aware of how much I was trying to propitiate this stranger. I was then more aware of feeling a dreamy contentment. I felt swaddled. The route and the process of driving were comfortingly familiar. The passenger had overlaid some other emotion which complemented this. I was going home, with a song in my head and a good deed in my heart. That, doubtless, was the explanation.

Suddenly I was struck by a doubt: was this person a woman? There was something about the line of the jaw and the delicacy of cheekbones and nose that was feminine. Something about the way they were sitting made me think of a man. The voice, I now, realised, offered no clue either way. There was also something familiar about them but I sensed this might have been because I was searching for something that could help me towards identification.

Did it matter? Probably not. The conversation was unlikely to enter sexually charged waters. But had I said anything so far that might have given offence? I shrugged to myself. People who appear androgynous often do so deliberately and so must be used to, even welcome, the confusion. Still, I like to know what gender I'm dealing with. I sensed, without being able to define how, that I talked differently to men and to women. Once again I felt on the back foot.

We were leaving Bracknell behind us and turning onto the M4.

My passenger stirred and half turned to face me. I was overtaking a lorry and so couldn't return the glance. "What was it that was on your mind just before you picked me up?" The last three words, so laden with double meaning, convinced me I was dealing with a female. Then there was a movement of the shoulder and I once again was unsure. I decided this didn't matter. My passenger's gender was a harmonic detail.

I related the story about the song and my charmed evening in 1986. "How interesting," was the completely sincere reply. "How do the lyrics go?"

It is rare for anyone to be asked to recite some of their own lyrics. I wasn't going to pass up the opportunity.

"'*I could have danced all night, there was an angel watching over me – silhouetted in the wine-light I could glimpse her, occasionally*'. That's the first verse. Enough to be going on with."

"Yes, that catches the moment."

I found this an astonishing remark.

"How do you mean? You weren't there." I realised this sounded rude so I turned it into a laugh.

The response was quick: not apologetic but more as if she – as I had now decided – had been caught out and was having to back-track. "You described the evening. Then you recited the lyric. I'd say that catches the essence of it."

"Good. It was an important day."

"Indeed."

"No, that's wrong. It wasn't important. It was..." I suddenly couldn't summarise my thoughts at all. "It was different. I wasn't really there. And yet I was."

"And a woman was involved."

"Oh, yes." I smiled to myself. Then I noticed the inflection. This had been a statement, not a question. My prose description had been general. Had the lyrics been that revealing?"

I expounded my theory about the beneficent presence I felt had watched over me that day. "I suppose," I said, probably sounding atrociously precious, "that writing songs makes some events seem more important or tragic or whatever than they really are. Emotions become exaggerated. We get a sense that...well, when something worthwhile comes of it that we've been inspired. Protected, perhaps. By some higher force." I realised I was in danger of talking drivel. "Well, it can seem that way," I added almost apologetically.

"Not at all. I think you were right first time. I've heard," – and here her voice took on a dreamy, almost ironical, tone that continued for the rest of our conversation and left me unsure if she was referring to her own experiences, to someone else's or to something hypothetical – "I've heard stories about guardian angels: would that be the right way of expressing it?"

"Quite possibly, yes."

She nodded. "People finding their life saved or altered by some intervention for which there's no obvious explanation."

"Or no purpose," I interrupted, deciding to throw myself into the philosophical tone the conversation had adopted, one that jived precisely with my state of mind. "For what purpose might someone be saved? And why? And, most of all, by whom?"

There was a long silence. "I don't know," she said at last, in a voice that appeared almost to be tinged with despair.

There followed an extraordinary moment.

What happened next struck me not as a memory but as a piece of real life. It was as if the event was unfolding behind me and I was seeing it all through another pair of eyes of which I was not normally aware.

It was about 11.30 on that night in May 1986. I was leaving the pub in Vauxhall with the woman my passenger had inferred. I stepped out into the road but for some reason turned my gaze back towards the open doorway. Standing there was a young woman I'd never seen before. She gave me a smile of intoxicating wistfulness and warmth. Then she was gone.

For a moment I froze, then turned back to the road. A number 77 bus, going far too fast, swung round the corner, missing me by inches. The whole incident had taken no more than five seconds. I should have been flattened.

Somehow I had forgotten all this until now, in the car with the hitch-hiker.

Just as the strange vision faded, we passed the junction at Theale after where the motorway lights stop until you get Swindon 30 miles further west. We were plunged into darkness.

The car's headlights sliced into the fog ahead. Shaken, I turned the radio on. It was a song I know and love well, Morrissey at his mawkish best. '*...and if a double-decker bus, crashes into us, to die by your side would be...*'

I turned the radio off.

The unexpected revelations, the co-incidence of the music and the darkened road changed the mood of the conversation and of the journey. I felt that we were hurtling towards something and that every second was precious. Perhaps responding to this, my passenger shook herself out of her reverie.

"Why do some people have to be saved? I don't know." The observation seemed personal. It was as if she'd been carefully considering the matter since our last exchange: a period of time which, I suspected, had seemed to last for me for longer than it had for her.

"Saved from a worse fate, perhaps," I suggested.

"In each life, there's only one fate."

Again I had the feeling I'd trapped her into saying more than she ought. A wave of scent sweep over me as she turned, something that called to mind other women in other places: then, as long-vanished scents will do, it vanished leaving nothing but a vague feeling of longing and regret.

"So," she said earnestly and with the air of someone changing the subject, "suppose there *were* these guardian angels. How do you think they'd behave?"

She hadn't changed the subject at all. In a way I was relieved. Even so, the question had caught me unawares.

"They'd have rules," I suggested. She twisted round in the seat. Encouraged by this reaction, I continued.

"There'd be certain things they couldn't do. Certain…interventions they couldn't make. It's like those time-travel films – *Back to the Future* and stuff – where you have to leave the past as you found it."

"And certain things they couldn't explain."

We had entered those strange waters, known to me mainly through flirtation, where every gesture or remark is charged with a secondary meaning unnoticeable to an observer passing by on less highly charged business of their own. Yet this conversation was unlike anything I'd ever experienced. We were discussing something vital. One part of me was in the car, driving blindly into the silver fog; another was back in 1986, seeing the situation from a different point of view. I was torn in two and yet feeling a sense of completeness; confronted with soul-stripping self-revelations and yet protected by heady, almost erotic, magic.

This strange composite had made me that purest of things, a person with an unshakable sense of the importance of the immediate. Every second counted. This was just like, and yet quite unlike, a mutual seduction. Part of me was viscerally engaged, both in the moment and the memory I was re-living: the other part was observing from another world in which every outcome bar one had been annihilated by predetermination. Though my highly charged confusion I sensed that my passenger, without being able to do so explicitly, was striving to guide me to some point of singularity.

We passed junction 13, Newbury. Mine was the next. The home leg. Perhaps seven minutes to go. The fog had cleared. The road was empty.

"I read somewhere," she continued, re-adopting her earlier dreamily ironic tone, "that such angels can do nothing directly, only indirectly."

On one level, this made no sense. Read somewhere? What kind of authority would, in this world, such a source have? The other part of my mind swung across to lock into her last remark. "But perhaps they can cheat the system?"

Her laugh was like pure water running from a mountain pool. It washed through my mind in a way that was both reassuringly familiar and also not of this world at all. The duality of my perceptions was now total. Everything inside the car existed automatically and necessarily on two different, parallel and almost simultaneous levels.

I was struck then by the strangest of feelings: the idea that these two parts of this strange harmony were slipping out of tempo, one being dragged behind the other. The effect was not unpleasant: the rhythms still meshed, but in unexpected ways. Between them, as might exist in the gap between two worlds, strange harmonics rose and died, never to be heard or sensed again.

"Indeed they can," she was saying in a voice filled with delight. "Take this journey. Hypothetical example. Even though you stopped to pick me up, I can't do anything to make you drive slower or faster. Not directly," she added as an afterthought.

"Assuming you are my guardian angel," I suggested.

"Always assuming that."

"Why not? You could say you needed a pee or something."

"You'd make the time up. You did before."

There was another highly charged pause.

"But you see," she went on, "you car's a tiny bit more inefficient now."

"Why?"

"You kept the engine running while you picked me up. It's a bit older, tireder, rustier." The phrases tugged at my sails, one erect in these strange winds, the other furled against the coming storm. "But you drove as if that weren't the case. Because…in one sense, you didn't stop for me. And in another, you did."

I began to have some vague glimmering of what was going on but was unable to speak.

"But it's me that's more important, perhaps."

"What?" I managed to ask.

"Just my being here. I have to exist, don't I?"

Yes, I thought, you do. No spirit, shade or phantom could engage my attention or change my life as much as a fully corporeal female informed by the same physical rules as was I. Anything else would just scare or confuse me. Perhaps God was right and his son had to be made flesh to get our full attention.

"*I always hoped I could rely on the father, son and holy ghost,*" I heard myself saying, "*but now, no matter how I try, my faith has run dry – just when I need it most…*"

Where had *that* come from?

"But me alone isn't enough. And there's only so much I can carry."

I glanced down at her bag. What the hell was in *that*?

"So, together, gravity and rust might work."

For a split second I lost control of the car. I should explain that 'Gravity and Rust is what gets us all in the end' was the remark my friend Mark had made the summer before in Upper Lambourn; that 'in the end it's gravity and rust that slows us down' was the coda of the song I'd just finished writing; and 'Gravity and Rust' was its title. Again, it was only half of my mind that was surprised. The other half nodded to itself.

My passenger kicked the backpack and gave me a bewitching smile that nearly lifted me out of my seat. I had seen it before, many years ago.

A few seconds later we passed over the bridge at Easton. Two miles to go. We cleared the last hill.

Just then everything went haywire.

From the opposite lane there was a flash of light. Something huge was moving towards us, swerving and crashing through the central reservation. I could see, in slow motion as accidents always are viewed, the front right tyre of the fuel lorry spinning madly, rubber peeling off like black sparks from a demonic Catherine wheel. I could see the driver in his cab, could see the Arsenal banner pinned on the panel behind him. I could see the driver grapple with the wheel.

Then I saw a red car, the same make and colour as mine, emerge out of the strange illumination that had thrown part of the scene into sharp relief and part into the darkest shadow and vanish under the oncoming wheels of the lorry.

This collision happened in my mind. The two parts of my brain fused back together. Now I was witnessing something indivisible. The lorry, toppling onto its side and trailing sparks like a comet, passed some twenty feet in front of us. The trailer whipped behind it, sliding away. My car shuddered in its slipstream then came to a swerving, skidding, uncontrolled halt a hundred yards down the motorway. It spun round to face the opposite direction.

I could see, now in a more normal slow motion, the lorry shudder as it reared against the barrier on the hard shoulder. I could see the driver jump out and tumble into the empty carriageway. I could see the toppling of the cab with its broken spine and then the trailer, rearing up against the black sky and hanging for a moment. Time seemed to hang in suspension.

"*In the end*," I heard several voices singing, "*it's gravity and rust that slows us down…*"

Time crashed back over me. The trailer slammed down into the verge. There was a second or two of monumental silence then a brilliant explosion.

I got out and staggered towards the blaze. Other cars had stopped. I could see the lorry driver being helped to his feet. I felt divorced from the scene. I was a witness, certainly: but a witness to what? I had been in two worlds at the same time.

I looked back at the part of the motorway where I had seen the red car crushed by the lorry. There was nothing there. My headlights were blinding me. I walked beyond my car and looked again. Still nothing. My senses were all to hell in any case. I turned back to the carnage.

The eastern sky was aflame. Other cars were backing up, their headlights blurred in the fog which had started to close in again. The people driving east were slowing. But on my westbound lane there was nothing. I was the last to have passed beyond the accident. Except for that other red car…I shook my head as if to dispel a dream.

I heard my tune, with an unexpected harmony, running back through my head. Yes, that would work. *"in the end…"*

I walked back to my car and pulled open the door. "Sorry, I…"

The car was empty. A faint smell of perfume swept past me and was gone. The backpack was still there. I poked at it and found the zip wasn't fastened.

It was full of stones. I picked it up. It weighed perhaps twenty pounds. Enough to make a difference. The backpack; and her; and a little bit of help from the slightly older engine. If you're dealing in split seconds and can make no direct intervention you need all the help you can get.

I didn't understand how or why all this had happened. I didn't understand anything. But here I was, standing on the empty motorway, surrounded by fire, fog and darkness – alone again but still alive.

Into the Dreamhouse

CATHERINE PAUSED AT the end of the street. The house loomed out of the grey, fried-egg hissing of rain, a monstrous gargoyle of patched stone and withered rafters. Sickly lights burned at the windows. It was without doubt the right place.

"Hardly a dream house,' she thought: then again, where was? Everywhere grew tongues at twilight, whispered secrets she knew too well until her pillow was sodden with sweat. Then it would be time to move on. One place was as good as another.

She pushed open the door.

The first ten minutes were the best because nobody knew her. People moved from room to room like wraiths, locked in their inscrutable communal concerns.

"I'm looking for Shebah," she said to two women as they floated past.

Shebah appeared: immensely old, chain-smoking, a crimson study of a scarecrow on the move. She apprised Catherine quickly, then reached forward and cupped her chin in her hand.

"Your room's at the top," she said. Catherine followed Shebah upstairs. Odours of musk and jasmine washed behind her, mingling at every landing with more earthy smells. Corridors stretched away, dark tunnels of gloom illuminated by flickering candlelight from half-open doorways.

"About twenty," Shebah said, answering Catherine's unspoken question. "Some come, some go." Catherine nodded, feeling more at ease in this shifting world. Shebah paused. "We've no secrets from each other, really," she said. Catherine's hand closed fearfully around a small glass cat in her pocket. "You won't come to harm here."

The room was in darkness and at points open to the sky. Rain drifted against the washbasin, wind tugged at the curtain like the sea on a net. At the far end was the bed. Shebah lit a candle and turned to leave. "You won't come to harm here," she repeated. "Whatever people know."

The house curled up like a snake and slept. Catherine knew she was the last person awake yet had a strong feeling of being watched. It took ten minutes to tip-toe to the door and peer into the windswept darkness of the top hallway. There was nothing to see. She turned back towards the guttering candle. Floorboards creaked; were answered up and down the building. She stood still for five minutes, then collapsed on the bed.

Catherine started dreaming. Never, not even since the murder, had she had such dreams. They tumbled out as if from the locker room of a lunatic. A babble of voices chased her down a candlelit hallway. At the far end...Catherine screamed, and woke up.

The house was alive. She heard the echo of her scream ringing down beam and gutter, across every rat-scuttling threshold. Candlelight flickered in the corridors: in the background she had the impression of other objects on the move. She found herself at the doorway, then halfway down the stairs.

The crumbling plaster soaked up reflections like a sponge. Below her, the house was adrift on a dozen sickly points of light. People moved back and forth talking of the scream but in a disjunctive way, as though it had been something collective. She tried to catch expressions but each face was hooded by a cowl of dark light. Far below, through a great rent in the stairwell, she saw Shebah waving her arms like a priestess.

Catherine crept back to bed.

She spent the next day in her room. The house seemed to shrink in the pale daylight. Rain fell without break. One day, Catherine thought, I'll be free of all this; but she couldn't see how. Every footfall made her shudder, recalling the night Dennis had returned.

As the daylight retreated the house grew larger, expanding into its truer personality. Catherine slunk downstairs and stole a piece of bread. She wondered how long life, even here, could be sustained without money. She had been told Shebah made no demands but there existed other necessities.

Shebah was standing on the stairs. Catherine forced the rest of the bread into her mouth.

"Share and share alike, dearie," she said. Catherine, masticating for air, nodded.

As the evening wore on, the house again settled down to its strange repose. Again Catherine dreamed. This time the images made more sense, even though little was to do with her own life. The jolly woman in the leaking boat, for example, was called Beth. Catherine had never met her but she was no random creation of her subconscious. Beth had a place in someone's life, if not yet in hers.

The following day she ventured into the front room to sit quietly and watch the rain from a different perspective. Two women were in the far corner.

Catherine mustered her courage to speak. "Sorry about the scream," she said.

They laughed. "We're all sorry," one said, but without malice.

"Did you like Beth's boat?" the other said.

"I…I dreamed about someone called Beth last night," she stammered.

"Yes, yes," the first woman said impatiently.

"But I've never met her."

Both women shrugged as if the distinction were meaningless. Catherine went back upstairs.

That night – the third night – her dream at last connected with experience but in an unexpected way. This was the dream of alternative memory. Now it was she who had come back to the darkened house, to find Dennis stalking her. Now and then she could see his green slitted eyes through gaps in the banisters or reflected in the windows of empty rooms as she crept by on all fours, the knife between her teeth. Hour after hour the chase went on, restarting, veering off from a previous pattern into another jumble of half-landings and echoing bathrooms.

Just before dawn the knife fell, but in his hand, not hers. She could feel his blade rasp against bone and sinew, as hers had on his. Pale daylight was breaking across the sodden eaves of the house before her body twitched for the last time. He fell forwards and vanished into her entrails, swallowed up like an ox in quicksand. As it did so the image blurred into a conscious vision of rain.

Catherine stood up. The house was holding its breath. She opened the door.

Everyone was there, staring at her with an identical expression, appalled and knowing. At the front stood Shebah.

"Too much, dearie," Shebah said. "Share and share alike, but..."

Catherine nodded. Even dreams could be common property. From each according to her needs, to each according to her wants: but nobody, it seemed, wanted any part of her awful, uncoagulated memories. She scanned the faces again, unable to blame them. Pity: she had liked Beth, would have liked to get to know her or talk about her with others in the rainy afternoons, maybe – in time – find out from whose life she had sprung. Three nights of safety were in the circumstances all she had a right to expect. She nodded again, then turned back into the room.

Ten minutes later she slipped out of the dreamhouse. No one said goodbye.

Heartburn

ONE OF THE advantages (or drawbacks) of living in London is that you rarely get to know or even meet your neighbours. Whether people crave anonymity or not, that's what they generally get. Even if you *do* get to know someone, and like them, chances are they or you will be gone in two months and you'll never see them again. In many ways it's easier not to start.

That's how I was until I moved into a flat in Kentish Town a year ago. By an extraordinary co-incidence, the person living opposite me on the first floor was the mother of my friend Paul. I ended up seeing more of her than he did, as he moved to Newcastle soon afterwards.

Her name was Mary and she was about 80 and pretty spry. She would go to bridge clubs and coffee mornings and seemed to lead an active life. The one thing she had trouble with was shopping. There were no supermarkets nearby and she didn't have a car so two or three times a week she would come back with as much as she could manage to carry. I did have a car but lived a fairly erratic existence and so wasn't much use.

To be honest, I was wary of getting too involved, of putting myself in the position where I was her lifeline. Having just ended a long-term relationship I didn't feel like taking on fresh responsibilities. Mainly, I was reactive. There might be a tentative knock on the door: next time I was out, could I be so kind as to pick up some chilli flakes, or a box of Earl Grey, or half a dozen eggs? These rarely seemed like urgent commissions so I didn't always do them straight away and sometimes forgot altogether.

I never asked myself whether these requests were strictly necessary and if what she really wanted was human contact. She told me once that she'd grown up in a village in Suffolk where people were in and out of each other's houses all the time. This sounded awful to me. I could never bring myself to ask if she wished that to be the case here. It was certainly not something I could provide. I was out most of the time, anyway. I did what I could and little more.

One day she had a fall – nothing serious she said, but it made the shopping difficult. She made no specific request of me. I was considering what to do about this and was about to call Paul when I heard someone coming up the stairs, quite slowly, and knock at her door.

"Oh, Jim, thank you," I heard her say. I couldn't hear what Jim said. "Come in, come in." The door closed. About ten minutes later I heard him leave.

A few days later, I saw Mary in the hallway. Jim, she told me – though I hadn't asked – was a friend from the bridge club who lived nearby and had a car, so he now did her shopping. Whether she told me this to explain the nature of their relationship, to absolve me from responsibility or merely to pass the time I wasn't sure. I told her that was great and happened to mention that I was going away the following Tuesday for a couple of weeks.

The next day, I met Jim as I was leaving the building. He was about to ring Mary's bell. He was about 70 and looked both prosperous and anxious, two things I vaguely imagined were rarely found together. I didn't then know what form his anxiety took.

"Hi," I said. "You must be Jim."

He put the bags down and looked at me. A fearful expression crossed his face so that I almost turned to see if there was a sinister figure silhouetted in the frosted glass door behind me.

"I'm Mike. Mary's neighbour. We haven't met."

At that, his expression cleared. "Ah, hello," he said. "She mentioned you. The helpful young gentleman." I smiled. I doubted if any of the descriptions were accurate but let it pass.

"We know each other from the bridge club," he went on, as keen as she had been to ensure their relationship was precisely understood. "Do you play?"

"No. I tried once but couldn't get the hang of the bidding. It seems you have to say the opposite of what you mean. It's all in code."

He gave a slow smile and made an odd movement with his thin hands, as if kneading bread. "It *is* in code," he conceded, "but one you can learn. Come and try one of these days. We have people of all ages – beginners are welcome."

"Perhaps," I said, moving down the steps towards the pavement. "I can always ask Mary. I think I'll stick to poker, though." As I said it, I realised that this was perhaps the worst game I could have mentioned. His reaction surprised me.

"Marvellous," he said. "Different, of course, very different. But thrilling. You know what they say – bet as if you had 'em and never draw on an inside straight." He beamed at me. "The thing about both poker and bridge is that you need to understand people."

"And have a good memory," I added.

There was a pause; a beat; a quaver of silence. "Indeed," he said. I raised my hand in farewell and went on my way, slightly uneasy.

The following week, the day before I was planning to go to Singapore, I made a curry and had quite a bit left over: the habit of cooking for one was taking time to adjust to. I remembered Mary had revealed a taste for spicy food. I put it in a dish and knocked on the door.

"Oh, hello Mike," she said. "I thought you might be Jim."

I wondered how Jim could have got into the building without ringing the bell. Did he have a key? If so, why for the outer door and not for hers? Did she, perhaps, only trust him so far? Was any of this my business anyway?

"I thought you might like this," I explained. "Vegetable curry. I cooked too much…that's to say, I thought you might like it. As I said, I'm going away tomorrow. I'm afraid there isn't any rice left, but…"

"Oh, you could *freeze* it," she said.

The thought struck me that she didn't actually want a vegetable curry. Or perhaps, in her world, offering food was a gesture made from older people to younger ones, and always by women. I suddenly felt foolish, and certainly un-London, by standing in this first-floor hallway having this conversation at all.

"I *could*," I admitted, "but I thought…"

"Well, that's very kind of you," she said. "And, as it happens, I have some rice. Thank you. How long will you be away?"

"Hopefully no more than two weeks. But with these printers, anything is possible."

We chatted for a bit longer. She made no move to invite me in, which I welcomed. We said goodbye.

And that, I thought, was that.

Later that evening I discovered there had been a mix-up with the reservation and my flight wasn't until 24 hours later. I was packing the next day when I heard Jim come up the stairs. Mary opened the door. As usual, I could hear her words more clearly than his.

"Oh, damn," he said, suddenly distinct, "I forgot the Rennies."

There was an edge to his voice which displayed a real concern. My mind was elsewhere. As it happened, I'd recently been shopping and had bought some Rennies, which I hadn't really wanted but needed to get the card payment up above the five-pound minimum. They were still in my pocket. This seemed like an ideal solution. I opened the door and stepped into the hallway.

At that moment, two things happened. The first was that Mary's door swung shut, though Jim's shopping bag was still in the corridor. The second was that my mobile rang.

"Hi,"

"Mike, it's Lucy." Lucy lived opposite and we'd met in the pub up the road a couple of times. Was there anything between us? Might there be? I couldn't say.

"Hi, Lucy."

"Traffic wardens about."

I should explain that since moving here I've been embroiled in a battle with Camden Council about my parking permit. This had already resulted in four tickets which I was contesting. I had no wish to add a fifth to the list just before going away. Fortunately I had a friend near Heathrow where I left the car when I went abroad.

"Thanks. Look, I'm away for a few weeks. I owe you a drink for this. I'll call when I get back."

"Sure. Go!"

As I put the phone in my pocket, my hand jostled against the Rennies. Without thinking, I dropped them into Jim's bag, nipped back to get the car keys and ran down the stairs.

I got the car out of the bay a few seconds before the warden latched onto me. The sequel involved, as it always did, driving around for twenty minutes until I thought the coast was clear and then returning to find that my space had been taken; then driving round for another twenty minutes to find somewhere else to park. Not for the first time, I wished I didn't have a car at all.

All of this had driven the thought of the Rennies from my mind by the time I'd got back nearly an hour later. I finished my packing and went to bed.

I was away for longer than I'd expected. As I'd feared, there were problems at the printers so I had to stay an extra week. The only flight I could get back was via Paris so I decided to stop off and see some friends there for a few days.

It was therefore nearly a month later before I returned to Kentish Town. For a while I sat slumped on the sofa, staring at the pile of letters in the hall, amongst which I recognised a final demand for the electricity bill and reflecting, as I had done before, that travel has the habit of creating more anxieties than it cures.

I was just making a start on the post when there was a knock on the door.

It was Mary. "Hi," I said. "Come in."

She looked awful: frail, thin and upset. "I…er…" There was a pause. She seemed to have forgotten why she'd knocked on my door at all.

I ushered her in. "Would you like a cup of tea?" She looked at me blankly. "I was about to make one," I added, untruthfully.

"Oh, yes. Thank you." She allowed herself to be sat down and I fussed about with kettles and teapots.

"Thank you," she said again as I poured the tea. There was a silence.

"I'm very glad to see you back," she said with surprising warmth.

I didn't know what to make of this. "Well," I said carefully, "it's good to *be* back."

"Yes." She looked at me wildly. I started to feel uneasy. Although my life was lived independently of hers, we were connected. Within limits. Did she feel that these connections were closer than I felt them to be? I'd done what I'd felt I should. Perhaps it would have been kinder and more honest for me to have done less. This was London, after all.

"How have things been?" I asked. There was a silence. "How's Jim?" I asked, desperate to fill it. "He wanted me to learn bridge but…"

"Jim isn't very well *at all*," Mary said in a rush. I realised that her unease had been focused on someone else, not herself.

"I'm sorry. What…?"

"He's had a breakdown. A mental breakdown," Mary explained. "And it's *all my fault*."

This opened up a new view of the situation. The only time when friends of mine had breakdowns was when they'd been ditched by someone. I looked at Mary: trim, agile but without doubt about 80. What emotional currents flowed at that age? What was going on here? What could I do?

"I'm sorry to ask but I wonder if, when you next go to the shops, you could get me some tea? This is the first cup I've had for a week. Did you know the corner shop has closed?"

I went into the kitchen and, having taken out a couple of tea bags for tomorrow, came back with the box.

"Oh, thank you," she said. Then she started to cry. This was a bit of a facer as well. Women of any age in tears always make my mind close down. They seem to be able to access gradations of misery that most men can't get close to understanding. I just stood there, really. After a while she stopped and dabbed her eyes.

"I'm sorry…"

"Not at all…"

"Poor Jim," she said at last. "He always prided himself on his *memory*, you see. 'Keeping his faculties', he called it. He had a scare a couple of years ago, a brain…you know. Tumour. Benign. But it made him realise. He used to be a lawyer, always having to remember things. Laws, court judgments…secrets, perhaps. He had something to lose. Then there was the bridge. It was a kind of test for all of us. You *have* to remember when you're playing that. Well, we all do, don't we? All the time. We are what we can remember. You'll see that when…well…" She sniffed again and took a sip of tea. "And it all started with that *silly* business with the Rennies."

At this point I started to pay serious attention. "The *Rennies*?"

"Yes – the day you left."

She left another pause, as if to give me the chance to say that it was the day *before* I'd left and that I remembered the Rennies very well. I said nothing.

"As you know, he used to do my shopping. When I called him that morning I read out my list – I try to keep it as short as possible – and added some Rennies." She gave a shy little laugh. "I think that curry you gave me…oh it was lovely, but perhaps a *bit* spicy…"

I felt a feeling not unlike heartburn gripping me. In fact, it *was* heartburn.

Mary took another mouthful of tea, put the cup down and continued.

"Something odd happened. He said he'd forgotten them. Well, *anyone* can do that. They weren't part of the normal stuff. But in fact, he *hadn't*. They were there in the bag." She started weeping again, then stopped. "Oh, I *wish* I hadn't mentioned it." She was now rocking back and forth in her distress. It was like listening to an eye-witness report of my own car crash. "He was upset, more upset than I thought was reasonable. Then I realised."

I closed my eyes.

"You see," she said, in a suddenly calm and quiet voice, like a schoolmistress explaining a parable at Sunday school, "Anyone can forget to do something. But to do something and then forget it is *very* different."

There was a long silence. I felt almost numb with shock. The moment when I could have said anything had passed.

"So," she continued, returning to her sorrowful tone, "it's been downhill ever since. He hasn't been to bridge. He hasn't been answering his phone. I found out a few days ago that he's in hospital. A mental collapse, they called it that in my day. The doctor – I spoke to the doctor – used another word, I can't remember what. He asked if I was next of kin. That's not good, is it? He told me not...not to be too hopeful. Apparently he isn't making much sense, talking about these blasted Rennies all the time. He's on pills, but – oh dear, aren't we all? They never seem to do much good..."

Her words seemed to be coming from underwater. I turned away, the pain in my chest now dominating all else. I took some deep breaths and swung round to face her.

"I'm *really* sorry about that," I said. "Would you like me to do any shopping for you? I'm going to go to the supermarket in a bit anyway." This was, I now saw, the expiation I deserved.

I sat down. "Well," she said, "that would be *very* nice. Thank you. There are just a few things. Let me think..." she sat back in the chair. There was a long pause. "Oh dear," she said, "now *what* was it?" She looked across at me. I looked back.

"I'm *so* sorry," I said again, very slowly, "about Jim."

Something in my manner communicated itself and she became once again alert.

"Oh, Mike," she said, for a moment resting her frail hand on mine. "Don't be upset. After all, it's not *your* fault."

So Much Time

"THIS IS QUITE normal," Doctor Finch said as he switched off the pen-light torch and sat down.

Mike blinked, waiting for his eyes to re-adjust. He could only rub them with his right hand because his left arm was in a sling.

"There's nothing wrong with you, apart from your arm, of course. That should be fine in a month or so. The head wound seems superficial. You're very lucky. How fast were you going?"

Mike could clearly remember the speedometer when the van hit him and the car started to spin. Even though it was not moving forward, it had taken the needle some time to come down to under thirty.

That was when the car had flipped over. It had happened very slowly, as if it were being gently picked up and turned by a giant. He remembered thinking it would be a good idea to pull his right arm into the car, which he did. He'd also noticed that his wristwatch showed the time as being exactly four o'clock. Things didn't often happen at exactly anything o'clock: except for the chimes of Big Ben, of course. Was it the first one or the last that marked the hour? He couldn't remember.

"I'm sorry – what did you say?"

"Your speed."

"Sixty-six miles an hour, when the van hit me."

Doctor Finch made a note. Mike wasn't sure if he was recording the figure or the fact that Mike had remembered it so accurately.

The pen moved slowly across the page as if the Doctor was considering what to write, or how to write it. Out of the window, Mike saw a pigeon glide onto the ledge and gently beat its wings. Then the flapping picked up speed: at the same moment, Doctor Finch concluded his note with a flourish and sat back in his chair.

The consultation was coming to an end but Mike felt it necessary to repeat his description of the accident.

"It was amazing how much time I had," he ended lamely. He felt he had come nowhere close to explaining what had happened.

"This is quite normal," Doctor Finch said again. "Many people experience this. No one's sure why. It might be caused by a rapid release of noradrenaline which makes the brain process choices and actions at many times the usual speed. Birds seem to have it."

He glanced at the window where the pigeon was strutting slowly up and down the ledge like a fat waiter and gestured at it with his chin. "It's very hard to run over one of those, for instance." His tone left open the question of whether he'd ever tried to.

Mike wondered if this might be something the Doctor would defend, if he ever pulled it off, on the grounds of medical research. Then again, Doctor Finch was an orthopaedic surgeon, not a psychologist, or a vet. Why should he want to run over a pigeon?

None the less, he was forced to accept the wisdom of the remark: pigeons did seem to get out of the way at the last moment. He tried to analyse his emotions when this happened while he was driving. What was foremost in his mind? Curiosity? Sympathy? Sadism?

Almost unmoving, Doctor Finch was watching him think about this. Then he turned his head and continued talking. "Or it might be to do with how we recall events. A trick of memory, if you like. Intense incidents make our brains gather a lot of data. Looking back, this makes us think it all happened over a much longer period."

Mike shook his head. As he did so he could feel his thoughts fly around his mind before settling like the artificial snow in a Christmas ornament. There were things he wanted to say about all the Doctor 's remarks but forced himself to deal just with the most recent.

"I'm not relying on a memory," he said at last. "It was all in slow motion. The memory of it was the same. So – well, it really happened, in just that way. Time stretched out. Do you understand what I mean? Since then, it sometimes does the same thing."

Doctor Finch shrugged and pointedly glanced at his watch. He was becoming bored with the conversation. He said all he could on the subject, perhaps strayed outside his area of competence by discussing it at all and at such length.

Mike felt drained. It was as if they had been talking for an hour and, far from struggling to keep up, he had been overwhelmed by more ideas than he could develop.

Time seemed to hang in suspension. It was only when Doctor Finch stood up that Mike was compelled to do the same.

* * *

Mike's first problem was with his girlfriend Sally. Things hadn't been going well. After six years, familiarity can easily turn, if not to contempt, then to a deadening sense that matters could not be otherwise. Imaginative in many ways, Mike could not see how he could either make the relationship better or end it.

A moment to assert, or even express, what they wanted had by both of them been missed. The relationship had settled into being its own thing, the definition of and yet also distinct from what they were. There were three of them in it: him, her, and the relationship itself; a kind of anthropomorphic hybrid of what they might once have been and which now dominated their lives with its hopelessly anachronistic or idealistic demands.

Mike was no longer sure of what he wanted but was sure it wasn't this. However, disentanglement would be worse. He was old enough to see that many relationships are held together by inertia, though still young enough to want something else.

The accident and its aftermath changed everything. One of the differences between them, which until then had merely been a point of occasional comment, was he liked to talk and she didn't. Following the crash, his talking – or so she told him – became at times hyper-active; her responses – or so he told her – became almost non-existent. The flat was sold, the books were divided up, the ornate wardrobe her aunt had given them was passed on to her sister; and all the rest.

Sally spent the first evening after the separation with her friend Ros. "The trouble was..." Sally explained.

"Yes, I can imagine..." Ros replied, and poured more wine.

* * *

"The trouble was..." Mike explained.

"Yes, I can imagine..." Pete replied, and poured more wine.

The trouble was, Mike could have said, but didn't, was that many conversations, including this one, were no longer making any sense. Sometimes everything was normal. At others, time moved back into accident mode. Then it seemed that people were carefully considering all their responses before replying, very slowly, as if he were a damaged child.

He became solitary, tense and watchful, like a sick animal in the undergrowth waiting for a fever to return. He never knew when this would happen. The collapse of time engineered by this goblin that had somehow got into his soul might happen at any moment. There was no trauma, or even stress, that triggered it.

He tried to fabricate such conditions, once stepping out in front of a bus and on another occasion driving towards a hairpin bend with his eyes closed. He knew, though, that he wasn't going to go through with these manoeuvres. The goblin knew it too. He was also aware that to cause an accident would be irresponsible. The needs of others were, however, of increasingly little importance to him.

Then, perhaps while sitting quietly at home, or in the supermarket, the brake would suddenly be applied. The first sensation was a jolt in his chest, followed by a roaring which soon died down to a kind of low tinnitus hum. If he were talking to someone, their words would slow but not in a way he could define. It was not as if they were coming from a tape run at half speed and nor were there long pauses between the words – it was more as if two separate passages of time were occurring, one for him and one for everyone else, both of which he could experience simultaneously.

Either gradually or suddenly, but always unexpectedly, the two strands would knit back together: the branch line and the express would merge, the dark tinnitus would vanish and he was once again running on a single track with the rest of creation.

During these episodes, Mike's mind crackled like a bonfire. The problem was that these insights could not be acted upon. If the goblin arrived while he was talking to someone – which he had, despite his fondness for chat, reduced to functional exchanges – he could not slow his mind down enough to continue the conversation. If this happened when he was alone or in a public place, there was nothing to do except marvel at how much he grasped about the world and those around him.

These insights never survived. Like dreams, dew or faerie gold, they melted away, leaving nothing but an unsettling memory. He tried to go everywhere with a pen and paper and his mobile ready to record but, once the goblin arrived, these were forgotten. There seemed no way of cheating it into revealing its true nature.

Eventually, he decided to see a psychotherapist he had found online, Dr John. He made the appointment, fretted for several days and twice nearly cancelled the session.

* * *

"It's as if something's happening, but isn't," he said into the near-darkness. "I don't know when it's going to come. It all started with the accident...well, that was just my arm that got damaged. That's fine now. The other one, though – I'd probably have lost it if I hadn't had the time to think. I had so much time. The car rolled over, you see. Ever since then, the moment comes back. Well, not the accident moment. But like it. Time playing tricks. Slowing down. I could out-think Einstein when it was going on. But I don't know when...worse than that, I don't know why. Where," he finished plaintively, "is it all going to end?"

There was a long, deep silence. He was sitting in a strange room in a strange house in Clapham. The furnishings were heavy, the lighting poor. There was no sound there or anywhere else in the house, apart from the distant ticking of a grandfather clock. He was aware, on thinking back, that what he had just said made him seem dangerously unhinged.

When he had arrived a tall, cadaverous, dark-jawed man had greeted him with an air of solemnity, led him upstairs, invited him with gestures to sit down. He supposed that the man was still in the room. One of the armchairs by the window had a shape in it which might have been the psychiatrist, but could as easily have been a rug, or a shadow, or a stuffed bear. The silence went on and on.

He decided that he may as well keep talking: it seemed impolite to do anything else. His life was going badly enough without his compounding matters with a professional solecism such as directly addressing Dr John, or looking at him, or acknowledging his presence in any way. Perhaps this was all a cunning part of the man's technique of disjunctive auto-analysis or whatever it was called. Whatever its purpose, it sure as hell wasn't making him feel relaxed.

"The trouble is, I can't remember what I thought when it was happening. Just that it was...oh, I don't know – I knew it all. But then I didn't. It's like it was just a drunken rant – the kind you forget the details of but remember the effect. Except there was no effect, only the shadow of one..."

Mike was willing the goblin to arrive so he could, perhaps, demonstrate to Dr John what he was dealing with. Nothing happened.

Finally, he stopped talking. This time he felt he had said all he could say without some kind of reaction. The invisible monster in the armchair, who may or may not have been there at all, had sucked him dry, but Mike felt as far away from a solution as before.

There was another long silence. Mike resolved to say nothing until he had at least received a sign that he wasn't alone in the room. He looked down at his feet, then focused his gaze with fierce concentration on the corner of an ornamental fire dog.

Two emotions, hope and dread, had vied for supremacy in his soul as the hour of the appointment had drawn closer. As the afternoon advanced, dread had held the upper hand. Nothing, however, had prepared him for this dark and silent ordeal. The almost complete lack of anything happening was reminiscent of his moments of temporal drift. Here, though, he had no hectic insights. This was inactivity of a qualitatively different kind.

Two minutes passed. He could feel the armchair's unseen strength of personality coaxing him into further revelations, urging him to give voice to his deepest anxieties. Eventually he could take it no longer.

"Hello?" he said.

He was aware of a slight movement of shadows in the far corner, the faintest displacement of dark air. It was as if Dr John had wished merely to say: "I am here. Speak to me more of your troubles" without actually doing so. An interview with Professor Stephen Hawking could hardly have produced less in the way of body language.

"I need help," Mike said with genuine desperation.

"Really," said Dr John.

It was now Mike's turn to fall silent, so surprised was he to hear the psychotherapist speak. This was the first word Dr John had said since he'd arrived. He allowed the sound to roll around his mind.

The voice was high-pitched, but also authoritative. Mike guessed that he had originally come from the west country but had since lived in the south east. The tone was guarded, but at the same time candid. The inflexion was confident, but betrayed a sense of self-consciousness. The owner of the voice did not seem to be happy. He had perhaps recently had a cold.

All of this Mike inferred, accurately or not, from a sentence containing only one word which he wasn't even sure had been a statement or a question.

At last Dr John spoke again. "I can see you have...troubles. Interesting troubles."

"Well, yes," Mike said. That was certainly one way of putting it.

"Make an appointment with Miss Manners, downstairs. My secretary, " he added, as if keen to make the relationship clear. Mike now realised that the man was Welsh. "I think I can do any day this week apart from Friday, but she'll know that. She knows everything."

This remark made Mike wonder if he shouldn't have been talking to her from the outset. From having said nothing for half an hour, Dr John could not stop talking. Perhaps this was because the discussion had moved to practical arrangements after the tedious business of the consultation.

Or – and here the madness really started to bite – was it possible that he and the omniscient Miss Manners had swapped jobs for the day, just for a laugh?

Mike was again aware of a hand waving in the gloom. "Talk to Miss Manners. She will make all the arrangements."

Mike stood up and went downstairs. Without being able to meet her eye, he gave Miss Manners forty pounds for the consultation and agreed to arrange another appointment if he needed to. She raised one elegant eyebrow, handed him a receipt and watched him shamble out of the building.

Five minutes later, as he was walking home down Nightingale Lane, the goblin descended. There was nothing but the swishing of a car and the slow passage of a mother and child to engage him, yet his mind moved into trauma mode. All manner of wisdoms overcame him as he staggered down the leafy street, the hum of action or reaction buzzing in his ears.

As he reached his flat and was fumbling for his keys, real life returned. He was left with nothing but the memory of Dr John's silences and the worse emptiness of things that might have happened but which, once again, had not.

* * *

Mike's second and penultimate shot at professional help was with a hyper-active Australian. He was out of the blocks immediately on the subject of his name.

"Look, it's just Craig, forget about the Malcolm, mate – some people get them the other way round, Malcom Craig, but I don't mind. Call me whatever you want to as long as I can help you – look, that's what's important. Craig, or Craigy, is fine. All a question of what you're happiest with. Listen – sit down, sit down. Do you want some water? No? You're sure? Now, I'm all ears. Look – whatever you want to say, just unload it. You talk and I'll listen, because..."

As the man prattled on, Mike wondered when, or if, an opening would present itself to bring about this state of affairs.

The silence in Dr John's room had provided him with an alternative view of time standing still. Craig, on the other hand, gave Mike an alarming glimpse of how he must have seemed to others when the goblin took over the controls. The words gushed out of him as if from a broken tap. He was clearly very nervous and Mike's alarming revelations, on the rare occasions he could get a word in, didn't make him any less so.

By the end of the session, Craig was visibly sweating and gabbling about his relationship with his mother. Just as Mike had the week before wondered if Dr John had swapped roles with Miss Manners, so he now reflected if he were really the therapist and Craig the patient.

He smiled wryly: if only he could get the time-brake to operate at his beck and call, he could earn a fortune as a therapist, or in most other professions. When this happened he had so much time to think: and, in so doing, he knew so much.

The trouble was that he couldn't control it. Also, the times of its arrival generally caught Mike when he was alone or, as now, during a conversation of pointless banality.

* * *

Then he tried his GP, a tired and unimaginative woman who had no idea what Mike was talking about. Although the goblin wasn't there, Mike knew he was babbling. This was enough to alarm her into giving him a prescription for tranquilisers. Still Mike talked on. By now completely overwhelmed, the GP reached for a pad and scribbled a name and phone number.

"You might want to have a chat with this man," she said, tearing off the sheet and handing it to Mike. "Not far away, in Nightingale Lane. A Dr John. Private, but reasonable rates, I'm told. I could refer you to someone on the NHS – but the waiting lists are, well..."

...by which time, Mike reflected, I'll be dead or stark raving mad or the world will have ended.

* * *

All three possibilities were seeming increasingly likely. The descents into the temporal abyss were becoming both longer and more frequent. Worse still, on each occasion he was sinking deeper. Sometimes the passage of external time seemed almost to have been annihilated, the hum of traffic noise or conversation almost slowed to a faintly rumbling silence.

Every sense, he was starting to realise, depended on combining a multitude of different stimuli into what a normal brain interpreted as a single event. Music, with the goblin, was a torture, tiny differences in execution between instruments being hideously arpeggiated. Even sight, that most rapid of senses, was starting to mislead him. It was now getting to a point where there was a short but perceptible gap between pressing a switch and seeing the light.

He now knew that no one could help him. His amputation from life was almost total. Increasingly, he watched the world around him wallowing on its sluggish and ill-connected tides while his own consciousness raced through every possibility like a quantum computer. Each perception was true and not-true: each conclusion was an infinity of possibilities, all of which he had the time to explore.

The trouble was, as there was no hard drive on which to save this data, there was nothing he could later recall. Each fresh descent was to re-embark on a rapid and dislocating plunge into the machinery of the universe from which he emerged both exhausted and unedified.

As well as time deceiving him, his memory was breaking down. Each incident cast disorientating shadows in his mind which the return to the sunlight did not completely dispel. He was turning into one of those unfortunate people who retain the shrapnel from dreams and nightmares which, through being remembered, turn into actual memories.

Then there was the question of why this was happening at all; and why to him.

He wasn't the only person who'd survived a car smash. The idea of the goblin taking over the levers was compelling but hardly scientific. He accepted that he hadn't made particularly prolonged attempts to answer this question. Part of him suspected that in any case it couldn't be cured.

Of all the times when he realised that this was only going one way, his *Pulp Fiction* moment was the most seminal.

He was idly flicking through channels, like David Bowie in *The Man Who Fell to Earth*, and had come across the scene where Butch Coolidge rescues his enemy Marcellus Wallace from the basement of the Mason-Dixon pawnshop.

The goblin returned just as Butch was fleeing upstairs. Mike was afterwards treated to his slowest insights yet. Everything that was going through the minds of all four participants in the harrowing scene were laid bare to him.

The realisation that he was now party to the detailed thoughts and emotions of fictional characters was a tipping point from which he never recovered.

He was reminded of the blind panic he had felt when snorkelling in the Maldives after a wave had pushed him to the edge of where the shallow reef dropped steeply to dark and impenetrable ocean depths. Flailing and gasping, he had finally made his way back to shore. The atavistic terror had never left him. Now it had returned: and now he was hurtling, with unexpectedly leaden limbs, towards a familiar abyss from which there could be no return.

* * *

And so the day came for Mike when external time stopped.

Sound, even the roaring in his head, ceased. The last thing he remembered was of tiny wave-particles of light – for a brief moment, he understood even this paradox – shimmering, slowing and then fading to nothing. Darkness closed around to match the silence. Deaf-blind in this moment of death or infinity, he had one fractional moment of total omniscience before everything switched off.

And there he perhaps remains, gifted or cursed by knowing what it is like to have all the time in the world and no time in which to spend it – as, maybe, in the final analysis, are we all...

Diversification

JOSEPH OF ARIMATHEA knocked on the door. For a moment nothing happened. He knocked again.

"Enter!" said the Supreme Being. Joseph did so.

The room was not large; not as large as it could have been. Nor was it small. For the millionth time, Joseph was frustrated at being unable to comprehend the concept of relative size in the infinite space in which they existed. He was still haunted by the fleeting moment on earth when he had been a builder, when exactitude to the fraction of a digitus or pollex was a vital part of his life.

Others seemed not to be so afflicted. Abraham, for instance, or Joan of Arc – both could effortlessly say that this was smaller than that and be right. Joseph had lost the knack. It was if an eternity of precision had been used up in forty-five short years on Earth…Earth. Yes. This was what he had come about.

The Supreme Being – Gudan as he currently liked to be called – was looking cross and worried. With good reason, Joseph thought.

"Well? What is this tumult outside? What is it?"

"It's Earth, sir."

"Earth? Yes, of course it's Earth. What about it?

Joseph delivered his message. There was a long silence.

"And they're *all* here?"

"Well, not yet, but…it's not looking good."

Gudan seemed to be having trouble comprehending this. Joseph continued.

"An *asteroid*?"

"So it seems. We're waiting for you, sir."

Joseph stood aside to let Gudan pass, then followed him out of the room, down a corridor and into the Disciples' Chamber. This – unlike the halls that (or so Joseph was told by Abraham and Joan of Arc) were "a million times the size and then a million more" than those used for the more formal convocations of the Saints and other formal assemblies – was comparatively snug. There was a table with thirteen places and a coffee machine on a table in the corner. Eleven places were occupied. Gudan took the place at the head of the table. Joseph sat down between Simon Peter and the Abbess of Crewe.

Gudan glanced around the room. The faces were familiar to him. To his left was Mary; to his right, Jesus. He sometimes felt that having two family members at his top table smacked of nepotism and, more faintly, of weakness; but everyone seemed to accept this. If they didn't then Iscariot, to Mary's left, would have learned about it. "My most successful double agent," Gudan referred to him when the supposed traitor was appointed Head of Intelligence: for it should not be supposed that Paradise, or Gudan's version of it, was harmonious and obedient in all respects. Free will was a hard habit to shake off.

Next to Iscariot was Samson, who was in charge of security. Unsurprisingly, he was looking twitchy. Not very bright but intensely loyal, Gudan reflected.

Exactly the reverse could be said about the Abbess of Crewe, one place beyond Samson. Gudan had at first been worried by having a fictional person amongst his closest advisors: but, as Simon Peter had pointed out, (a) many of them were at least partially fictional in any case and (b) what did it matter now?

Gudan had also wondered, but somehow had never dared to enquire, how a fictional person had acquired an immortal soul. Increasingly he suspected many of his subjects had been created by humans rather than by him.

There were several grey areas. Falstaff and Macbeth, for instance, had existed but Gudan could not say for sure which soul he was enveloping with his infinite love, those of the obscure real-life humans or of the grotesque versions created by that troublesome Englishman. Othello was another enigma: had he in fact existed at all? Gudan didn't know. There was, he now realised, much he didn't know. Omniscience only went so far. He could peer into people's thoughts and know when a war was going to erupt: but up here, with everyone shed of corporeal ties, matters were less certain. Was he in fact ruling over, if that was the right phrase, a legion of fictional imposters?

His gaze flicked on to honest Joseph and, beyond him, to solid Simon Peter. SP always insisted on sitting in the most junior place, having never got over that evening in the bar in Jerusalem when he had denied Jesus three times. Even though this had been part of the plan, SP abjectly continued to blame himself.

This frequently annoyed Gudan to an extent he hoped he was able to conceal. The extra space also gave SP room for the voluminous scrolls and ledgers he brought to every meeting. He was anxiously flicking through them now as if searching for a precedent for the catastrophe they were here to discuss. Gudan quailed at the thought of this, then moved his gaze to the right.

Jesus was, as ever, immaculately dressed: very *à la mode,* very *BCBG.* Gudan could, just, indulge this: he was, after all, an eternal Dauphin, forever young. He tried to imagine how he would feel were their situation to be reversed but, once again, found the required level of empathy impossible. All he saw was a trim, alert thirty-something-year-old checking the messages on his phone.

Next to his son was Eve who was, as usual, dressed in a way which seemed less than appropriate. Why had he decided to make sure that the first humans were naked? Prurience? Curiosity? It had all gone horribly wrong, as it transpired there were two others there before them: Satan; and Genesis, the tabloid journalist.

It had taken all Gudan's threats of eternal damnation to get Genesis to write an even half-way acceptable version of the story of the priapic devil and the naked woman in the orchard. Even now, it pained Gudan to think that his first dabbling with humans had resulted in such a staggering misjudgement. They were a tricky and contrary lot, as his son had discovered. Certainly with regard to Satan, he'd been on the back foot ever since. The least he could do was invite Eve into his inner sanctum, not that she ever contributed much.

To the right of her was Moses, who could always be relied on to contribute plenty. The business with the tablets of stone had given him a self-importance that not even forty years wandering in the desert had undermined. Suffering, Gudan had always tried to explain, was the purest form of love. It seemed Moses had learned this lesson all too well and remained passionately, and at times almost irritatingly, devoted. He also had all the facts at his fingertips and often spent an age in articulating them.

Next to him was Pope Joan, another fictional, or quasi-fictional, character but, like the Abbess, one whose clarity of thought and crispness of expression often spoke to Gudan more clearly than the mutterings and mumblings of his old guard. He allowed himself only a second – a fraction of a moment of infinity – to reflect that the two people whose opinions were most incisive were female and fictional before flicking his all-seeing gaze at the last two members of his inner circle.

To the right of Pope Joan was Otto von Bismarck. Gudan had been impressed with his conduct on Earth and had marked him down as someone who could get things done. So far, he had not been disappointed. He had certainly kept Satan in check: until now, perhaps.

Finally there was Mother Theresa. It had been a toss-up between her and Princess Di, both of whom had arrived at about the same time, so sparking an uprising of emotion that even Iscariot's cunning and Samson's ruthlessness had barely been able to suppress. It had been clear one or other would need to be accepted into the inner circle to quell the unrest. Francis of Assisi had sportingly said he would step down to spend more time with his aviary.

Gudan had been left with the choice and decided on Theresa. This was mainly because he suspected Di knew the journalist Genesis and he could do without every deliberation being leaked: also because Theresa had actually believed in him during her life, which seemed worth rewarding.

All these reflections passed through Gudan's relatively omniscient soul in a period of time so short that it could not be measured. He had, in any case, had had a relatively infinite number of opportunities to observe most of them before. The rest were relative newcomers, appointed as a result of the diversification crisis.

"So," Gudan said, "what exactly has happened?"

"An asteroid about four hundred kilometres wide crashed into the Pacific about thirty minutes ago," Joseph of Arimathea said as if reading from a script, which he was.

"Didn't they see it coming? Haven't they got *telescopes*?"

"It seems not. There was no particular distress." 'Distress' was something that could be felt in Paradise whenever the population was particularly exercised about something such as a global pandemic, a major war or the immediate aftermath of a World Cup final.

"So how many are…up here?" Gudan went on.

"About half," Jesus said.

"Plus three on the International Space Station," Joseph of Arimathea said. Jesus shrugged. "Not that…" Joseph wondered now why he had mentioned this. His search for precision, in this place of billions, still tormented him. He had tried to introduce a census some time ago but no one had cared. Exactitude – still he craved it; increasingly it eluded him. Joseph, more keenly than the rest, felt the souls now swarming around the gates, uncounted proof that something more terrible had happened than any of the assembled group had yet understood.

Gudan, indeed all of them, fed on emotions that arose from the human curiosity about the existence of an afterlife and what form this might take. For billions of years, Paradise had been a cold and lonely place, inhabited by Gudan and a few others who had little to do except prosecute their pointless wrangle with Satan.

The genetic accident that enabled humans to achieve sentience was a game-changer. The resulting aspirations gave Gudan a purpose he had immediately exploited. He realised that certainty was the enemy of emotional energy. It was the not-knowing that kept the pot boiling.

This was supported by what Gudan still rated as his finest idea, the concept of faith. If the existence and nature of the afterlife had been an established fact, it would have created no more emotional reaction than would a train timetable. Neurotic thoughts might then have drifted toward some other mystery which, being more immediate and terrestrial, Paradise would have received little benefit from.

For this reason, it was decided that manifestations be kept to a minimum. There had been long and acrimonious debates about the wisdom of Jesus – who, Gudan realised, was not wrought quite as much in his own image as Gudan would have liked – being made flesh and going down to stir things up when it looked as if Hellenic-Roman pantheism was getting too strong a grip.

The mission had achieved its ends. His son had proved adept at making remarks which, on later examination, were shown to be in direct contradiction. This was vital to prolonging terrestrial debate. He was also careful to provide subtly different information to his four biographers and eleven disciples: the twelfth, Iscariot, was the only one in on the business from the beginning and had an essential role to play at the denouement.

Gudan recognised the success of his son's adventure and was also aware that this had created a duality of views about his nature. Previously, he had been a wintery hardliner; just but not merciful; avenging rather than forgiving. Jesus had portrayed a meeker, more accommodating deity offering pragmatic observations about life as it was lived, rather than handing down invariable precepts and sweeping off in a roll of thunder. This was good in that his son's activities had been responsible for fissures such as Islam and the Reformation. These had done much to increase spiritual and emotional neurosis on earth and thus the amount of warmth, comfort and, frankly, purpose which Gudan and the rest derived.

As regards day-to-day life in Paradise, however, Gudan was less happy. Jesus had, perhaps without meaning to be, become a second centre of authority. Some seemed happier receiving orders from him.

There was the slight appearance of two camps. This was reflected in the current membership of the Inner Council, with the five non-family members being drawn from what even Gudan sometimes referred to as 'the old days' and five from those of Christian vintage. It was also impossible to ignore the fact that the religion was named not after him, but his son.

These reflections were a waste of time. Gudan rapped on the table to call the meeting to order, even though no one was talking. Immediately several began doing so.

Gudan put his hand up. Moses, as ever spluttered on for some moments. "Diversification…" was his last word before silence descended again.

Jesus took up the cue. "Yes," shooting his cuffs. "We've been into that before. Water under the bridge." He was careful not to look at Gudan, who was careful not to look at anyone.

The diversification "crisis", as it was now clear it was, had been Gudan's biggest single error: proof, if proof be needed, that infallibility was not given even to the great. It had provoked several resignations, including Martin Luther, Henry VII and Harriet Beecher Stowe, as well as the sacking of H.P. Lovecraft.

On a personal level, Gudan had had no regrets. They had been a miserable bunch, though he was more than once reminded by his son that the disciples did not exist as an adjunct of Gudan's social life. It was now clear they had been right.

The issue was one of striking simplicity. Most deities – whose number was legion – had many planets from which they and the souls in their care derived sustenance. Prayer was one form of this, though not the best. Any intense emotional activity would generate spiritual energy on which each after-life community thrived. It was human hopes and fears that brought Paradise to life, rather than the other way round.

Some deities had over two hundred planets. His ever-energetic son had visited some of these and reported on the diversity of the spiritual offerings provided by an assortment of worlds with varying kinds of dominant and sentient life. In one case, this was creatures with legs and arms who breathed gasses; in another, a hyper-intelligent kind of enormous dolphin; in a third, highly socialised termites in pressurised methane lakes a few degrees above absolute zero. Jesus had referred to several extinction events which, with a large number of planets, were of little consequence: for those with only one, however...for greater emphasis, the young man – Gudan was incapable of thinking of Jesus in any other way – would leave this point hanging.

The matter had been debated many times. The problem was that diversification needed time and investment. It also required wheeling and dealing to acquire or swap planets like some cosmic game of Risk, or else expending even more energy in appropriating hitherto un-deified planets where sentient life had recently emerged.

Gudan, who was lazy, had missed several opportunities. The moment had now all but passed. Like Africa in the 1850s, most of the best bits had been snapped up by energetic colonialists, leaving latecomers to fight over scraps. Each new opportunity was now rare, required more work and offered fewer returns. Eventually, a weary fatalism settled on the disciples. Most accepted that the situation was beyond redemption.

There was another reason why Gudan was unwilling to absent himself. Travel, for a deity, was not a problem as regarded distance. Time was another matter. Even a short trip might provide both the reason and the opportunity for a coup d'état. In this matter, Jesus was the focus of his concern.

Gudan was, as he had allowed matters to work out out, a one-planet god. He was sure there must be others but had never met any. That was another thing Jesus had often banged on about: networking. Opportunities had been suggested but each presented, or so Gudan had argued, insuperable obstacles. As he had no planets to swap, he would have to make the advances. Even Jesus' salesmanship could rarely convince him of a favourable reception nor what his angle in any discussion might be.

The one exception had involved a deity called Kaddesh who had needed help with manifestations similar to those Jesus had performed on Earth. He had indicated he was prepared to offer a planet in return. Jesus and his team had put together an impressive presentation and Kaddesh was sold.

Then, at the last minute, Gudan had vetoed the plan. Things were, Gudan judged, shaky on Earth and had argued – though had not fully believed – that a brief and ambiguous second coming might be the answer. He had dangled this possibility before his son for long enough for Kaddesh to go cold. His real reason had been a fear that Jesus would, in the time-honoured fashion of sons, use the opportunity to mount a hostile takeover.

In his more honest moments, Gudan admitted this error of judgment. His relations with his son had never fully recovered. He had since sensed a reserve on the part of the young man, a suspicion that he said less than he knew or felt about any matter and that their interests were not always aligned. Gudan found himself wondering if he had, by thwarting the Kaddesh deal, in fact created the very doubts about his competence that he was trying to avoid.

Gudan was thus a frightened and indolent deity trapped in a prison of his own devising. Now, the day of reckoning had arrived.

"As Jesus has observed," he said crisply, "we are where we are. Otto – your views?"

Von Bismarck blinked a couple of times. "We at a critical point have arrived at, majesty. Over half the souls currently awaiting clearance. As for the rest, a good deal of – upheaval."

Gudan inhaled. Yes, he could sense it. Young love, power frenzy, creative delight, spiritual anguish, theological debate – all of these could feed Paradise. Nothing, however, was as potent as immediate, naked fear. Of that there was, at present, a lot: a huge rush of a drug that might not be available again.

"The problem," said Joseph, as if reading Gudan's thoughts, "is that this is very short-term." He glanced round the room. Gudan noticed hyper-bright expressions on everyone's faces. Joseph gestured towards the curtained windows. Beyond them, as everyone knew, was chaos.

"So, what's the situation?"

There was a pause. Eventually Simon Peter cleared his throat. "It's a question of processing."

"Yes," Gudan said impatiently.

"This normally takes," Simon Peter ploughed on, "about 300 Earth years. Of course, in exceptional cases…"

He began a recitation of statistics that he delighted in compiling which, until now, he had never had the opportunity to offer to a captive audience. Joseph gave him a nudge, just as Gudan raised his hand.

"Quite. Look – how many processors do we have?"

"Sixty thousand. Each processing takes, obviously, about a lifetime to complete and normally…well, people don't mind waiting."

"Don't *mind*?"

"Well…no. In the circumstances."

"Circumstances?"

"Well – eternity and so forth."

"Of course, yes," Gudan said quickly. "Because they know they won't have long to wait and because…"

"Because time doesn't matter anymore," put in the Abbess of Crewe.

"Quite, yes," Gudan said, beaming down the table.

"But," she went on relentlessly, "until they're processed, it *does* matter. It's because they're still informed by the idea of time it was decided to have so many processors. Pre-processing, they would see themselves as being in queue and react accordingly." She turned to Simon Peter. "What's the normal number of arrivals each day?"

Gudan felt he was losing control of the meeting but said nothing.

"The average…oh the *average* – well, the *peacetime* average is around one hundred and fifty five thousand each day." Simon Peter shuffled his papers. "to be precise, one hundred and…"

"Good enough," said the Abbess. "A queue of a hundred and fifty thousand people looks daunting if you've not been acclimatised to eternity. It was felt this might cause…'negative energy' I believe the phrase is."

Gudan nodded. Processing had been one of his better ideas. All humans had, after death, residual emotions which could be extracted to power the furnaces of Paradise. Nothing provided as much spiritual anguish as a thorough and pitiless examination of every aspect of a life. It was also recognised that human emotions needed to be stripped away were Paradise to continue to be the peaceful, if bland, place that it was. Processing, by trained inquisitors, was therefore vital both to feed Paradise and preserve its sanity. The question was how long the deceased would be made to wait.

Simon Peter had given the clue to this, describing the time he had spent before his post-Gethsemane interrogation as "the worst three hours of my life." As his interrogation had lasted one hour, and as three seemed to be a propitious number, it had been decided three lifetimes was a suitable time for people to wait.

Experiments had supported this. Anything less, the emotional input was diminished; anything more, the post-human but pre-processing impatience produced negative energy and disruptive emotions requiring, as Samson had menacingly explained, "tough measures."

Gudan didn't want to know the details of these "tough measures". It seemed easier to hit upon about sixty thousand processors who were able to do the work of processing about one hundred and fifty thousand people who arrived each day. So matters had been arranged and so they had remained, adjusted for population increase.

"How many people do we have awaiting processing at present?" Gudan asked.

Simon Peter mumbled something.

"Yes?"

"About four billion," the voice of Moses thundered from across the table.

Gudan picked up his fountain pen and put it down again, this time at an exact right angle to the edge of the table. "And how many years' processing is that? Not three hundred, I imagine?"

As he expected, Jesus was first with the answer, his fingers flying across his smartphone before Moses, Simon Peter or von Bismarck had managed to pick up their pens.

"Sixty-six thousand six hundred and sixty six years."

Gudan frowned. "Not a very auspicious number."

There was a silence. From behind the thick curtains the sound of wailing was becoming louder.

"Do we feel," Gudan said, addressing a familiar theme which had sustained him through numerous difficulties, "that we detect a familiar hand here?"

Gudan had been quick to realise the power of an adversary. Every setback could be laid at the door of this jumped-up sprite who was, if only Gudan had seen it, of less threat to Paradise than the consequences of Gudan's own inadequacies. Introducing him to humans as a creature of equivalent worth to himself had been a calculated gamble but one which had paid dividends in terms of the fear, and thus the emotional energy, this created.

Gudan had become increasingly convinced of Satan's power. It became hard to separate the monster he had created from the one he believed existed. His tendency to blame Satan for misfortunes had not helped. Did this catastrophe have a Satanic cause or was it an act of chance? Gudan's instinctive suspicion that it was the former showed how far he had become lulled into believing in an implacable and powerful enemy. This gave him an empathy with the billions now beating their heads outside his gates, many of whom saw just this power at work in their premature change of status. Gudan had the awful, vertiginous, feeling that he had created a situation he was now unable to manage. Instinctively, he shot a glance to his right.

"If I could make a suggestion…" Jesus said.

"Please," Gudan said.

"We need to reduce the processing time by a factor of about two hundred., to a year or so. If people see that they're moving forward they get less twitchy, right?" Moses, who had spent a fair bit of his time on earth hanging around, nodded. "Deal with problems as they crop up."

At the mention of "problems" everyone looked first at Samson and then at Iscariot. Their combination of brawn and guile had solved every problem that Paradise had so far encountered. Whether they would be up to this one was another matter.

"I think..." Iscariot began: but at that moment, there was a huge surge that washed through them all: a crazy high of warmth and elation followed by a gathering of the clouds and a vision of growing darkness.

"That's that," Pope Joan said. Her voice seemed to be coming from under the floor.

Nobody questioned this. They had all felt the results. From outside, the wailing had doubled in volume. Inside the room, no one could bring themselves to speak.

Jesus glanced down at his phone and read a message which had just appeared. He typed a quick reply. He gave a grim smile, put the device in his pocket and stood up. As he did so, von Bismarck, the Abbess and Pope Joan got to their feet as well. There was a surprised pause. Then, looking slightly shamefaced, Iscariot stood up too.

"Well?" Gudan said.

"That's it," his son replied. "We're finished." He looked round the room and read in the haggard faces of the seven people still seated the confirmation of his remark. The temperature had already dropped. Everyone felt themselves slow down and grow dimmer, like stars burning out their reserves: no longer raging but now going gentle into that good night.

"Where are you going?" Simon Peter asked.

For the first time, Jesus looked shame-faced. "A better offer. They wanted the...well, the top team as well," he added, indicating the other four. "No offence."

"Who did?"

"Kaddesh." There was a pause. "I suggested you meet him, several times. There was always some reason why it couldn't happen," he added dryly. "He has over thirty planets, more than he's been able to service. He needed to organise manifestations to get attention. He liked what I'd done on earth…"

Gudan opened his mouth to suggest that "what *we'd* done," would be fairer but the young man had beaten him to the correction.

"What *we'd* done," Jesus said.

Gudan was shocked to see Jesus was indicating not him, but Judas Iscariot.

"In exchange, you'll recall he promised us a world – young, sentient and almost un-deified. The best deal we were ever going to get. I think you thought that – what was it…?" Jesus could clearly remember perfectly well but was milking the moment. "'that you didn't want me to be away for so long.'"

"The Fourth Crusade…" Gudan muttered.

"I know. We went over it. It seemed like a disaster at the time. Excommunicated armies, sacked cities, broken promises – negative energy everywhere. But it worked out. You just had to keep Innocent III in the Vatican for another few years – you took my advice about *that* – and everything was fine. It's what I always said," Jesus went on, now less in valedictory mode than rehearsing his keynote address at the board he was about to join, "we can deal with anything except indifference. There was a lot of that in 1204, but it passed. People didn't know any better. They've got cleverer now, sure – but there are more of them and they're at each other's throats half the time, fighting over resources, beliefs, tiny differences in ideas."

Gudan was forced to acknowledge the truth of these remarks. As the populations had multiplied and sundered, Gudan was at first all for using these differences as a basis for encouraging the strife on which emotional energy depended. Jesus had pushed the other way: the more people had in common, he argued, the more they could find to disagree about. Events had proved him right. Tiny doctrinal divisions, often resulting from no more than a mis-translation of one line of text, had produced conflicts that had raged amongst neighbouring and intermingled cultures for centuries.

"Why do you think," his son continued, now warming to his task, "I made all those ridiculously contradictory remarks? You have to keep theology inaccessible. That lot have supple brains – nothing to do with us, just the way things worked out. Give them a paradox and they'll turn it into schism, then you'll have fifty denominations, each claiming they're right and raining hell-fire on the rest. That's all we needed to do."

At this point, he seemed to be struck by a genuine sense of sorrow.

"Fifty-odd years of mostly misery in exchange for eternity in Paradise. It wasn't a bad deal. They just had to worry and bicker and reproduce, to feed us and keep the whole thing going. Granted, it's not the most exciting paradise I've been to but at least it's safe and warm. At least," he added, "it *was*..."

"So you're upping and leaving, you...traitors," Simon Peter said, pulling himself to his feet. Moses did likewise. The others seemed undecided whether to make a stand. Gudan gave them no lead but shot Jesus a glance that would have frozen hydrogen.

"Look," Jesus said in a more conciliatory tone. "I've *got* to go for this. What are we going to do otherwise? We don't know what's going to happen. I suspect we'll run out of fuel. If we go to Kaddesh and do what he's asked we'll see about re-locating."

"Starting," Iscariot put in, "with the ones that haven't been fully processed. Still energy there to be tapped."

Von Bismarck nodded. "More energy Kaddesh to warm his Paradise now needs," he explained lugubriously.

"That's it," Jesus said. "Or maybe pick up one of his planets. It's not a great time to do a deal but what's the option?" He gave a glance to each of his accomplices. All nodded but in a way that suggested they had been taken by surprise. This condition of departure, which they hadn't discussed – for the offer had been made some time before the asteroid – was a piece of improvisation. It needn't come to anything, of course. As Jesus himself had pointed out, it was best never to be too specific.

"I'll text you," Jesus said to Gudan. "Keep it going 'til I get in touch."

Then, with a nod at his divine father and his corporeal mother – who, perhaps sensing what was about to happen, had throughout the meeting remained as blandly and tragically trance-like as she had so often been portrayed in Renaissance paintings – he and his accomplices were gone.

Before any of the remaining disciples had had a chance to speak, Gudan reached for his pen and scribbled some names on a sheet of paper. He tore it off and gave it to Joseph of Arimathea. "Summon these to our council," he said in his most official tone.

Joseph scanned the names, his eyes widening. "'Mohammed, David Ben-Gurion, the Dalai Lama...Richard Dawkins' – are you *sure*?"

"Absolutely," Gudan said.

"Dawkins isn't...that's to say, he hasn't been processed yet."

"All the better. Show us what we're dealing with." There was a collective sigh of doubt around the remains of the meeting which Gudan realised he had to deal with now or never at all.

"Look," he said, bringing his fist down on the table, "we're *in extremis*, as my dear son has pointed out. We've nine billion applicants and have to keep the lid on this until he can sort this out." He briefly considered whether he should claim pre-knowledge of, or even complicity in, this filial betrayal. Better not, he thought. As his son had said, keep it ambiguous. He smiled to himself. Finally, he was starting to get it.

"We need to get everyone onside. So – we go ecumenical, big time." There were groans from Moses, Simon Peter and Mother T. Joseph, as ever the perfect diplomat, made no comment . Nor did Eve who, understandably, had never fully grasped the concept of human diversity. To his left, Mary seemed even more locked in her private sorrow. Fair enough, Gudan reflected: she'd just seen her only son walk out without so much as giving her a peck on the cheek. One had to make allowances.

Gudan turned to the groaners. "Any other suggestions? Good," he added after the briefest of pauses. "Joseph, see to it. Have them here immediately and we'll get to work to keep this show on the road." From beyond the windows, the sound of lamentation – now mixed with anger – was getting louder. "We've no time to waste."

"There's one name I can't read," Joseph said, "Derek Cameroon, is it?"

"David Cameron," Gudan explained.

"Who's he?"

"The hapless former Prime Minister of the United Kingdom," Gudan explained.

"Jesus," Simon Peter exclaimed, glad that for the first time in two thousand years he could take the name in vain without getting a cold look. "What do we want *him* here for?"

"Because," Gudan said, "I need someone who has failed. I need a loser." He might have added he needed a smoothie-chops who reminded him of his son but carried none of his son's threat. "I need someone to remind us that, even when things seem impossible, we can triumph, just as he failed when failure seemed impossible. I need someone full of glib phrases that sound well but mean nothing. We're going to be needing a lot of those. Do you remember the "big society"?"

No one did.

"So few do. But he believed in it, for a while. Its time may have come. That's what we need here now – a bit of the "all for one and one for all" mentality."

"Communism?" Mother Theresa asked in alarm.

"No, no," Gudan reassured her, "just a form of words."

He glanced round the table, satisfied that he had, for now, quelled any flicker of rebellion.

"Ecumenical," he repeated. "Inclusive. Global." He intoned these last three words with carefully judged pauses, emphasising both their connection and their capital letters. "For we must not forget," he concluded, putting his fountain pen in his pocket and standing up, "that we're all in this together."

Heal Thyself

"SO, HOW DOES that make you feel?"

The question appeared to have asked itself. I looked across the desk at the familiar face that seemed to be lightly smiling at me. How *did* it make me feel?

Loss was palpable, I said. It took up space inside me like a tumour, like anti-matter. It was there and not-there, like a phantom limb. It was growing alongside me, like two plants, now so entwined and co-dependant that it was hard to tell which was the host and which the parasite.

There was a long silence. I looked round at the consulting room: at the framed certificates, the bookcase, the low, comfortable chairs, the coffee table with, as usual, a box of tissues and beaker of water. I heard a slight tapping as rain started softly tumbling against the panes that I could glimpse through the half-drawn curtains. Dusk was falling.

"I don't think..." I began, and then stopped. I found that indeed I could *not* think; only feel. Nothing I said mattered. I might as well not speak at all. For a while I didn't.

Silence can have a peculiar quality of action. So it was here. Every beat of it left me craving something to fill the void. Nothing being said left me passionate for words yet unable to engage with them. Loss was an absolute change of tense from any verb yet encountered. Past; present; future – all were annihilated into fragments of time which rearranged into alarmingly personal conjugations: before we met; we together; after you died. None operated in a way anyone else could grasp.

I was in my own place with everyone else rushing or ambling past me in a way I could not adapt to. My needs were uncompromising but invisible. The oceans needed to have been poured away. They had not.

So, what about needing to get over it? Well, I said, you never do. I can talk all day and it won't make any difference. I shift my point of view, while I'm talking; rationalise myself into another state of mind. Then, when the working day is finally over, I walk back down familiar streets, taking whatever long-cuts most disguise my fondest and most casually adopted associations.

There was another silence. Then further words were said.

"You might well wonder," I said with an atrocious attempt at dignity, "how I view my future." What future? As a half-person? Twenty-four years; just about half my life. So, a quarter perhaps. As a quarter of a person.

This was no way to think. I looked across again at the face I knew so well, the hair as dark as mine is fair, the eyes as blue as mine are brown.

What would you have me do? What can I even do myself?

Despite everything, I'm trapped in a cycle of despair that horribly resembles self-pity. Except I'm big enough and well-informed enough to know it isn't that. It's just a relentless and overwhelming failure to adapt to this awful reality. Six months ago – six months and three days – you were here. Now you're not. My clock has stopped. It's still measuring the seconds though it's no longer telling me the time.

There was no movement from the other side of the room, merely what seemed to be a change of expression in the face that was regarding me with such fixed devotion.

"Oh, what did I most value?" I said, before any other suggestions could intrude. "Well, the fact that he was there. He was always there. Not always…there. But with me. He was safety, and danger. He was bloody annoying. He was…who he was. We argued…" I allowed myself a light smile that was more than just one of remorse. "But he always took my side when it came to it. Now – well, it's like life after an amputation."

I looked defiantly across the room. Was this enough? I'd just de-personalised him, which might serve to remove some of the pain. My eyes were misting with the tears I'd long held back. Ignoring the tissues on the low table, I shifted my gaze towards the window.

The sumptuous and hectic light of the late afternoon had collapsed into something soiled and wintery. Now the rain had stopped, there was a stark and mysterious silence to it that reminded me of waking from a luminous dream and being briefly unsure from what horrors I'd been dragged. Then, once again, they washed over me. No dream could release me from this.

Slowly, my view of the room returned to a desperate focus.

What, I wondered, did I find myself thinking about? It was something I'd asked enough and had often heard some surprising answers. As little as possible, when I could. Chardonnay, swimming, work, repetitive tasks and the hoped-for oblivion of a few hours' sleep if the right combination of these had been achieved. That was about it.

And then there was the awful, impossible business of other people.

I thought about and watched them all the time. Did they know about Steve dying in that stupid accident? Did they feel that enough time had passed so it didn't need to be mentioned? Did those who unspokenly sought my company do so because I had a grief more intense than theirs? Did those who shunned me do so because they couldn't winnow the emotions I might express? Were they even aware that Steve had existed?

This was the worst of all: that I was just me, the sorrowed shade I am now, without the person who made me whole; as, I felt with what increasingly seemed only a fragile certainty, that I made him.

Outside, the last light faded into mist. I heard the clip-clop of two pairs of shoes on the street outside, the growl of the 73 pulling away from the stop at Newington Green, the cry of a man at the junction calling a friend who had passed out of earshot.

"When there was so little I could do?" I found myself shouting. "So *little*? There was *nothing*! I wasn't there. He just...He..." I reached for the tissues as the face across the desk faded away into a damp shadow.

The buzzer called me back to order. I stumbled forwards and managed to press the button. "Yes? Yes?"

Who was it?

"Claire – your 5.30 client is here." A pause. "Are you OK?"

"Yes…yes. I'm fine." I blew my nose. A whisper of hair had displaced itself and I stroked it back behind my ear. "Yes."

"Adam Lucian."

"Of course…send him in, please."

I went across to the desk and carefully brushed my finger against the almost life-sized photo of Steve's face which had been facing me. Then I gently turned it down onto the leather top. I moved to the low sofa just as the door opened.

"Adam," I said, extending my hand. I gestured for him to sit. Slowly, on opposite sides of the coffee table, we both did so. There was a long silence.

He started to talk about the voices in his head, how no one could ever understand what this was like. No one could know, he told me.

"So," I asked him after a pause, "how does this make you feel?"

The Millennium Clocks

FACT IS, GEOFF and I needed to find some money and quick. We were on our uppers – he'd been laid off and the company I'd been working for had gone bust. We'd been through our savings and out the other side. So, there we were, sitting in a bar and making two halves of bitter go as far as they could.

This was back in August 1999. The big thing then was the millennium bug. This would, according to the stories, make every computer explode on the stroke of midnight, as many programmes only used two numbers for the year rather than four. Planes would fall out the sky, telephone systems would fail and the internet, which was only just getting going, would collapse.

Geoff put down the *Standard* and pointed at a headline. "'Y2K meltdown fears,'" he quoted, then looked up reflectively at the grimy ceiling. "How many things have most people got in their homes with a timer on it?"

"A few."

"More than a few. Microwave, oven, TV… central-heating system, bedside clock. If they have a car, that's got one. Watches…"

"Watches won't…"

He held up his hand. "It's not what's true. It's what people believe. Look at the paper. We don't have to convince them of anything. They're sold already. They just need a solution."

Geoff worked in sales. I was an editor. So, poles apart when it came to caution.

He explained what he had in mind. "You can be the boffin with the clipboard. I'll do the pitch."

I had a few objections but Geoff was off again. "We're going to need business cards and certificates. I know a bloke – leave it to me."

Without being at all sure about this, I nodded.

He got up. "See you back here tomorrow evening."

I nodded again.

* * *

"What's a chronological consultant?"

"What it says on the card. You know what 'chronological' means? We fix people's clock…stuff. Make them Y2K compliant."

"It should be 'chronometrical.' That's to do with clocks." He looked at me blankly. "My uncle was a clockmaker," I explained. "'Chronological' is to do with the passing of time."

"Too late now," Geoff said.

We hadn't even started with this lie and already we were telling the wrong one. Precision of words has always mattered to me. For Geoff, the best word was the one that created the biggest short-term effect, regardless of its meaning.

"What are these letters after your name," I asked, glancing at his card. "BSC? No, don't tell me – "British Society of Chronologists. Or Chronometrical…ists."

"Whatever. And, look – you're one too but you've got '(Tech)' after it. That makes you the boffin. I've also got you this," he added, passing me a small and rattling satchel. "Your box of tricks." I couldn't immediately face looking inside.

"Drink up," he said. "We're off to our first client. Islington way, twenty minutes' walk. Lady Louisa Dunbar."

"Who's she?"

"Friend of a friend of my mother's."

* * *

Lady Louisa Dunbar was about seventy and greeted us with a mixture of trepidation and relief. She lived in a beautiful but dilapidated house in Barnsbury that had probably been immaculate in 1965. There was no sign of poverty but rather of a failing to come to terms with the implacable workings of gravity and rust. I intuited that the departure of her children about twenty years before and the more recent death of her husband had made these things inevitable. During our conversations, I learned that these guesses were correct.

"It's *terrible* what they say in the papers," she said once the conversation had worked its way from the tenuous connection between her and Geoff to the matter in hand. "This 2YK germ…" She shivered slightly.

Geoff had been right. She and many others were frightened by something they neither welcomed nor understood yet which had, like a colony of rats, infested their homes. The papers had been short on detail but long on menace. And now here we were with a solution.

Geoff didn't overplay his hand. "A lot of it *is* rubbish," he said. Lady Louisa nodded vigorously. "They want to sell papers."

"Well, of *course* they do."

He mentioned other issues – the National Front, Ugandan Asians, the Cold War, hippies, the unions and football hooligans all came trotting out. He was building up a picture of her from her reactions. I felt uneasy and looked at my shoes and, more occasionally, at the form on my clipboard. Lady Louisa talked on. She wasn't a stupid woman, just lonely and slightly rattled.

Then he pounced.

"Well," he said, standing up and looking at his watch. As if we were connected by wires, I stood up too. "We'd better look at the devices."

More slowly, Lady Louisa got to her feet. The change from general to specific, from anecdotal to commercial, had been abrupt. I could see the thought crossing her mind that she'd wasted the valuable time of these professionals with tittle-tattle. With a horrible fascination I waited for Geoff's next move.

He smiled, now in control. "Perhaps we could start in the kitchen," he said. He gave me a glance to show I should take over.

"Do you have a microwave, Lady Louisa?" I asked. She clasped her hand to her chest.

"A microwave oven," I explained, thinking she thought I'd meant a cardiological implant.

"Oh, yes…I don't really use it – it doesn't seem natural…of course when my grandchildren…ah, here we are…" She swung open a cupboard door.

I don't know when the first microwave was sold in the UK but this might have been it. It had three controls: on/off, four power settings and a timer. It was as far removed from the Y2K nightmare as a rocking horse. I swivelled the dial. Immediately there was a 'ping'.

"Classic sign," Geoff said.

There was no escape. I turned round to face him. "Looks like an RKG," I said at random.

For the benefit of Lady Louisa, Geoff twisted his face into an expression that could have conveyed any emotion from despair to amazement. "Try the chrono valve on it."

I reached into my satchel and pulled out something that looked like a distributor cap for an Austin Seven. I pressed a lead against the front of the microwave, made the dial go 'ping' again and turned round, writing on my clipboard. Lady Louisa seemed about to speak but Geoff was too quick.

"On to the next," he said, then swivelled round. "Ah, an oven timer." He moved towards it, squinting theatrically, drawing Lady Louisa forward with his interest. "Looks like our old friend the C-14."

"Could be," I said.

It went on like this for about twenty minutes. While I was doing my pointless fiddling, Lady Louisa engaged Geoff in chat about children, families, politics and the arts. She established that he had read no books for pleasure, played no musical instrument and had no partner. In his confident mood he was unaware the tables were turning. She was now getting as much from him as he had earlier done from her.

We were in her bedroom, me poking at her Teasmaid with a 1980s guitar tuner. This marked the end of my awful inventory. Although I'd said little apart from invented acronyms, I felt drained. I passed the clipboard to Geoff. He glanced at it. Again he did this thing with his face, squirming his mouth and eyes but finishing with a hopeful raising of the eyebrows.

"Tell you what," Geoff said. "Why don't you go and do the rectifications. I'll have a chat with Lady Louisa about the commercials."

I nodded weakly as they went into the living room. More for the form of the thing, I went back to the bedroom.

The furniture was beautiful but faded. The chest of drawers was, I was sure, a Hepplewhite, though sunlight-stained in one corner and with one drawer-front chipped. The bed, with its high, curved headboard, looked eighteenth-century Venetian. It was made up for two though only one side had recently been slept in.

I glanced at the paintings, recognising a Hockney and a Sickert. Everything had been furnished with the help of not only money but taste and style. I, however, was a fraud, creeping around while my mate ripped off the owner over a cup of Lapsang. I re-set the Teasmaid clock to the correct time by my watch, nine minutes ahead of where it had been.

I fiddled around for another five minutes while Geoff worked his awful alchemy, then paused in the hall. I checked my watch: ten past four. At that moment, there was a breathy, arthritic sound from over my shoulder. I swivelled round. There was a pause when, as always happens after such chronometrical preambles, the air seems to be sucked clean away, followed by a mechanical exhalation and the release of a glorious chime in a B flat. The wonderful grandfather clock stood at the far end of the hall was striking four.

My uncle had owned one like this. Seven feet tall, it had the elegance of a cheetah and the symmetry of a cathedral. I stood back to admire it. As I heard the living room door open, a name rose unbidden to my lips.

"Is that a John Calver?" I said to Lady Louisa.

She froze in amazement.

I was now ten years old again, dragging up what I could remember of my uncle's passion. "No, it's too tall. Perhaps a Thomas Webb? No, it's a bit later than that. Bullock?" I turned round, almost breathless.

She gave me a surprised and appraising glance as if she was seeing me for the first time. "Almost," she said. "Not far away. Samuel Bowles, Dorset, 1799." She ran her hand down the right side of it. Unbidden, I did the same on the left. "My grandfather bought it. My grandfather's grandfather clock – what do you think of that?"

I smiled but could think of nothing to say. Nor, in the background, could Geoff.

"Do you know how to wind it?"

* * *

"That was smart of you, making that stuff up about winding it," Geoff said.

I was annoyed that, in his world, everything was seat-of-the-pants. "I knew."

"Really? And she said she might know some other clients."

We parted at the end of the street. I accepted a hundred pounds as I needed to pay the rent but it seemed like blood money. I was certain this was less than half of what Lady Louisa had given him.

We got a similar gig a few days later, a Mrs Crowbridge in Gospel Oak, seemingly another friend of a friend of Geoff's mother. She used to be a concert pianist but could no longer play as her hands were gnarled by arthritis. She had a clock, this time in her living room, which she was unable to wind properly. "It should be a seven-day clock," she said, "but…"

"Eight-day," I said automatically. "That's what they're called."

From over her shoulder, Geoff rolled his eyes.

"Eight-day?" Mrs Crowbridge mused. "How nice. So they throw in an extra day. Like a baker's dozen."

"Yes. Since about 1720."

"Goodness me." She appraised first me and then the clock with fresh eyes. "It doesn't go for more than three or four days. I don't like it when it stops. Even if it's in the middle of the night I hear it and have to get up and wind it as quickly as I can. Silly, I know." She paused again. "My husband bought it. Nearly fifty years ago. Twenty-five guineas, more than we could afford. He died three months ago. He used to do the winding, of course – I don't know why I say of *course*. Just because I'm a woman it doesn't mean I can't wind a clock. Except it seems I can't. At least, my *hands* can't, not now."

Geoff made a dumb-show gesture of looking at a watch.

She smiled again, now back in the present. "It's important to keep the clock going," she said, "though I can't say *why*. I mean it's not as if I'm *connected* to it..."

The room was suddenly silent. Mrs Crowbridge lurched forward and I thought she was about to faint. She gathered herself together, her hand on her chest, and pointed. The clock had stopped.

I crossed the room and pulled open the door. The crank key was on a dusty ledge inside. The clock was English, probably from about 1790, so wouldn't have an opposing winding. I turned the crank clockwise and, like a paramedic doing CPR, felt the mechanism turn. With each wind, the wheels and cogs seemed to gain strength. After twelve the turning became harder.

"You mustn't over-wind it," Mrs Crowbridge said. I held up my hand: I needed to count. After five more I could feel the stop work lock into place. I replaced the key, opened the top glass and moved the long hand forward for the minute or so we'd missed. I shut the door and, dusting my hands, turned back to face my client. "Sorry," I said. "I was concentrating. It needs seventeen turns." I looked down at her hands. "I'm guessing you give it, what, ten? Eleven?"

"Ten, normally. After that it's too hard. Anyway, Andrew said I must *never* over-wind it."

"You can't," I said. "It's a fusée. It's got a mechanism to prevent it. Your husband might have been used to older clocks, which you *could* over-wind."

"Yes, he was. His father had a – what was it called? Foil?"

"Foliat."

"Yes, a Foliat. How clever of you," she said. "I don't suppose...could you come back next week and wind it for me? How much would that cost?"

At the mention of money, Geoff came to life. "Perhaps we could discuss the commercials in the kitchen," he said, ushering her towards the door.

She looked at him narrowly. "The kitchen is *that* way," she said, pointing at the door on the far side of the room. "But why do we have to discuss money *there*?"

Geoff had no answer to this. Mrs Crowbridge manoeuvred me into a corner and had persuaded me to agree to return in a week's time. "Would you think twenty-five pounds enough?" she asked under her breath, glancing at Geoff over my shoulder as she pressed some banknotes on me, conjured up by god-knows-what unlikely dexterity.

"Fine," I said, retracting at the last moment the temptation to shake her arthritic hand.

"I have friends who'd like to meet you," she added with a smile. "You have to keep the clocks going."

Something about her earnestness confused and discomfited me. I nodded.

Geoff, sensing he was being excluded, was stalking round the room. He picked up a TV remote control. "Is this Y2K compliant?" he asked. He pointed it at the television and pressed some buttons. Nothing happened. He threw it down. "If not, it's a death-trap," he muttered.

"This time next week, then," Kate Crowbridge said, ignoring him. She reached out her hand to seal the deal. Hesitantly, I took it. She grimaced slightly. Then we left.

* * *

That was the end of my direct relationship with Geoff. I gave him one of Kate Crowbridge's tenners but he was too busy bitching about my "smarmy-pants act" to question the division of spoils. At the end of the street he turned left, I turned right. I had the vague idea he might be able to cause me trouble but was wrong about what form this might take.

* * *

Over the next few weeks, I found myself seemingly the only practitioner – certainly in the swathe of London between Chelsea Embankment and Hampstead Heath – of a craft that I never knew existed: clock-winder to rich widows. I soon had about twenty weekly clients, including Lady Louisa and Kate Crowbridge. This gave me the best part of two grand a month, cash in hand. Each session took about an hour, not including travelling from Vauxhall. About ten minutes was spent winding, the rest listening to the stories told over many cups of tea.

I comforted myself that this was an act of corporeal charity. The women were lonely and needed to talk about their glories and triumphs, war-time memories and lost loves. My skill, which I took care to improve through research, was valued. The good workman is worth his wage. I was prepared to indulge their recollections.

After a few weeks, however, a number of clouds began to gather. I was becoming struck by recurring threads in their behaviour and narratives that made me question what I had got myself involved with.

In the first place, the clock-winding itself was a moment of high anxiety. Most were concerned lest I over-wind. More surprising was the fear that I under-wind, something which they frequently did as the mechanisms were often stiff. Although they expressed it in different ways, all shared Kate Crowbridge's apprehension about the clock stopping.

After the winding they relaxed and, this major worry removed, the talk flowed. I had developed various ways of delicately extricating myself. Few excuses worked better than the suggestion that I might otherwise be late for a similar appointment elsewhere.

When you have less of something you perhaps count it all the more carefully: but that shouldn't mean you start to feel an affinity with the abacus. There was, however, an alignment between their own well-being and that of the clocks which went beyond normal apprehension about the consequences of what these measured. All had grown up in houses where the clock management had been a matter for the paterfamilias. All had had husbands – or in one case a brother and, in another, a female partner – who had performed this role. Time in this digital age was more democratic but they were still lumbered with implacable remnants of their past. Not to maintain, cherish and observe them would be a betrayal.

And now the millennium was about to descend, shattering the old century and, through the half-understood Y2K threat, undermining all their assumptions of the certainty of time.

* * *

The next thing was that I learned that Geoff had been impersonating me to take the less subtle route of conning elderly people out of their savings. We looked quite similar: a carefully led and impressionable witness could convince a jury that it had in fact been me. I couldn't concoct alibis as I didn't know where or when he'd been doing this.

I thought about going to the police but this risked creating a worse muddle and solving nothing. We had, after all, conceived a mutual and dishonest project, from which is there is rarely any escape.

* * *

My problems really started on a Monday in late November. I had two calls. The first was to Mary Gaynor-West. She was probably the richest of my clients, inhabiting an immaculate town house in Primrose Hill filled with beautiful furniture and decorations, including a Chippendale cabinet, two sumptuous oriental rugs, what seemed to be a genuine Degas and several Sisleys. She had a number of younger relatives, she told me more than once, all of whom were constantly "chivvying me about my will." I was reminded of the stoats and weasels "chivvying" poor Mole in the Wild Wood.

The will was much on her mind and she returned to it several times during a long session of tea and biscuits after dealing with her clocks, which included a French *Verge* probably worth more than many of the cars parked outside along Fitzroy Road. The document was on the walnut coffee table when I arrived.

More than once she would pick it up and read part of a clause to illustrate her point. "...and of course, Cynthia *always* believed...", "...I've never trusted Martin *one inch*...", "...naturally, Marjorie thought she was being cut out...". It was like unwittingly and unwillingly eavesdropping on a private conversation.

At one point, I saw a figure in a long list of bequests: £80,000. Whatever was going on clearly involved high stakes.

The doorbell rang and she went to answer it. She returned with a man of about forty whom she introduced as "my nephew James." I was simply "the man who winds the clocks." There was a minute of desultory and increasingly embarrassing chat, during which I stood up to make a meaningless adjustment to the carriage clock on the mantlepiece. James had a way of making one feel remarkably ill at ease. I moved towards the doorway, keen to be gone.

"My word, what's this?," he said, gesturing to the will on the table. "Has the lawyer been?" His tone was jocular, his expression anything but.

Mary shuffled the papers back into the envelope. "I've been considering a few changes."

James' glance swivelled round to meet mine. The inference was clear: I, a stranger, was privy to her will: he, a relative, was not.

I said goodbye, promising to return at the same time next week.

I had hardly turned into the street when I heard footsteps behind me. I turned to face James. He was breathing heavily as if he'd just run from Chalk Farm station.

"The hell are you playing at?"

I denied any sinister motive: I was, I reminded him, just the man who winds the clocks.

"Oh yeah? Well, let me tell you that no one needs help winding a clock. You just wind them." He poked me in the chest. I pulled back, a gesture he interpreted as weakness. He did it again. "I was watching you, you greasy little chancer," he hissed. "I don't want anyone trying to…to trick her into something she might not mean, like you did with Louisa Dunbar."

Again, I repeated my innocence and made to turn away. As I did so, I caught sight of Mary Gaynor-West observing our confrontation from the living room window. The curve of her mouth suggested a mixture of excitement and satisfaction. I watched James stalk back into the house, feeling that his last accusation had been directed at the wrong person. Someone was playing games but it wasn't me.

Having made one enemy, within two hours I had made another. This debacle took place at Amanda Gosling's house near the Royal Free. On this occasion we were interrupted, again as I was about to leave, by a man who was not a nephew but a son, in his late fifties. He too was called James. He had the spindly frame, nine-months-gone belly, paunchy cheeks and bloodshot eyes of a man who had been in the pub since about 1972.

His mother was obviously afraid of him but at least managed to introduce me by name, adding that I was kind enough to drop in "to wind her clocks."

He looked at me suspiciously. "*Wind* them? Does he get paid for winding them?"

"Thirty pounds."

"For winding a *clock*?"

"Three clocks."

He strode over to the nearest one, a lovely Seth Thomas mantel, and savagely pulled open the case. The crank key was on the right-hand ledge. He grabbed it, causing the clock to shudder on the marble, and inserted it into the left winding point.

"Excuse me," I said, speaking for the first time. "That one doesn't need to be wound. Also, you're about to wind it the wrong way."

Without paying any attention to me, he gave the key a good turn, this time counter-clockwise.

"It doesn't need to be wound," I said again.

He turned to face me, flushed with a self-righteous rage. "Who the *hell* are you to tell me what to do?" he said. "Anyway I thought you said you wound clocks. Now you say this doesn't *need* to be wound. So what are you doing here? Snooping around? Casing the joint?"

"James…" his mother began.

"It has two winding mechanisms," I said, trying to keep calm. "The right one does the hands, the left one the chime. Your mother doesn't want the chime, as it wakes her up at night. That's the one you've started winding."

He put down the key and looked first at me, then his mother, as if he expected signs of collusion.

"I've heard about you," he said at last. "I'm going to make enquiries. This isn't the only house you prey on, is it? Kate Crowbridge? She's another of your victims, isn't she? You better watch your step." Then he gave his mother a perfunctory kiss and swept out, slamming the door behind him. It was just four o'clock.

At that moment, with a wheezy gasp, the Seth Thomas gathered itself together, struck four times and relapsed into slumber. As before, this seemed like a good time to leave.

I walked down Malden Road and into the human zoo of Camden Town deep in thought. The enterprise was involving me in things that went way beyond clocks or even conversation. I was walking, blindfolded, into a series of domestic typhoons. I had annoyed one James and humiliated another. Neither was likely to forget this.

Nothing I had done in these last few weeks had been reprehensible but the fact remained that the first visits Geoff and I had made, particularly to Lady Louisa, had been predicated on deceit, which could yet come back to haunt me. That many of my clients had been recommended by her transferred the original sin. I was a sinner who had not formally renounced his crime. I wondered if returning the hundred and twenty pounds which had been my share of our only two gigs would assuage this. I doubted it. In any case, my immediate problems were more pressing.

Both Jameses were aware I had other clients. Word had obviously spread in more ways than I'd hoped. I was viewed as a real obstacle to many people's financial security. I'd been threatened and poked in the chest, accused of mind games and testamentary ambitions. Would it end there?

Worse still, the necessary regularity of my various visits gave me a problem. Should I go back to Amanda Gosling and Mary Gaynor-West this time next week or not? To do so might be to walk into an ambush; not to do so would admit my complicity in what I was now starting to see as guilt.

Eventually, I decided on a kind of compromise and gave myself the next day off. I had two appointments, both inconveniently timed and a long way apart: Mrs Crowbridge in Gospel Oak and Mrs Daphne Mercier in what she called Brompton but everyone else called Earls Court.

I left messages with both saying I was sorry but something had come up and I could fit them in on Thursday morning. True, the clocks might have stopped by then but I reflected uncharitably that this would make my service all the more important as well as proving that it wasn't a matter of life or death. Either that or they could find someone else to wind them. I'd had enough of clocks for a bit. I turned into Royal College Street where I was due to have a drink with a friend.

I arrived at Mrs Mercier's house on Thursday just as the ambulance was preparing to leave. A paramedic ushered me inside, perhaps thinking I was a member of the household. I found myself alone in the hall. The door of the living room was ajar.

"...Daphne called me this morning at about nine," a woman sniffed. "I live across the road. She was worried it was going to stop." A mumbled question. "No, not her heart...her clock." Another mumble. "I don't know why it bothered her. I came and helped. We've always had old clocks in our house." She sniffed again.

"Take your time," the policewoman said.

"Well," the neighbour continued. "We caught it just a few minutes before it would have stopped, or so she told me. At quarter past nine."

I nodded: this was true.

"My, it was hard work. I can see why she got the young man to come to do it." Mumble, mumble. "No, I *don't* know his name. Then she stood up to put the kettle on when the clock struck the quarter. She just keeled over and…" There was more sobbing and more mumbling.

I didn't like this. I was about to get mixed up in something which looked alarmingly like an unexplained death. I pushed open the front door. I turned left, so walking past the living room window. I looked over my shoulder, just as the policewoman was looking out. Our gazes briefly locked. Click-click went the mental shutter behind her eyes, or so I assumed. Feeling now both guilty and foolish, I hurried down to the end of the street towards the bus stop.

Half an hour later, Mrs Crowbridge's house seemed quiet. I hovered by the gate for a few moments, so conveying to anyone who might have been watching the very impression of shiftiness I was so keen to avoid. As I reached for the knocker the front door was suddenly pulled open, revealing a police officer, male this time. I stammered my introduction.

"To wind the clocks?" said the officer, who had introduced himself as Detective Sergeant Briggs. "How interesting. May I ask you a couple of questions?" He gestured towards the kitchen.

I told him just about everything I'd been doing for the last six weeks, omitting Geoff and today's visit to Mrs Mercier's house. He told me that, about an hour before, the cleaning woman had heard a thump from the living room and discovered Mrs Crowbridge dead on the floor, a winding key in her hand. The clock had stopped.

"What time was this?" I said.

"Why do you ask?"

I felt a sense of increasing dread. "If it hadn't been wound, it would have stopped at about half-past ten."

He nodded slowly. "Could you see if it *has* been wound?

I went over to the clock and inserted the key. "No, not for about a week – so, since I last did it."

"It looks like she was *trying* to wind it," Briggs said.

"It does."

"And couldn't."

"No. I usually come every Tuesday. Yesterday I couldn't."

"Unfortunate." He gave me a level stare. "That's all, for now. We'll be in touch if we need to ask anything else." I got up and made for the door. "One more thing," he said. "Are you aware of any of your other 'clients' having had similar problems?"

I thought quickly. Did he know about Mrs Mercier, or that I'd been to her house? If so, or if it came out later, my furtive departure would need some explaining. Would this not be a good time to do this? I wasn't sure.

The confusion must have shown in my face because, after a few seconds, Briggs raised his eyebrows. "I don't think so," I said.

"Any problems at all?"

Wondering if I should mention the two Jameses and again deciding to stay silent, I shook my head.

There was a pause. "Are you going to keep on with your other 'clients'?" he asked, the sarcasm still all too evident.

The question was unexpected, appearing to be more human curiosity than part of the interrogation. "I hadn't thought about it. I suppose so."

"They seem to need you."

There was nothing I could think of to say to that.

"That's all for now, sir."

I did my normal calls for the rest of the week and wound the clocks with particular care. On the last call on Saturday I was half an hour late and was alarmed to see that Lady Louisa had a doctor with her, taking her pulse. She jumped to her feet when she saw me. "At *last*," she said plaintively, her face unhealthily pale.

"Dear Lady Louisa, *please*…" the doctor said.

I wound the clock, conscious of the tension behind me. When I turned back to face them the colour had returned to her skin and the doctor was packing up his case. He handed her a small jar of tablets.

"Now, if the faintness returns, take two of these…" She wasn't listening to him but looking at the clock, then at me. She knew what had caused her seizure. Now, beyond all possible doubt, so did I.

On Monday I returned to Mary Gaynor-Clark's, an hour earlier than usual in the hope of fooling James. He wasn't in the house but was waiting for me afterwards outside on the street.

"I warned you before," he said. "And yet here you are again."

"I'm here to wind the clocks," I replied neutrally.

"Oh, yeah? Winding up my aunt, more like. Getting her to change her will."

"I don't know anything about that."

"Oh, no. Butter wouldn't melt in your…mechanism." For a moment I thought this was a joke. I found myself thinking of the Mad Hatter's tea party when the March Hare admitted to putting butter into his watch, making it stop – "but it was the *best* butter."

Then I looked at James and realised he was, once again, beside himself with rage. "The police might be interested. Do you do this to all your clients? Charm them, wind them up…then kill them," he hissed.

I should have laughed but, after yesterday's events, I couldn't. I suspect I stared at him with a wide-eyed horror which might have made him think he'd got me taped. I couldn't explain to anyone, and certainly not to him, that my coming round every week would produce exactly the opposite result.

As before, I observed Mary Gaynor-Clark watching us from the first-floor window. Again she seemed excited and satisfied. God knows how many other people had been used by her to keep his expectations dangling. What James didn't understand was that I was as much trapped in this as he was.

So, there I was. I had eighteen clients, each of whom it seemed would die if I didn't wind their clocks every week. No one else's winding would suffice. To abandon them would be morally impossible and would lead to deaths that even the thickest detective could connect with me: and perhaps with Geoff, so ensnaring me still deeper. To continue would be to expose myself to a lifetime of drudgery and to increasing physical threats from nervous relatives.

Nor was it certain for how long this would go on. All the women were old. Would I, twenty years hence, be ministering to a group of wraiths, forced to play God and to decide when a life should end? Would deaths from other causes prove more potent than the strange and unwelcome power that I had come to wield? When, if ever, might I be released?

All that was certain was that I was firmly trapped in the consequences of a crime that I had casually entertained three months before: a practical reminder that no one should try dishonestly to interfere with the passage of time, whether measured by the turn of a key or by computers at the turn of a millennium.

So you, my reader, rich with hindsight, twenty-five long years on from my dilemma; so you, wise with your modern certainties; so you, *hypocrite lecteur, mon semblable, mon frère* – what would *you* have me do now?

A Rotten Borough

As the unfortunate candidate says, you won't find any of the places mentioned here on any map, nor any of the people in any directory. In addition, the regulations for electing parish councillors may not accord with those that apply in this universe: but they do with those in the one in which this story is set.

THE HOUSE I lived in when this happened was at the end of a street. Beyond this, there was nothing but a common. Little remarkable about that, you might say. The town is called Thatchbury but don't go looking for it on a map. I've changed the names, for reasons that should become clear. I've moved away as well. So would you have done.

I said "nothing but a common" but in fact there's also the remains of an old cricket pavilion. I can't think of it without being reminded of that awful day, at the start of which the pavilion had been, if not in good nick, then at least standing. I was standing then as well. I'm not now – never again.

I also say "at the end of the street" but there was quite a big gap between me and my only next-door neighbour. There was no one opposite. My house was almost an afterthought.

I can see I'm not telling the story very well. Let me start again.

The thing about my house you must grasp is that, in the common I mentioned, there was going to be big housing development. Greendale it was to be called, after the old farm just over the brow of the hill. I only discovered this a few weeks after I'd bought the place. I thought the vendor was being a bit easy with the price and the terms – he wanted out.

I had a half-hearted go at my solicitor but she said that "OPP hadn't been applied for so it didn't show up on the search.'" I said that, as I'd later discovered, the story of the impending development had been all over the *Thatchbury Gazette* for months before I'd bought the house:

she said, sniffily, that she could only base searches on official records, not on newspaper tittle-tattle.

I wasn't sure where I stood with this and the moment passed. My neighbours were jealous of my vendor's quick thinking. The road would, they promised me darkly, be turned into a roaring, mud-splattered highway for the construction traffic. As for the view – well, enjoy it while you can.

That was five years ago but, in the end, the plans never got off the ground. I find these things hard to follow but it seems there were two developers and they couldn't agree on anything. The project stalled, opposition became more focussed. I signed petitions, even went to a meeting. Everyone seemed more switched on than me, talking about "calling in" and '"the Inspectorate", "them local plan", "the climate emergency" and "obviously, the ombudsman…" It seemed that I had a team of strangers fighting my corner and in a language I didn't speak.

Meanwhile, I'd got £20,000 off the asking price, some of which I spent on triple-glazing the house. Aside from that, I sat tight, waiting for the storm to break.

And then, about six months ago, I'd got a letter marked "important – change of ward boundary" to which I should have paid more attention. Live and learn.

This story really started a few days after I'd got, and lost, this letter, when there was a rat-tat on the door. There was a thin, bald man in his sixties on the doorstep, a big smile on his face. I remembered him from the meeting. He introduced himself as Tim Gregory and he said he was a local Lib Dem councillor. I assumed that there was an election coming up and started to make my excuses.

"I don't want your vote," he said, sensing my unease. "I couldn't have it anyway." I pondered this paradox. "Perhaps I could come in."

Fifteen minutes later he was finishing explaining his proposition. I wasn't sure I had it straight. "So the parish council is the one that decides the plans? You know, for the houses?"

"No. The…"

"Oh, that's the other one – East Brockshire."

"Yes – but..."

"So...hang on, the MP – Lucy Farrell, right?"

"Yes, although...

"So she runs that council, does she?"

He went through it again. I don't have the mental hooks on which I can hang this kind of stuff so everything kept slipping off and getting muddled up. I was reminded of Christopher Robin explaining Brazil, Factors and Pumps to Winnie-the-Pooh, a bear of very little brain.

He grabbed some paper and drew a chart. It looked like a cross between a circuit diagram and the royal family tree during the Wars of the Roses.

"Right," I said, really trying to understand. "So the ward is where the people go to vote?"

He explained it a third time – he was a very patient man – and I finally got what he was on about. It seemed rather alarming. I told him I'd think about it. He drained his tea and said he'd pop back in a couple of days.

Later that afternoon there was another rat-tat on the door and a very different person was standing on the threshold: younger, more forceful and with the manner of a salesman at the end of the month who's still several sets of brushes short of his target. His searchlight gaze locked onto mine from time to time but it seemed to be an act.

He identified himself as Rupert Donald, Conservative ward member for wherever, portfolio holder for this and that. He kind of backed me into my living room. Two minutes later he was sat in the chair Tim Gregory had occupied shortly before, making me an identical proposition.

He assumed I had a perfect working knowledge of municipal life and politics and so made no effort to explain anything. Fortunately, Tim's summary was still fresh in my head so I was able to conceal my ignorance and even to ask a couple of intelligent questions. The conclusion was also identical, except that he had no tea to drain as I hadn't offered him any. I said I'd think about it and he said he'd be in touch in a couple of days. Then he was gone.

These two unexpected and parallel conversations had shaken me out of my torpor. The situation, which I only partly understood, had given me the chance to make a difference. I felt hemmed in by destiny. The only real choice I seemed to have was between blue and orange. As Tim had explained things to me and Rupert had not, there was only one answer to that.

So it was that, a few weeks later, I was at the Lib Dem Headquarters in Thatchbury, signing papers confirming that I, as the sole elector in Greendale, was nominating myself to stand in the forthcoming local council elections.

* * *

Tim never failed to delight in explaining the extraordinary circumstances which had led to my candidature. One evening in the Lamb and Flag in Thatchbury he was tracked down by Paula Harvey, a journalist from *The Brockshire Gazette,* based about thirty miles away, whose editor had got wind of some tangled election story. She brought back the drinks and sat down, pen poised. "So…"

It had started about three years before, Tim explained, when the Greendale development still seemed like a done deal. The Boundary Commissioners has sent their usual letter to East Brockshire asking if any ward boundaries needed changing. "Well, actually, yes," Tim said, slipping into a Belgravia-Cockney drawl that was, I think, a parody of the Council's CEO, "there is *one* place…"

The Commissioners had looked at the site and the planning documents and had agreed that, yes, by the time of the next election sufficient houses would have been built and occupied to justify the creation of a Greendale Ward, to which they allocated one seat in addition to the 16 that already existed in the rest of the parish.

"They drew up the plans and they were passed. However," Tim went on with relish, "three months later the Greendale plan hit the buffers. That's a different story," he added slowly, half-hoping Paula would ask him to relate it. She didn't. "The ward business was forgotten about. It would only come up when there was an election. As it has."

Paula made it clear from her expression that there were some dots she needed to have joined up.

The point was, Tim explained, the new parish-council seat assumed the housing estate would have been built and people moved in. But it hadn't even been started.

"Oh," Paula said, the light starting to dawn, "so there were no electors."

"Well, yes and no," Tim said. "There was one." And he clapped me on the back. I felt I should take up the story.

"There was an error on the map," I said. "My house got put the wrong side of the boundary, in the Greendale ward. There's a gap between me and the one next door and no one opposite. Perhaps it was the edge of a map sheet, I don't know..."

"More incompetence from Linda Conway, probably," Tim muttered, referring to East Brockshire's CEO. "Anyway, there he was. The only elector." They looked at me: she with curiosity, he with something resembling fatherly pride.

"So, whoever he votes for gets in?"

"It's even better than that," Tim said. "The law's changed. Now, parish councillors have to have been resident in the parish in which they're standing for three months before election day."

"So he's the only person who can stand?"

"That's right."

"Doesn't he have to be nominated?"

"Ah-ha," Tim said, warming to her municipal knowledge. "Indeed. Fortunately, that aspect of the law was changed at the same time. You now need two nominees but only one needs to be resident in the parish." He sat back in his chair and beamed at her.

"So, to re-cap, he's the only person who can stand and the only person who can vote. Plus, he can nominate himself. That's a bit odd, isn't it? A candidate nominating themselves?"

This was the bit Tim enjoyed most, I felt. As he then explained, when the law was altered, the stipulation that a candidate could not self-nominate had somehow got lost. "It's been tested. A few months ago there was a by-election near Leeds. A candidate spotted this and put herself down as one of her nominees. Labour challenged it but the judge ruled that the law as it stood was perfectly clear. If the law were changed, that would be different – but it hasn't been. In most cases it's not an issue."

"But it is here," said Paula. "Who was the other nominee?"

"Me," Tim said.

"In other words," Paula said, "you two represent the entire democratic machine for the election of this possibly decisive candidate in this…what's the phrase – rotten borough?"

Tim started backpedalling. His delight in explaining legalistic and procedural points had seemingly allowed him to stray the wrong side of a moral line. He talked of incompetence by East Brockshire, the Boundary Commissioners and parliament, the law of unintended consequences and playing by the rules as they existed. She nodded, then turned to me.

"How long have you been a member of the Lib Dems?" she asked.

I didn't know the best answer. A confident "twenty years" could be disproved. "Three weeks" sounded feeble. Then I wondered if I was actually a member at all. Did I even need to be in order to contest – if that was the right word – the seat? I had signed so many things without understanding what most were. Had this been one of them?

"Erm…" I said in a recollecting sort of way, looking at Tim.

"He recently confirmed his membership," he said crisply.

"So, what made you pick the Lib Dems?"

"Well…" I began.

"Were you approached by the Conservatives? I understand it's going to be a tight contest. They must have contacted you."

"Erm…" I said again. I sensed I was not doing very well in this latest grilling. How fortunate, therefore, that I had no voters I needed to impress; apart from myself, obviously. I wasn't sure I was achieving even this goal.

"I understand overtures were made, later," Tim put in, "but wisely..."

Paula drained her pint, snapped her notebook shut and gave us both the benefit of an electrifying smile that I hadn't previously suspected she possessed. "I'm not that interested in the political intrigue, odd though that might seem." I could sense Tim wanting to take issue with "intrigue" but deciding not to. "What gets me is the procedural stuff, the one-elector, one-candidate business. It's probably unprecedented."

"Almost certainly," Tim said.

"The thing I don't get is why this matters. I mean, you're only a parish council."

Tim resisted the temptation to say, as he had said to me several times before, that one of the aims had been to pull one over on the Tories. "That's true," he said carefully, "but we're about to become rather rich."

Paula opened her notebook again. "How so?"

"There was a large development at the opposite end of the parish. There'll be a significant developer contribution..."

"A CIL payment?"

"Exactly. Most goes to East Brockshire, of course, but we've just finished our neighbourhood development plan." He gave me a wolfish grin. I smiled weakly back, resolving to ask him again what these things were. "As a result, we get to keep a quarter of it. There are differing ideas how this should be spent. Our plan, for a green energy centre, could revolutionise the way the district council thinks about this kind of thing. The Conservative majority has been...well, luke-warm, at best. If we can make it work here, it could change policy. Here and elsewhere."

His eyes started to glint. "For the first time, we'll have enough money in the parish to do this. Whoever controls the council gets to say how it's spent. As you say, it's knife-edge."

I hadn't been aware of this. I wasn't sure if I welcomed the idea that I was a pawn in a serious event, however beneficial. My election could influence decisions over a far wider area than I'd imagined.

"What would happen if there were no election here, if your loyal candidate hadn't decided to stand?"

Tim explained that the new law decreed that the filling of seats left vacant because there were no candidates "would be decided by the higher authority": East Brockshire in this case, though it was unclear whether this would be made by the leader, who was political, or by the CEO, who was – nominally, Tim implied sarcastically – not.

It was for that reason that this particular seat, which could hold the key to the election, was so vital. A greater good was at stake. He was quick to add that the rules and the laws were being followed by the book. The Lib Dems had struck first.

Paula thought about all of this for a moment and then shut her notebook again. "Very interesting to meet you both," she said. She flashed a couple of cards across the table as she stood up. "If any more tangles emerge, let me know." She gave us a level stare. "However, our local democracy correspondent might want to take up the political angle."

I could see Tim slump and tense at the same time. "Particularly about your affiliation," she added to me. She stood smiling down at us. "Mind you, he's busy with another election. A nasty story with a Labour candidate – depends how that plays out."

You little tease, I thought.

"Anyway, thanks for your time." And she swept out.

I looked at Tim. "I could do with another drink," I said. "Then you can explain again what a neighbourhood development plan is."

* * *

Tim was right when he said the election was likely to be knife-edge. For a start, it was political, which elections for parish councils rarely are. The politicisation had happened about a year ago when the scale of the developer funds had become clear. The sixteen councillors, all previously apolitical, had turned into eight Conservatives, seven Lib Dems and one person who said he was independent but was later proved to be a member of the Labour Party. As a compromise which pleased no one, he called himself "Labour Independent."

There was nothing particular for these groupings to do except growl at each other until the CIL payment was made: and, before that, it so happened that there needed to be an election.

This polarisation attracted some interest. Party battles were usually only fought out at the election for East Brockshire District Council and at the Town Councils of Thatchbury and Melbridge, which between them accounted for nearly half of the district's population.

The rest of the district was comprised of small town and rural parish councils which co-opted members from those willing to stand, or able to be cajoled into doing so, and rarely managed to fill their available seats. And then there was Greendale.

* * *

The week before the election I met Tim, once again in the Lamb and Flag. I'd got to know him fairly well by now: well enough, certainly, to tell from his expression of nervous good humour that he had bad news.

We circled around this during the first pint. Unless I was going to harangue myself in the bathroom mirror there was no point in campaigning so it couldn't be about that. Eventually the conversation focused on the election day, 13 January.

Tim shifted in his chair. Here it comes, I thought.

"Do you remember Rupert Donald?"

"Yes. The Conservative who tried to recruit me."

Tim nodded. "A nasty piece of work. I suppose we should have expected something like this. Pure spite. Although," he added more judiciously, "it's all in the regulations. Maybe better we know now. I'm surprised he didn't leave it until afterwards and then shout foul. We were slow on the uptake with checking the new rules. In fact," he went on, now cheered up, "he's done us a favour."

Then his expression clouded again. "Unless it's a trick, of course." His brow furrowed as he tried to peer through the smoke that his opponent had possibly put up, or possibly not.

This, I thought, is why I couldn't be a politician, or a journalist, or a spy. You had to be constantly on the lookout for snares, disinformation and double-dealing and ready to hit your enemies in the same way. This could become an end in itself, rather than pursuing whatever noble cause had led you to the profession in the first place. All too easily, the means become more important, and certainly more attainable, than the ends. Social equality, world peace or ultimate truth are impossible goals to accomplish. Luring and trapping your opponents into indiscretions or errors are not.

I waited for Tim to get to the point.

Here was the thing, he said. Rupert Donald had discovered that, under the new regulations, the presiding officer had to be a resident of the parish.

"That's me, right? So, what does he do the presiding officer? Announce the result? I can do that now."

"No, that's the *returning* officer. The presiding officer sits in the polling station and ticks off the electors…"

"Elector, in this case."

Tim waved his hand impatiently. I could tell he was rattled. "He has to stay there all day, I'm afraid."

"Oh. How long do they have to open for?"

Tim coughed. "7am to 10pm."

"That doesn't seem too bad. It'll be in the Lib Dem office in Thatchbury, won't it?"

"Well, no. It has to be in the ward."

"But there aren't any buildings in the ward, apart from my house."

"It can't be a private house."

It was like playing a game of twenty questions.

"So? Is this a new regulation as well?"

"No," Tim said. I said nothing.

"We messed up, I'm afraid," Tim said: then, as so often is the way with apologies, his mood lightened. "It's not the sort of thing you normally think about. We only realised a couple of days ago." He grinned, aiming for a man-to-man expression to which I returned a neutral stare

"East Brockshire contacted us to ask which building in the ward we were going to be using. The same day, Rupert Donald asked the same thing." He took a pull of his beer. "Impossible to believe the two weren't connected. EBC doesn't want us to win. Well, they wouldn't, would they?" Now back in the world of political cut-and-thrust, Tim seemed more assured.

I pushed my empty glass across the table. "I think I'm going to need another one of these," I said.

"So, where's it going to happen?" I asked when he'd returned from the bar. A surge of hope ran through me which I did my best to conceal. "Will it have to be called off?"

Tim frowned. "Oh, no – there's too much at stake." With a politician's poise he paused, daring me to object. I didn't object. He nodded crisply, confirming my commitment. "There *is* a building. The old pavilion."

I couldn't place this. Tim explained that about a mile from my house, in the middle of what would have been the Greendale Estate were things to have worked out differently, there had once been a cricket pitch. Other nearby structures, mainly old farm buildings, had been demolished in the early, hopeful days of the development project: but there had been a question as to whether the pavilion had some kind of heritage status. It had therefore survived pending an investigation which, having been overtaken by events, never materialised. So there the pavilion still was, waiting for me.

I now remembered a picture in the *Brockshire Gazette* a few years back of a derelict, haunted-looking building surrounded on three sides by windswept fields and on the fourth by a dark and menacing wood. It might have been, and perhaps had been, the lead photo for a story about a local serial killer.

"So, we'll use that." Tim's remark was a statement, not a suggestion.

"Does it have electricity?"

He looked at me as if I were simple. "It doesn't have anything except a bloody great lock on the door which EBC put on. The windows are all boarded up so it shouldn't be too draughty. I'd bring some warm clothes, though. We'll sort a table and chair out.

What the hell did I want a table and chair for? Did he think I was going to use the opportunity to start work on a novel?

"For the paperwork. You're the presiding officer. We'll come over and bring you some food."

"Can't someone relieve me for an hour or so?

"Well, no, I'm afraid not. Rupert Donald said he'll drop in to check. I'm sure he will. The presiding officer or their deputy must be there at all times."

"And the deputy..."

"Has to be a resident of the ward as well. So, there can't be one." Tim paused and sat back in the chair. He was now relaxed and as normal. The bad news seemed to be over. "All clear?"

I pushed my empty glass across the table at him. It was a small protest but the best I could muster.

* * *

At twenty to seven in the morning on the long-awaited election day of Thursday 13 January, I set off across the field towards the pavilion. The air was damp and bitingly cold, suggesting a freezing and foggy day to come. The eastern sky was lit with the first signs of a pale, sickly dawn. One moment, my torch would show flat, tussocked ground for a hundred yards ahead; the next, the mist would sweep across the landscape so the light reflected back at me as if from a fogged mirror.

I trudged on. Surely I must be there? I have a poor sense of direction and the conditions were making it worse. Had I gone past it, or was I walking round in circles? I started shining my torch in a widening arc. Just when I was starting to get alarmed, I saw the pavilion about a hundred yards away. If the mist had not just then cleared I would have missed it. Without reflecting on where that might have left me – Greendale Heath is a large and featureless place – I turned towards the building. I was half-expecting to see Rupert Donald lurking in the gloom, stop-watch in hand.

However, I was bang on time. As I turned the keys in the padlock and in the door and stepped across the threshold, I heard the tolling of a church bell striking the hour. As the last peal of seven faded away I had the storm lantern on the desk and was applying a flame to the wick. This was the last thing that was to go right that day.

The next ten minutes were spent arranging the pointless paraphernalia of my day's work. Tim had been keen everything be done by the book, including fixing a "Polling Station" sign to the door. He had even arranged for a booth to be brought over. There were two folding tables, one for the impressive locked voting box sitting by the door and one for me, the presiding officer. There was a folding chair. There was a clipboard with the list of voters (or voter) and a sheet of paper listing the regulations. There was a pad of voting slips. I got all this sorted out but had at the back of my mind the sense something was missing

It was now ten past seven. I looked around me. As Tim had said, all the windows were boarded up except for one Velux in the roof. It was a dreary scene. I wondered how many people had already cast their vote and were now speeding off to a productive day's work. My day ahead promised no such rewards.

I unpacked my backpack. It contained a large thermos of black coffee, a small water bottle, a large bar of chocolate, a half bottle of scotch, a copy of *Our Man in Havana* (which I'd always meant to read), my fully charged mobile, an extra jumper, a pair of gloves and a scarf. I was already wearing three layers of clothes on the top, two on the bottom and a woolly hat. They didn't seem nearly enough. I put on the scarf and put everything else apart from the thermos and the mobile back in the bag.

I love coffee: the smell, the taste, the effect; perhaps most of all, the quiet and unvarying formalities of its preparation, much like a Catholic priest finds comfort in the rituals when making ready for the eucharist. I'd spent fifteen minutes this morning grinding Kenyan beans and drip-filtering the results, then gently bringing it back to near boiling on the stove before decanting it into the thermos. I'd so far not had a sip, just as the priest would decline a nip of the communion wine before donning his cassock: that was a pleasure to be savoured. I realised now that I needed it rather badly.

I unscrewed the thermos and inhaled the aroma. It was a moment straight from an advert, although probably no coffee advert had ever been filmed in a location like this. I put the cup down and started to pour.

The next few seconds have replayed themselves countless times in my mind, sometimes when I'm asleep. Either because of the extra weight, or because I knocked the leg, or due to some fault in the design, the right part of the table gave way and the half-full cup of coffee, and my phone, slid onto the floor.

Instinctively I put the thermos down, but on a surface that was longer flat. It toppled over and boiling coffee poured over my hands. I made a grab for the flask but missed. It bounced down the reclining table and landed on the floor with the unmistakable crack of a serious breakage. There was the faint and tantalising aroma of perfectly-brewed coffee, soon replaced by the previous smell of mildew and tom cats.

It was an ugly moment. Worse was to come. Both my hands, particularly the left, were scalded. Water was needed, but I had only the small bottle I'd brought with me. I hadn't anticipated this emergency. I'd have to ask Tim to bring me water, quite a lot of it, as well as the lunch and dinner he'd promised. And coffee.

I picked up the phone from the floor next to the thermos and pressed the on button. Nothing happened.

There were two likely reasons for this. One was that the screen was cracked from top to bottom. The second was that cold coffee was dripping out of it. I pressed the button several times, in the increasingly savage way you do. Dead as Dillinger.

I was also pressing my mental command-Z button to undo the idiotic sequence of events: here in a polling station on election day, with me as the presiding officer. Presiding over, so far, a fiasco. I checked my watch. Not even quarter past seven. What a start.

Soon it became impossible to ignore the pain in my hands. I dug out the bottle of water and, very carefully, poured a few drops on the back of my left hand. It felt briefly better, then worse. The skin was starting to blister. I remembered that scalds carry on heating from the inside and getting the injured area cold was of first importance. The water in the bottle was at about blood temperature. There was no running water in the pavilion. Where might be cold water be found?

Of course – outside. I pushed the door open and plunged my hands into the dew on clumps of grass and weeds. I had to get down on my knees, crawling from one tuft to the next. After ten minutes of this, the pain had abated but I sensed I would need to do this every fifteen minutes or so. Mind you, what else did I have to do?

I went back inside. I could hardly look at the thermos and cup on the floor but eventually put them in the backpack. This seemed a good moment to have some chocolate. I broke off a large chunk and chewed it greedily. This stimulated rather than sated my appetite. Why had I not brought more food? I'd had one piece of toast while making the coffee.

What was needed, I now saw, was several rounds of cheese sandwiches, slabs of fruit cake and shiny red apples. I had had weeks – months, in fact – to prepare for this moment. I looked in the bag. The only other thing in there was the bottle of scotch. It was not yet seven thirty in the morning but this was no ordinary day. I unscrewed the bottle and raised it to my lips.

"Hello, hello," a familiar voice said.

I gulped. Some of the whisky spilled onto my scarf. I looked up to see Rupert Donald in the doorway. He shone his torch around in an arrogantly proprietorial way, finishing with it straight into my eyes. Then he flicked it off. For a moment I could see nothing.

"Nice place you've got here," he drawled.

"The only place," I corrected him.

"Well, not quite." He offered me a chuckle. "You could have done this at your house, you know. If there are no 'suitable public premises' and fewer than something like 30 electors a private house can be used. Didn't Tim say? Four-week notice period but, even so."

I had no way of knowing if this was true. His remarks fed the nagging feeling that Tim hadn't looked after me as well as he might. It seemed safer to say nothing, not even ask him what he was doing there.

He continued to pace up and down. I saw now that he had a takeaway cup of coffee from which he from time to time took little sips. "Bloody cold, as well. I can see you've got something to keep the chill out," he added, gesturing to the bottle.

I felt unequal to describing the sequence of events that had led to my drinking scotch at half seven in the morning.

"I think I'll stick to coffee," he said. He gave me a searching look. I began to wonder if he had perhaps been lurking outside and had seen the catastrophe through a chink in the window: perhaps filmed it. In politics, anything was possible.

"Don't forget to vote."

Facetiously, I indicated the clipboard, the voting slips, the booth and the ballot box. Then I realised what was missing. I had no pen or pencil. Unless it was well hidden, Tim had not provided one either.

Rupert seemed to pick up on my unease. "Not sure who to vote for? I think there's only one choice, isn't there?"

I was about to tell him to piss off but realised I needed his help. Tim had said he would come down with some food: but he had also said he'd provide pencils and appeared to have screwed up over the venue. Could I trust him to arrive with a hot lunch? Particularly on election day, doubtless spent driving pensioners to warm polling stations, comparing exit polls and preparing victory speeches, I could have slipped his mind. As well as food, I also needed water, coffee, something for the throbbing scalds on my hands and a pencil. My phone being bust I had no way of reaching him. Could I trust Rupert to remind him? Their paths would probably cross during the day.

"Look," I said, trying to appeal to him on a human level. "Can we forget the politics for a moment..."

"On election day?"

"It seems I have to stay here all day. Fair enough. But I need a blanket and…and stuff. Tim said he'd bring me some food at lunchtime. Could you tell him that…"

"Can't you call him yourself?" My broken phone was still lying on the floor. Had he seen it? If so, had he seen it was broken? Would admitting something that he may or may not have known weaken or strengthen my hand? Was the human factor in any case enough, on this day of all? I realised I hadn't answered his question.

"I…er, don't have his number."

Rupert raised his eyebrows. The statement was clearly preposterous.

"I'll tell him how you're fixed," he said ambiguously. Then he turned on his heel; which immediately disappeared as the rotten floorboard gave way. He toppled forward. For the second time that morning a spray of hot coffee arced its way across the room, missing me by inches. Once again I caught a faint whiff; once again, the sensation didn't last.

In the moments that followed, I wondered if I could blame the scalds on this latest spill and use this as a way of leveraging help. However, a scream would have been needed and it was too late for that now.

As Rupert Donald still sprawled, grunting, on the floor, I also briefly wondered if I could, in helping him up, relieve him of his phone and, perhaps, the elegant fountain pen which I suspected people of his type kept in the breast pocket of their suit, which he was doubtless wearing under the Barbour jacket.

Come to think of it, I could do with that too. In fact, if he were to have been killed or at least knocked out, this would present a way out of many of my immediate problems.

He was neither of these things, however. If I wasn't going to beat him to death with my thermos I had to help him to his feet. This I did, but received no gratitude.

"Jesus," he said. "Was that some kind of trap?"

"I'm sorry," I said, unthinkingly admitting liability. "I think the floorboard gave way."

"Damn right it did." He flexed his ankle. Many people's reaction when anything unexpected happens is to reach for their mobile so they can photograph the incident and post it on Facebook. He started to do this, then cursed. "My bloody mobile's broken." He glared at me. I said nothing.

It seemed he could walk. If he wasn't going to be dead or unconscious, what I most needed was him out of here and heading back to Thatchbury. There he would hunt down Tim, if only to present him with a bill for a torn trouser leg and a new iPhone. What I didn't need was him huddled in the corner, with nothing between us except two busted mobiles, two spilled cups of coffee and half a bottle of scotch.

"Unsafe building," he muttered as he limped towards the door. "Could invalidate everything."

He might have been right for all I knew. Matters had got so badly out of control that this threat meant nothing to me. It was clear the day was to be a trial of more than just political survival.

"I would give you a hand," I couldn't resist saying as he stepped across the threshold. "But, as you know, I can't leave the building."

I was unsure if I had gone too far. Instead, he laughed. In a mad way, I felt I'd gained his respect. Then he scowled and shuffled away. I went inside and shut the door. As I did so, the church clock chimed. Eight o'clock. Fourteen to go.

There was nothing else to do, I poured a large shot of scotch, the main effect of which was to make me realise how badly I wanted another one: which I had. I sat down on the floor. I'd hardly slept the night before. The day had already given me more unpleasant experiences than I normally encounter in a month: and the sun had barely risen. I shut my eyes.

* * *

I awoke with a jolt and for a moment had no idea where I was. Fusty-headed, I got up and walked across the room. Even from the chinks of light coming through the cracks in the boarded-up windows I could sense something unexpected outside. I pulled open the door.

My forecast for a day of mist had been wrong. While I had slept the weather had changed. The snow was falling in every direction, including up, and lay banked against the side of the building up to about two feet deep. There was no movement, no sound and no light except what came from the swirling, silvery flakes, softly falling and billowing across the universe. It was impossible to discern any horizon, or even any features much further away than my own outstretched hand.

For a time I stood there, transfixed by the change. Then I stepped back inside and pulled the door shut. The pavilion, lit only by the storm lantern's sickly and sulphurous light, now seemed even more dank and dreary. I opened the door again. This made no appreciable difference to the temperature inside.

Snow fluttered in and started to settle in an arc inside the doorway but I doubted that this would do any more damage to the building than had the last five years of neglect. I wrapped myself up in all my clothes and sat there, waiting.

Waiting for what? I realised that I was waiting for Tim to bring me my promised meal; also, that this would probably not now be happening. Somebody was coming at ten o'clock – still over eight hours away – to pick up the box but until then I was on my own. Not even Rupert Donald would be venturing out again in this. The sensation was alarming and liberating in roughly equal measure.

I sat watching the snow fall: there was nothing else to look at, nothing else to do. The doorway was directly in front of the table at which I was sitting. The classic formality of the composition – the perfect square opening filled with tumbling shards of icy light, the semi-circle of snow on the floor, the waxy glow from my lantern and the dismal, mouldy walls which, away from the entrance, faded into ever-deepening shadow – made me feel as if I were becoming part of this austere, near-monochrome tableau, rather than an observer.

I felt at peace. It was almost like being slightly drunk. Then I realised that I was in fact slightly drunk. I was also aware that I wasn't feeling cold and that my scalded hands weren't hurting. Might these, and my inappropriate elation, be the first warning signs of hypothermia?

I looked at my watch. Could it be half-past five already?

I decided to stand up but my legs were reluctant to obey. This didn't seem like a good sign either. I lurched over to the doorway. The need to get out of this awful, depressing building was now overwhelming. I stepped across the threshold, pulling the door behind me.

I was in a world in motion. The snow rushed at me from every direction. My footsteps crunched, the sound appearing slightly delayed in the freezing air. Then I took one more step and there was no answering noise. I was falling forwards into a void. The world was no longer brightly crystalline but dark and full of menace. A moment later I found myself sprawled on the ground, gasping for breath and with a sharp pain in my leg.

How long I lay here I have no idea. By the time I managed to move, the sky had become darker and the snow heavier. I blundered around for a while but kept coming up against a wall of snow. It was impossible to tell if these were large drifts or the side of some kind of pit. I tried to think. How far had I fallen? Ten feet? Twenty? The accident seemed to have happened hours ago, and in slow motion.

Round and round I went, all sense of direction lost. The pain in my leg was subsiding, but so too was all the feeling below my knees.

Then I saw a pale light above me. I swung round. The clouds had parted and a sickly moon had appeared. Just ahead, there was a gap in the mounds of snow against which I'd been stumbling.

I scrambled towards it, hoping to get up onto open ground before the moon vanished. The snow was deep and slowed me down, as in a dream. I had just reached the top of the slope and could see a few bare trees silhouetted in the far distance when the clouds closed again and I was plunged back into near darkness.

A number of thoughts struck me. Firstly, why was it dark? I looked at my watch but couldn't make out the hands. In any case, a tinkling sound as I raised it to my ear suggested it had been broken in the fall.

Secondly, now that I was in the open again I realised the snow had grown still heavier and the wind had got up. Thirdly, my clothes were soaked, on the outside with snow and on the inside from cooling sweat. My hands and feet were numb and my teeth were chattering erratically. My left leg was starting to throb. Finally, there was the matter of the pavilion. From being somewhere from which, twenty minutes or several hours ago, I had wanted to escape, it had now become a place of refuge: but where was it?

Having accepted that I was under-dressed, partly-drunk, injured and lost in the middle of a howling blizzard I began to feel genuine alarm. For the inexperienced adventurer – and if anyone qualified for this title, I did – the next station on this line is blind panic.

I took a few deep breaths and tried to think rationally. As I didn't know where I was in relation to the pavilion, it didn't matter in which way I walked. The Common was only a few square miles so, if I kept going in the same direction for long enough, I'd eventually find a house. The trick was not to go round in circles.

How I could avoid that? I didn't know.

As my left leg was injured, it seemed best to steer slightly to the right to compensate. There was nothing else to decide. After being buffeted by a ferocious blast of snow that nearly knocked me off my feet, I set off. It was now dark although, as is the way in heavy snow, faint areas of light appeared for a few seconds here and there, mirages in the storm: maybe they were transitory reflections of some car headlight or street lamps several miles away, transmitted from flake to flake like reflections in an infinitely complex and ever-changing hall of mirrors. It was hard not to veer towards each one.

Once again, time seemed to have lost its meaning. I had no idea how long this journey lasted nor how far I walked. I do recall that there came a time when the lights took on different hues, although none were colours I could identify.

I heard strange tunes which might have been made by wind in the bare branches of trees or perhaps from the flickering figures I could see on the edge of my field of vision. Once, a huge and silent horse rushed past me, was caught by a blast of wind and vanished in a flurry of snow.

Then, without warning, these hallucinations were interrupted by the clouds parting again to reveal the moon, higher in the sky than it had been before. The pavilion was on my right. I was standing in almost the same place as when the mists had parted at five to seven. Odd. Then the clouds closed again.

I staggered towards the building. I half expected it to have vanished into the blizzard like so much else: but there it was. I even managed to find the door. I turned the handle but it didn't open. Had I pulled it shut behind me when I'd left? If so, it must have locked itself. I could try to break it down but I doubted my frozen limbs had the strength. I half collapsed against the door.

Finding the pavilion had been my goal: now arrived there, I was little better off. The wind whipped snow in every direction so it made no difference on which side of the building I sheltered. The thought struck me that unless I could get inside I would die.

Looking to my left, I saw a water butt against the wall. The building's sloping roof started about six feet off the ground: and, set into the roof was a Velux window. I remembered it from the morning when it allowed a few rays of pale sunlight into the building. I could recognise it now because the snow on the rectangle of the window was an inch or two lower than that on the surrounding roof. This was, I reasoned groggily, good news as it suggested some snow had melted because the inside of the pavilion was warmer. It seemed worth giving it a go.

As I stood up, I had about two seconds of the moon which confirmed all this in an over-exposed flash photograph. Then the snowstorm descended again and I was once more alone in the high Arctic's polar night, barely a mile from home.

Climbing onto the water butt was more of a challenge than I'd expected. Once on top, by leaning forward I was able to reach almost to the bottom edge of the window. I hoped it could be opened from the outside. First I had to get to it. I pushed forward.

Several things happened immediately.

The water butt ripped away from whatever was fastening it to the wall and collapsed onto the snow with a dull thud. I managed to get a handhold on the lower frame of the window and pulled myself forward so I was now wholly resting on the roof.

As I did this, I more or less disappeared into snow. There was a lot more of it on the roof than I had thought. Still holding onto the frame, I hauled myself further up until I was half kneeling over the window. I started scraping away the snow to reach the glass. I shifted my position, putting most of my weight on my left knee.

There was a loud crack followed by the realisation that I was falling. I landed, mostly on my right hand. The pain was dulled by the cold and by a rush of adrenaline: it seemed amazing I had any left. Then there was a rumbling, tearing sound as other things started to fall about me.

Last of all there was a roar of flame and a searing heat that shot me backwards against what remained of the wall. Then something hit me on the head and I toppled backwards into oblivion.

* * *

"How are you?"

I opened my eyes. I was lying in a bed in a white room: a hospital, probably. My left hand was bandaged. It felt like there was a bandage on my head. I couldn't see my right arm at all. I started to panic.

Tim put his hand lightly on my chest. "Relax," he said. "You're in one piece, except for a toe."

"A toe?"

"One of the little ones. Frostbite."

I thought about this for a moment. I then realised the reason I couldn't see my right arm was because it was suspended on a pulley above me.

"What the hell am I doing with my arms tied up and minus a toe?"

Tim chuckled. "For someone who's been unconscious for two days, you've woken up quickly." My expression must have caused his levity to evaporate. “Can you remember anything about what happened?”

I reflected. “Not really. The last thing was Rupert Donald coming over.” Tim raised his eyebrows but said nothing. “More than you did,” I added waspishly.

“There were problems,” he said.

“You’re telling me.”

“Perhaps I’d better come back when you’re…” he left the sentence unfinished. Stronger? In a better mood?

“I’d rather you told me now. Otherwise I’m going to lie here and fret.”

“OK. I only know what I saw. The gaps you’ll have to fill in, if your memory returns.” There was a pause. He seemed to be deciding how to tell the story. He went for the deep end. “At about half past seven in the evening on election day, we got a report that the pavilion had blown up.”

“Blown up?”

“Yes. Do you know why?”

“Not at the moment, no.”

“It seems there were some gas cylinders stored there. We didn’t know about this of course. It appears the roof collapsed and fractured one of them. You had a storm lantern, didn’t you?”

“Yes. You knew that. In fact, I think you advised it.”

“Possibly, yes…yes, I think I did. Perfectly safe – if used properly.” I couldn’t see where this was leading. “The doctors said,” Tim continued, “that your injuries were consistent with your having fallen through the roof.” He paused for a moment. “*Were* you on the roof?”

“Why should I have been on the roof?” As I said this, I had a flicker of a memory of being on the roof of just such a building in a blizzard. Had it been *that* building? The recollection faded.

Tim spread his arms. “I’m asking you.”

Suddenly this seemed less like a chat between an election candidate and his agent than an interrogation.

“So, you turned up and the building had exploded and I was lying there like…well, like this?”

"More or less," Tim said.

I decided to leave it at that. "I'm tired," I said. Tim left. I was fretful for a while but a nurse came in and gave me a couple of pills after which I slept.

When I woke up my mind was clearer. I had a dream-like memory of the events until the time I reached the pavilion but these were slender, like a spider's web in a hailstorm, and threatening to disintegrate if I thought about them too hard. I drifted off again. When I came to, Tim was once again sitting at my bedside.

This time he was less confrontational and I was stronger. We went over again the bits that he knew and I could remember. The entire story was only mine to tell but my mind had, perhaps charitably, erased parts of it: whether permanently or not, time would tell. I sensed that the complete narrative would not show me up in a good light. Amnesia would probably be my friend.

Eventually – and it seemed impossible to avoid the subject any longer, although for passages of our conversation I had forgotten that this was why I had been there at all – I asked how the election had gone. His expression hardened again.

"We lost," he said at last.

"Lost? How?"

"You didn't vote. At least," he continued in a less bitter tone, "there was no evidence from the remains of the ballot box that you had."

I frowned to myself. Was this possible? "I'm sure I did." As I said it, I wasn't sure. There was something I had been missing but I couldn't remember what. I felt my head starting to throb.

"Also," he added, "the polling station had been destroyed." I could see why it might invalidate the votes cast there, if any.

"Unfortunately," Tim went on remorselessly, "if no valid votes are cast the returning officer has to decide what to do. The seats in the other wards were split, eight to us and eight to the Conservatives." He paused to let this sink in. "The returning officer who is, you'll remember, Linda Conway, our impartial Chief Executive, decided she would give the seat to the party which had won most votes overall across the parish." He stopped again. I could see what was coming.

"And they did," I said.

"Yes. By 12 votes. It was that tight. Actually, it's hard to blame her." Then he twisted the knife a bit further. "So, now they have control of the parish." For a moment I couldn't remember why this was so important. "And the CIL money. If it's paid," Tim added slowly. "We've got a trick up our sleeves on that one. You see, I think that the developer could claim that…"

I waved my hand. My headache was getting worse; but the real reason was that I had become sickened by the political machinations in which I had played so disastrous a part. The episode belonged to a part of my life from which I had been severed. I could recall our pre-election conversations with perfect clarity but they didn't seem to have anything to do with me.

I knew then I would soon leave this town. I now had less than no reason at all to stay in Thatchbury. The place was dead to me: a rotten borough.

"One question," I said. "You said you were going to bring me some food. Why didn't you?"

"The weather…"

"All the more reason."

"Well," he added quickly, looking away from me, "I ran into Rupert Donald and he said he'd been to see you and you had everything you needed."

I could have asked why Tim believed this when he had several times said Rupert was not to be trusted but let it pass. There was also something else Rupert had said – that the election could have been held in my house if Tim had got his act together – but I couldn't be bothered. I was too bored and ashamed by it all. Perhaps it was better that it had ended this way, in snow, fire and oblivion. For some reason, I remembered Enoch Powell's famous remark that all political careers end in failure. Never did this seem so true.

Tim stood up, rather awkwardly. "I'll come back tomorrow," he said. I gave him a look that must have made him realise there was nothing more to say.

He didn't come back and I never saw or heard from him again.

* * *

Two weeks later I was packing up my house as well as I could with one arm in plaster having arranged with an agent to rent it on any terms while I moved back to the anonymity of London.

There was a knock on the door. I opened it and found myself looking at Paula Harvey, the journalist from the *Gazette*.

"Hi. Do you remember me? We met in…"

"I remember you well, the stuff that happened on election day rather less well. So, if you want to do a feature on that, forget it."

"Oh no," she said. Although I hadn't opened a paper since, I'd been aware that the fiasco and the procedural wrangles it had produced had been widely covered. My phone and doorbell had been ringing constantly until I'd had the former disconnected and started ignoring the latter. I'm sure she had played her part in this but I bore no ill will. It was all part of the process. I'd only opened the door now because it had all been quiet for the last few days. The story had gone cold and the newshounds would be hunting for fresher flesh elsewhere. None the less, here she was.

During these reflections I realised she'd gone into the living room and sat down. I followed her.

"No, all that's over with." She gave me a look which seemed almost pitying. I shrugged. Anything was preferable to an interest in my political career. "I've just been at East Brockshire Council. I thought you might be interested to know what's just been decided."

I sat down and ran my hand through my hair. There was a lump where the beam had hit me. My right arm was still in plaster. My missing toe hurt at times and this was one of them. The skin on my left hand was still raw. There also seemed to be a lump of ice in the centre of my body which refused to melt so that I never felt completely warm, even in an overheated room. Apart from that, I was fine.

"I'm really not sure I *am* interested," I said slowly. "I haven't been following local affairs since then. But since you've come over I suppose you might as well tell me."

She gave a brittle smile. "There was an appeal against the CIL payment. It succeeded. It's a kick in the teeth for Linda Conway and East Brockshire Council. The developers will pay a notional sum but the parish will get next to nothing. So, no green-energy system – the developers win again. It turned out there was a problem with the way EBC's planning department had handled the application, so when…"

My head was buzzing. Everything about that terrible day, or what I could remember of it, was now doubly pointless.

It was possible Tim and his cronies had orchestrated this coup; or that the revenue would in any case have melted away like faerie gold or been diverted for purposes for which it had not been intended. Paula's pat phrases, gloating over this latest example of municipal disaster, revolted me, in much the same way as had Tim's in the hospital .

My experience of political life, the details of which I could barely remember, had at least been swift. My political career had ended: there was no point in listening to anything more she had to say. I stood up.

"I'm sorry," I said, just as she was babbling about a motion at the next Executive meeting, "but I've had enough of all this. Please – go."

She stood up, surprised. This was perhaps her scoop of the year and she was sharing it with me as a gift which I had not asked for and did not want.

"But…"

"Yes, I know. But please – that's it."

She left.

I couldn't spend another hour in this town. I packed a suitcase, sent an email to the agent saying I'd make arrangements for clearing the house in the next week and called a taxi. Half an hour later I was at Thatchbury station. On the train I spoke to a friend in Camden and agreed I could crash with him for a few nights until I'd got my head sorted out. The clickety-clack of the train soon sent me to sleep.

It was getting dark when we arrived at Paddington. I stood, for a moment bemused in the centre of the concourse, trying to remember which of the two tube entrances I should head for. Then someone tapped me on the arm.

"Excuse me, sir," a perky young man said, "are you interested in joining the Labour Party?" He thrust a leaflet towards me. In his other hand was a tablet.

I gave him a steady gaze. "All political careers end in failure," I said.

"No, they don't!" He was sharper than I'd bargained for. "Look at Atlee, for example – and, of course, at a *local* level, we can *all* make a big difference…"

"Don't take this personally," I said, "but piss off."

Then I stalked away: towards the tube station; towards Camden; and towards the oblivion that all our misfortunes crave and into which all things, the laudable as well as the unworthy, eventually slide.

By the same author

Unaccustomed as I Am

The locations range from the Lambourn Valley to Las Vegas, from the Hundred Acre Wood to a dark and secret basement, from a steam train to a drug den and from Suffolk to Provence.

The cast includes the Earl of Berkshire, Mr Chivers from Planning, Sherlock Holmes, Winnie-the-Pooh, thirteen crime writers, a distracted mother, an enraged greengrocer, a hopeless salesman, a sinister collector, a lonely pharmacist, a professor of Neological Linguistics, a municipal inspector, a sentient racehorse and an inner yak.

The book offers a chaotic interview, an inept public performance, an unexpected wedding, a messed-up exam and a good deed gone wrong; a burning telephone, a murder mystery without a body, a trip to the seaside in the 1950s, Richard IV's map, two doses of broken glass and four famous sleuths in search of some lost teaspoons – twenty-six tales of confusion, misunderstanding, tragedy, parody and farce.

"What a truly delightful collection Unaccustomed As I Am *is. There is such pleasure in being in Brian Quinn's company as he ranges thoughtfully, insightfully and often comically over subjects major and minor, from vivid childhood and student memories and pitch-perfect parodies of Hemingway and Shakespeare to short stories of real power and punch."*
Stephen Fry

RRP: £9.95
Published by: Penny Post
ISBN: 978-1-8382580-0-9